Iridescence

Sensuous Shades of Lesbian Erotica

edited by
Jolie du Pré

NEW YORK

Manufactured in the United States of America

This trade paperback original is published by Alyson Books
245 West 17th Street, New York, New York 10011
Distribution in the United Kingdom by
Turnaround Publisher Services Ltd.
Unit 3, Olympia Trading Estate, Coburg Road, Wood Green
London N22 6TZ England

First Edition: June 2007

07 08 09 10 11 a 10 9 8 7 6 5 4 3 2 1

ISBN: 1-59350-004-1
ISBN-13: 978-1-59350-004-7

Library of Congress Cataloging-in-Publication data are on file.

Cover design by Victor Mingovits
Interior design by Charles Annis

CONTENTS

Contents

INTRODUCTION

In 2001, I was seduced by lesbian erotica and I quickly fell in love with it. The relationship has been effortless; after all, I'm a bisexual woman with a fondness for all things female. These days lesbian erotica and lesbian erotic romance is all I desire to write.

Literary erotica is a fascinating genre and there are some wonderful stories to be found. But what I've also found is that a majority of those stories contain a white cast, which wouldn't be a problem for me if it weren't for the fact that lesbian sex isn't just for white folks and not all lesbians are white. Our world is a diverse world, and our erotica should reflect that.

So, I had an idea: why not combine my love for lesbian erotica with my desire to see more characters of color? The result is a representation of lesbians from every color of the rainbow and stories in every shade of sexy—from hot to hardcore. But there are more reasons to be proud of this collection. You will find that in addition to the exquisite sexual depictions, the quality of these stories is exceptional and the varied themes will keep every lover of lesbian erotica eagerly turning the pages!

There's the delicate flow of Fiona Zedde's *Night Music* and JT Langdon's historic *Water Gatherer*, and the scorching heat of Dylynn DeSaint's *Shopping in New York* and Shanel Odum's *Lick 'Er License*. CB Potts's *Test Your Luck* and Tawanna Sullivan's *The Getaway* give us action and plenty of grit. Sofía Quintero spins a highly entertaining drama in

On Her Terms, and Cheyenne Blue's *Glory B.* will haunt you long after you've finished reading it.

Indeed, I applaud all of the contributors of *Iridescence* for turning this book into a rare gem, one that I know you will treasure.

—*Jolie du Pré*

Night Music

Fiona Zedde

With the concert hall's stage lights flooding over her sunset-colored dreadlocks and the ascetic lines of her face hewn in rich tones of rosewood, Zoya was breathtaking. The violin's bow in her hands stroked the instrument, making it sing. Even beneath the other instruments—cello, harp, flute, piano—I could still hear her. A silken noise of breath and movement, spirit and flesh.

During her solo, my thighs trembled as I watched her fingers slide over the violin's strings, imagining them on me, inside me. In the sea of dark clothes and pale faces, she stood out in her tuxedo, elegant and ramrod straight in her chair, her mouth hard with concentration. When the show ended, her features softened and became human again.

I'd seen her before, once, at a party in New York. Back then her hair was shorter and she hadn't yet made it as far as the Philharmonic. I had been too intimidated by her striking looks to even so much as introduce myself. That night I was content to drift around the room, watching her. And now she was here in my sleepy Florida town, quaking my insides just like she did five years ago.

After the concert, I walked out of the symphony hall and left my friends behind, pleading an early morning appointment. The truth was that I wanted a moment alone to savor

Zoya's beautiful music that was still singing in my head. It didn't matter that it was raining and I hadn't brought a thing to cover myself with. My short Afro wouldn't wilt in the rain.

I stood on the rain-splashed steps of the symphony hall staring at the misted cityscape, remembering the tilt of Zoya's head under the house lights, the smiling curve of her mouth when the applause came.

"Are you waiting for someone?"

She appeared around the soaring Roman column, her fingers trailing along its textured surface. When our eyes met, her hand stilled on the marble. She was smiling. Rain fell around her like diamonds, splashing against her tuxedo jacket.

"I saw you in the audience." She stepped closer, pulling her hair free of its black silk ribbon. The thick mass of dreads spilled down her shoulders and back in a cascade of reds, browns, and golds. She slid the ribbon into her pocket. "I'm Zoya."

"Rhiannon." I offered my hand to shake but she kissed it instead, brushing her mouth lightly across my knuckles. A slow, steady pulse began to drum between my thighs.

"So, Rhiannon, what are you doing all alone out here in the rain?" Her voice was low and deep. "Isn't it dangerous for you to be hanging outside this place so late at night?"

"Not at all. The most dangerous thing that could happen to me around here would be a drive-by flower delivery. Meadowlark is a peaceful town." I shrugged. "Anyway, the music inside was so perfect, I didn't want to ruin it by going off somewhere noisy and spoil my afterglow."

Zoya chuckled. "You definitely wouldn't want to do that."

She was still as charming as ever, just as desirable. Only

this time I was the one being watched—my face, my neck, the tightening of my nipples against the red silk blouse in the warm August night. Her eyes searched my face again.

"Would you like to come back into the hall and share a meal with me? To prolong your musical experience?"

Although I'd already eaten dinner barely two hours before, I didn't have to think about it. My body loosened in response to her words, saying yes for me. "Of course. It would be a pleasure."

She swept her hand before her, inviting me to walk ahead.

"I don't know where I'm going," I said.

"There's a back door straight ahead and to the left."

As I walked in front of her I could feel her eyes on me, following the shift of my ass under the black skirt. At the door, we stopped for her to put in an electronic code. Her arm brushed my breast and her scent, of sandalwood and lavender, overwhelmed me. In the cool hallway, she pointed out the small treasures that the symphony hall had on its wood-lined walls. Black-and-white photos of the Alvin Ailey Dance troupe, of Marion Anderson, and Maria Tallchief, the Osage ballerina. An antique Stradivarius violin gleamed in the light from its thick glass case mounted high on the wall, beautiful and untouchable.

"There's an old picture of the Philharmonic somewhere around here too," she said with a dismissive wave.

The hallway spilled us into a thinning crowd of musicians. Some looked up as Zoya walked past, greeting her with wide smiles and the echo of her name among the clamor of them packing up to leave. I knew they would be back tomorrow evening for a final performance, before leaving Meadowlark for Sarasota and another crowd of impressionable, seducible women. We soon left the crowd behind for another hallway, one that was not as brightly lit, or as impressive, as the first.

"This is it."

Zoya led me into a small room. It was quiet, acoustically sound with bare walls and a smooth ceiling. In one corner next to a thin, iron-worked chair sat a violin, its wood glowing a deep cherry in the silk-lined case. A long fold of burgundy velvet was draped over a tall oval shape in the opposite corner and in the center of the room a covered dish waited. Beside it was an unopened bottle of water.

She gestured toward the dish. "My lonely meal that I would love for you to share with me."

Zoya took off her shoes and set them in the corner by the violin. I did the same. We sat on the floor, facing each other over her dinner—a bowl of chilled fruit and curried chicken salad sprinkled with cranberries and almond slivers. There was only one fork.

"Please, help yourself to whatever you want," she said, picking up the fork. "Although I would be more than happy to feed you."

I bit into a strawberry to hide my smile. We ate quietly together, exchanging long, flirtatious glances. She forked the exotically spiced salad into her mouth with an economy of movement, intent yet elegant.

"I've seen you before," she said after her more immediate hunger was satisfied.

"Yes, you have. New York. Five years ago. Mandla and Kai's party in the Village."

"Ah, I knew it. That was a long time ago. I'm surprised that you remember me."

I smiled around a bite of fruit. "You're not the forgettable type."

"Thank you." She smiled.

"You don't have anything to thank me for. Yet."

Her eyes widened in surprise, but she said nothing.

"Was that too bold of me?" I asked.

"Not at all, I like a woman who's not afraid to set the tone for the evening." She took a deep swallow of her water. "Can I tie you up?"

My skin quivered at her unexpected words. As I opened my mouth to answer, she held up her hand and laughed softly. "No, don't answer that."

I linked my fingers with hers. "But I want to." Her hand was hot and hard against mine.

A smile of surprised pleasure curved her mouth. Zoya pulled me against her. "Then allow me to thank you in advance."

She tasted of curry and cranberries, spice and tartness that seduced my tongue and made my pussy tingle. After a long moment, she released me and stood up. I pushed our unfinished meal to the side then turned as I heard the sound of the door being locked.

"Just in case," she said, dropping the key near her violin.

On the other side of the room, she dragged the thick swells of velvet away from the long oval shape it hid. It was a mirror.

"I don't like to see myself while I play, but for you I'll make an exception." She spread the fabric on the floor.

"Clothes on or off?" I asked, already with a hand on the top button of my blouse.

Her voice dropped lower. "Off, please."

I stripped off my blouse, allowing it to drag over my already hard nipples. The skirt followed next, falling gracefully from my bare hips with the sound of a whisper.

A low noise came from Zoya. "Very nice." She cleared her throat. "On your knees for me, love. Now lean back on your elbows. Spread your legs. Wider, please." Zoya bit her bottom lip and smiled. "Perfect."

She pulled the black silk ribbon from her pocket. Up close I noticed that it wasn't silk but rather a piece of softened leather. She tied my wrists together then bound them to my ankles. The bonds were tight when I tried them, but not painful. In the mirror I could see myself curled backward on the burgundy velvet like a bow, breasts lifted and taut, body spread out like a prize for her, cunt hairs already wet.

"Comfortable?" Her face was beginning to harden, becoming that mask of concentration that I'd seen earlier on the stage. I knew a rhetorical question when I heard one. She brushed my belly with her fingertips.

"I'm sure you already know how beautiful you are," she said. "How fuckable. Your breasts, that sweet pussy that's wide open to me. I had no idea I'd be this lucky, not here, not with you." She took off her jacket and jerked her bow tie loose. "I do remember you from that party. Thought about that mousy little dress you had on, wondering what was hidden under all that cotton. Did you have panties on then? Could I have reached under your dress and touched your naked cunt? Maybe even invited you to a dark corner so I could fuck you with the dick I was packing? You seemed out of place there, and fresh. I wanted to get my hands on you then, wanted to do this."

Zoya touched my face, my trembling lips and throat, with their faint dusting of perfumed talc and sweat. The mirror reflected my body-shaking sigh of pleasure, the greedy widening of my legs. When it became too much to hold my head up, I let my neck fall back and drowned in the sensations she stirred in me. Her fingers drifted over my breasts, barely touching the aching peaks that begged for fuller contact. With a soft teasing laugh she licked my nipples. Her long pink tongue enfolded them, wet them, making me squirm against the velvet. She pulled my nipples deep into her mouth. Each suck sent a current of electricity bolting to my cunt.

"I like the noise you just made," she said.

Her fingers slid over my hip, down to cup my ass, then

slipped between. "But I like that one even better. I love to see you spread out like that for me. I wish you could see yourself, dripping and wet, pink like a conch shell. Do you know what you taste like?" She slid two fingers inside me. "Here, taste." The fingers hovered above my mouth, glistening.

I stretched my neck to lick her fingers. She touched my clit, rubbed it in slow circles. Already I was breathless, hot. I sucked her fingers into my mouth, its salt, its wet, its link to her other fingers pressing against and into me, fucking deep shuddering gasps from my body. Her mouth fed on my breasts again, suckling and licking in rhythm to her fingers inside me. My belly trembled and clenched.

"Not yet." She pulled away. My body hummed with frustration, tingling in her absence. "Don't worry. I won't leave you wanting."

Zoya quickly undressed then folded her clothes neatly over the chair near the violin. She wore white thong panties. Her body was well-made, strong with smooth rippling muscles in her belly, small dark-tipped breasts like up-turned teacups, and long runner's legs.

She dropped to her knees in front of me. "I've wanted a taste of you all night." Her hands cupped my hips. "Arch your back for me, baby. Put that pussy in my face."

She devoured me, her tongue sliding quickly and deeply inside, as if intent on licking every ounce of moisture from my cunt. I pushed myself against her face, trembling, wishing I could bury my hands in her hair and pull her closer and harder against me.

In the mirror I could see us, her head bent, lapping hungrily between my thighs, the high curve of her ass, her fingers slipping past the string of her white thong to fuck her own drenched pussy. She moaned against me, fucking me with her tongue. Her fingers squeezed and pulled at my nipple. Sweat dripped in hot rivulets down my breasts and throat.

The sounds of our playing were amplified in the room—the lap and slurp of her mouth on my pussy, my panting gasps, the muffled sound of her moans, even the wet slide of her fingers in her own cunt. They tilted me over the edge. I gasped her name, straining against the leather ties, jerking against her mouth. Still she wouldn't release me; instead she licked and sucked at my twitching pussy until she came in loud, breathless gasps.

Zoya slowly raised her head and began to kiss her way up my body, triggering delicious aftershocks all over my skin. While her deft fingers released my bonds she tasted my mouth again, sharing the flavor of my cunt. I groaned as my body uncurled from its awkward position and needles of returning sensation slid through me.

"Sorry." She kissed me again and lowered us to the velvet. "Is now the proper time to thank you?"

I laughed, stretching my body against the cloth. Lassitude invaded my limbs, making it difficult to move. "Absolutely. Play something for me."

"Of course." Zoya smiled and stood up to retrieve her instrument. She sat beside me with her legs tucked under her, beautifully naked with her long, varicolored dreads tumbling down her broad, powerful back. She leaned into the violin, her cheek caressing the glowing cherry wood like an attentive lover. Her fingers touched the bow, the bow touched the violin, and a little night music began to play.

Test Your Luck

CB Potts

"You change when you put that on, you know?" Marlee's eyes were barely open as she watched her lover button the front of her Tribal Police uniform.

Sesi's smile was quick, the arch of her smooth black eyebrow flirtatious. "Is that a good thing or a bad thing?"

"I'm not sure. You naked?" Marlee shut her eyes and grinned at the thought. "A very good thing."

"And me dressed?" The shirt was tucked in now, quick fingers working the heavy black belt.

One eye opened, slid slowly from her shoulders to her shins and back again. "The handcuffs are nice."

"Perv." Sesi turned toward the door. "I'm on till three. Catch you up later?"

Marlee smiled. "Unless the bingo bitches wear me out!"

In some parts, being part of the Tribal Police meant patrolling open countryside and breaking up domestic disputes. Not so here, not among the Akwesasne. If Sesi was going to run into trouble, there was only one place it was going to happen: the casino.

Tonight was no different. Some yahoo came up on the bus, dropped a cool five G at the tables, and had a meltdown when he lost it all. A few choice words from Sesi and Everett, her six-foot tall, 250-pound partner, had been enough to assuage that situation.

Then she'd had to have a little conversation with Susan, the reservation's wannabe whore.

"You need to go on home, Sue." Sesi had shouldered the teenager out of the casino after dispatch got an irate call from management. "It's not right, what you're trying to do."

"What? Find me a man? Get the hell out of this place?" Susan had been in rare form, spitting at Sesi's boots. "We can't all turn queer like you did."

"That's enough, Sue." Everett had stepped in. "Either start walking home or we're gonna have to bring you in for soliciting."

"Asshole." She started stomping away, sending gravel flying with every step. "You think she's gonna switch back, give it up for you?" The look she shot Sesi was pure hatred. "Not gonna happen. She likes rug munching too much."

They'd watched her go half a mile down the road before either spoke.

'Good thing," Everett replied. "Becky'd kick my ass I step out on her." His joke helped, but Sesi was still pissed.

"Fuckin' kids. Where the hell does she get off being like that?"

"I don't know. You wouldn't think you two were sisters."

"Half the time I don't think we are, either." Sesi turned on her heel, headed back to the patrol car. "Other half I know we're not."

The rest of the night slid by without incident. One local woman locked her keys in her car, and another needed to be persuaded that driving home was not the most brilliant idea she'd ever had, but it was nothing out of the ordinary.

And then trouble arrived.

A pair of them, on motorcycles. Bandanas and leather

jackets, boots and mirrored sunglasses, despite the fact that it was nearly midnight.

"Hoo boy," said Everett. "Looks like a couple of fun guys."

"Let's step inside with them," Sesi said. "Just to be a presence."

From the grateful glance they got from the floor manager, Sesi knew it had been a good idea. The biker boys weren't playing any slots, nor had they settled at one of the gaming tables. Instead, they were pacing the floor, obviously scoping for exits and the cashier's cage.

"They on?" Sesi asked her partner. Lots of hardcore drugs had come down via Quebec lately, cranking their users up to new levels of stupidity.

"I don't think so." Everett shook his head. "If they were, they would have done something by—"

The first shot came out of nowhere, catching Everett clean through the back, just below the ribcage.

"Everybody get down!" Sesi shouted the direction at the same time one of the bikers bellowed, an odd synchronicity that brought assailant and defender squarely into each other's sights.

"Freeze!" Sesi yelled. Everett was moaning at her feet, a thick crimson ribbon pooling out from his stomach.

"Young lady," a voice said from behind her, an ominous clicking in her ear sounding louder than any thunder she'd ever heard, "you're in no position to be giving orders."

"Fuck," she breathed, suddenly cold.

"Maybe later, darlin'. But right now, I want you to drop the gun."

Her service pistol clattered to the floor, near Everett's head. He wasn't moaning anymore, having moved rapidly onto rumbling, bubbly breaths.

"You and you,' the voice ordered, "go get the cash." The cold metal pressed against the side of Sesi's head, an O-ring of death next to her scalp. "Or you'll have to scrape Pocahontas here off the walls."

"Sesi."

"What?" The gunman leaned forward. "What did you say?"

"My name is Sesi. If you're gonna kill me, use my name."

"Sesi." It slid through the gunman's mouth, coming out dirty and soiled. "That's a pretty name."

Pretty enough to give me half a second, Sesi thought. Taking advantage of the gunman's momentary distraction, she dropped a shoulder, reached behind her, and pulled.

The gunman was big—nearly the size of Everett—but he was also completely surprised. He went sprawling onto the casino floor, one booted foot kicking her injured partner squarely in the head.

Sesi was on his back in a minute, her own recovered pistol pressed in the back of his neck.

"Don't fool yourself," she said. "I have absolutely no problem blowing your fucking head off right now." Underneath her, she could feel his muscles tensing, a motion that stopped when she cocked the pistol.

She looked up at the two astonished bikers. "Drop the bag or I kill your boss."

"Hands in the air!" Juala, one of the blackjack dealers, was pointing a rifle straight at the nearest biker. "I may not be as good a shot as her, but I'll still hit your skanky ass."

"Me too." Much to Sesi's astonishment, a tiny grandmother pulled a pearl-handled .38 Special out of her handbag. "This is the only place I go anymore and I'm not going to have you ruin it for me."

"Oh, yeah, Granny?" One of the bikers lurched toward

the old woman, nothing but crazy showing on his face. "We'll see about that!"

Time froze. In that split second, Sesi yanked her gun upward toward the threatening biker. Granny pulled the trigger. A violet-red bloom of spray erupted on the biker's upper left shoulder, resembling nothing more than a bizarre boutonnière. Another, larger spray resulted from Sesi's shot, dropping the biker in his tracks.

"Son of a bitch! You shot him!" There was no way the gunman was staying on his stomach now. He reared to his feet, sending Sesi flying. "I'm gonna kill you . . ."

His knee dissolved into bone fragments and pain.

"Not until you kill me first," Everett replied. "Not until then."

Sesi's next shot ensured that didn't happen.

The third biker dropped the bag and stood wide-eyed. "What the fuck?" he said. "This was supposed to be an easy off."

There was nothing easy about it, Sesi mused.

It was nearly dawn before Sesi could leave the station house, and well past dawn by the time she'd made it off the reservation to the trauma center, checked on Everett, and talked with his wife. He was going to make it, but the doctors wouldn't say much more than that. It wasn't until the noon fire bells were sounding that she made it back home. Marlee was waiting.

She'd heard everything, of course. Sesi could tell that half the town had been there, just from the new layers of tire tracks messing up their driveway.

"Don't start." Sesi held up one hand, begging for silence. "I'm too tired."

"Too dead is what you're gonna be, keep this shit up." Marlee pushed the door open. "Bath's waiting."

The water was still steaming hot. Sesi sank into it gratefully, leaning back against the cool curved edge of the tub. "This feels so good."

"Shut up and let me wash your hair." Marlee's hands were possessive on her shoulders. "I'm still mad at you."

"Baby, it's my job."

A long stream of hot water served as Marlee's reply, soaking into her scalp and cascading over her shoulders.

"I have to do it."

Clouds of bubbles, tinged faintly pink by the debris of the day, slid from her tresses.

"And . . ."

"And when you're gone," Marlee asked, voice breaking, but just barely, "what am I supposed to do then?"

Sesi closed her eyes. "I don't know. But it wasn't my time, this time."

"Barely."

"Everett . . ."

"Won't be around to be your partner no more." Marlee's grief was real. She loved Sesi's partner like a brother. "He'll be riding the desk, if he can come back at all. Who can you count on like that?"

"Only you."

Another flood of hot water, drowning out the need for words. "But is that enough?"

"It is for me," Sesi replied. She stood up and stepped out of the tub, dripping everywhere. "Always."

It was all in Marlee's kiss: all the anger, all the fear, all the sorrow and all the terror.

"I can't lose you." Her lips were soft against Sesi's neck.

"You won't." Promises buried in soft black hair, endearments given soul to soul. "You're part of me."

Breasts tightened, nipples rising to meet lips that needed

assurance. Smooth bellies flat against each other, thighs parting before demanding knees.

"Look at me." Sesi's eyes were wide. "I want you to see me."

Marlee looked back, eyes shining. "Don't leave me."

Fingers slid in, slick and knowing. "Here I am. Right here."

Hips rose to meet every thrust, rocking in time. "Here I am. Here I am." Their words joined, a chant, a magic between them, growing deeper and faster in time.

A dance of the fingers, a rub, a twist, a long, slow shudder. Sesi knew the road that had to be traveled, and raced along the trail.

"I have to taste you." Sesi slid downward, one hand still caught in Marlee's grasp. "Drink you dry."

"Here I am." Thighs spread wide, fresh juice glistening on the bronzed folds. "Here I am."

The first touch of her tongue was enough to push Marlee over again, but Sesi couldn't stop. She slurped and licked, teased and taunted some more. Fingers slid back inside, pushing deeper and deeper while thumbs drummed on the freely offered clitoris. Marlee gave it up a second time, thrashing on the sheets like a wild thing.

But Sesi didn't stop. A thing possessed, she plunged her tongue deep inside Marlee, slithering twin fingers up her rear passageway, determined to wring every bit of sensation out of her lover. Marlee's thighs closed tight round Sesi's head, pinning her in place while she panted through a third orgasm.

When her legs opened, she felt Sesi's fingers start to move again.

"Enough." Marlee's hand was soft on the back of Sesi's head. "Darlin', enough."

Sesi looked up, tears running down her face. "Is it enough? Enough for forever?"

She started shaking uncontrollably, long tremors rocking through her slender frame. "Because what if? What if . . ."

Marlee sat up, scooping Sesi in her arms. She'd seen enough shock in her day to know what was happening. "Enough. You stop that." She pushed Sesi's hair back from her face, settling the raven strands back into some semblance of their normal order. "That's not your job to worry. That's mine."

"But . . ."

"I said enough." There was no brooking that tone. "Close your eyes."

Sesi did. Sleep claimed her quickly, leaving Marlee to face the long afternoon alone. Or not, as the case may be, she thought, planting a tender kiss on the side of Sesi's face. At least not yet.

Grease

Isabelle Gray

My girlfriend calls me a grease monkey. She hates the fact that I'm a mechanic because the mess of the job offends her sensibilities. That she does my laundry might also have something to do with it. My boss, Gus, claims that he prefers cars to women, but only old cars—really old cars, because, in his words, you can't trust a car that doesn't need a carburetor. I work about fifteen miles out of town at an old-fashioned garage, because in many ways, I'm an old-fashioned girl. I can appreciate the instant gratification of say, Jiffy Lube, with the super clean garages and high-tech equipment and fancy computers and all, but I like the fact that I have to manually hoist a car up and slide under to work on her. The work is more honest and I sleep well at night knowing I do my part to put food on the table. I also sleep well knowing that Tia is lying next to me. Most people would call her abrasive, but I think of her as an acquired taste, like opera or sushi.

It is sticky hot today. Nebraska summers are like that—so hot that you have to put real effort into breathing, and your skin always feels thick and damp. I'm lying under a 1976 Jeep Wrangler that needs a new Pitman arm and an oil change. I'm sweating beneath my coveralls, and I can feel rivulets of sweat trailing between my breasts and down my thighs. It's a terrible feeling, but once I finish this car, I can go home. Gus called in today and decided he wouldn't be working. He does that sometimes, when he's too disgusted with life to leave his house. I regularly encourage Gus to leave his television off and avoid the newspaper at all costs, but he is ornery and willfully punishes himself by watching and reading things that will inevitably make him more cantankerous.

Tia is like that too. She doesn't like people, not even kids. Her job as a divorce lawyer requires that she immerse herself in the problems of other people, all day, every day. When she comes home, she often locks herself in our bedroom closet with nothing but her iPod, listening to La Bohème until she's regained enough sanity to deal with the rest of the evening. When I come home from work and find the closet door closed, I know that it's best to stay out of the bedroom altogether. I'll tinker around in the garage workshop, until she comes for me. When I get home and she's out of the closet—alas, she never sees the irony of her little ritual—she'll wait for me in the living room watching *Jeopardy* while she nurses a martini. It is her life's ambition to get on the show, and she has determined that the best way to practice is to watch the show as often as humanly possible. I find the whole thing irritating because I'd like to think of myself as smart but I can never make sense of the concept of answering a question or answer with a question, however it goes.

The best part about coming home most days is that I am immediately directed to the laundry room where Tia will undress me and sit on the washer, watching me wash the grease and grime from my hands before shuttling me off to the shower. Once I'm out of the shower, she greets me with a kiss and a Pepsi, and I sit on the kitchen counter while she makes dinner. Like I said, Tia is very much into rituals.

We met when she brought her car into my garage. The engine had started to make funny noises, as she put it, on her way back to Lincoln from Omaha. I was leaning against one of the gas pumps, reading a book on meditation, because I was going through a self-improvement phase. While Tia has rituals, I have phases. When she stepped out of the car I dropped my book, which sounds trite, unoriginal even, but that moment became my saving grace, because I had time to breathe while I leaned down to pick it up. When I stood up, I wiped my hands on my thighs, but my palms still felt sweaty. She stepped out of her car with such confidence, extending first one leg then the other, as if she was expecting a valet to take her hand and assist her. I turned my baseball cap around and smiled to little effect, so I shrugged and shoved my hands in my pockets. She looked around with a slight sneer on her face, and in that moment, as her upper lip curled slightly on the left side, I felt my heart pound and I knew that—okay, I'm not sure what I knew—but I knew something.

"My car's making a funny sound," she said.

I nodded, popped the hood, peering at the engine for an inordinate amount of time.

"Do you have any idea what you're doing?" she snapped, when she decided I was taking too long.

I quickly stood up, banging my head against the hood of the car. Wincing, I rubbed my head and grumbled, "Yeah, I know what I'm doing. Your fan belt is loose."

She leaned against the car, running her fingers through her hair. "Is that going to take long to fix?"

I leaned back under the hood. "No, just a minute. There, it's fixed," I finally said, stepping away from her car.

"What's the name of this place?"

"Gus's Garage."

"Catchy."

Again, I shrugged. My body didn't know what else to do.

"How much do I owe you?"

I shook my head. "This one is on the house." I slammed down the hood and returned to my book, pretending to be absorbed while eyeing her over the pages.

She paused, looking me up and down. "I thought that chick mechanics were only a thing of myth."

I looked up from my book. "Well, now you know."

"Mmm," she said, and got into her car, speeding back onto Highway 6.

The Jeep has clearly not had the oil changed in about ten thousand miles. I reach to my side and grab a drain pan, and watch as thick globs of oil slowly drip into the pan. I notice that my breathing matches the pace of the oil falling, thick and shallow. In a few hours, I'll be bathed in the cool of a controlled climate, so I wipe a few drops of sweat from my eyelids and continue working.

The second time Tia and I met, she called me at the garage. It only took me a few seconds to recognize her voice with its timbre and thick accent coloring her words.

"Do you remember me?" she asked.

"You're the loose fan belt."

"I wouldn't have put it in those words."

I blushed even though no one was around. "I often think in automotive speak."

"I wanted to thank you for helping me out."

"It was no problem, ma'am."

"I'm no ma'am."

"I'm sorry. It's the way I was raised."

"I see," she said again. "Can you come to dinner, this evening?"

I looked at my watch. "What time?"

"Make it seven, bring wine—good wine."

I mentally reviewed the rest of my day and decided I would cut out early. "I don't even know your name."

"Conchita Esperanza de la Fuera, but you can call me Tia."

"What a beautiful name," I said breathlessly.

After giving me her address, we hung up and I flopped into the rickety chair behind the only desk in the garage. It was only then that I realized she had never asked me my name.

I can't remember what all I did after that, but I was useless at work and Gus sent me home early. I showered slowly, taking extra time to clean behind my ears, under my fingernails. She seemed like a woman who would pay attention to such details. After picking up a bottle of red wine and a bottle of white, I showed up at her front door, my hair still wet, wearing a pair of loose linen slacks, a scoop-necked T-shirt, the fancy kind, and sandals. When Tia opened the door, I tripped backward, my face a flushed red. There she stood, one hand on her hip, wearing a red spaghetti-strapped top that ended just above her navel and a pair of matching silk boxers. As I regained my composure, I thrust the bottles of wine toward her, my eyes traveling down her brown thighs, muscled calves, dangerously attractive ankles, and pair of stiletto heels wrapped around her feet.

I stepped into the foyer and she closed the door, inspecting the wines.

"Good choices. Follow me."

I nodded, looking around as she led me to the kitchen where several pots sat in the sink. Dinner was already on a small Formica table with two chairs.

"I didn't feel like setting the dining room table, so we're eating in here."

"I usually eat on my couch."

She turned toward me, brushing her hand under my chin.

"So many rough edges, *querida*. What am I going to do about that?"

I smiled a little. "Whatever you want."

It feels thirty degrees hotter when you're underneath a car during the dog days of summer. Before finishing with the oil change, I shrug out of the top of my coveralls, relaxing slightly. I quickly clean the drain plug and replace it, using a torque wrench, one of my favorite toys. Sighing, I grip the outside of the filter housing and pull it off, grumbling as oil resting in it splashes across the front of my wifebeater. Humming to myself, I start rocking back and forth on the dolly. For some reason, I can't concentrate today. I keep thinking of Tia . . . Tia de la Fuera. I love saying her name, the way it rolls off my tongue with a slight vibration, as my lips part around each letter. Without realizing it, my hands have crawled under my T-shirt, easily sliding up my stomach, slick with sweat and now streaked with grease. My breath quickens, and I feel a light tingling dancing up my legs from my toes. As I begin brushing my thumbs across my nipples, I bite my tongue. I think of the curve of my woman's ass in the silk boxers she wore the second time we met. I think of her brown skin and her dark, shining eyes. I think of Tia de la Fuera.

To thank me properly, Tia prepared tamales and rice—authentic cuisine, she told me, and not that shit I would find at most restaurants around here. I opened the white wine with the bottle opener resting on the edge of the table. She served each of us while I filled our glasses, then sat, crossing her legs, one shoe dangling from her toes.

"I hope you like spicy food," she said, taking a bite of rice.

"The hotter the better."

"Oh," she replied, arching an eyebrow. She reached across to the counter and handed me a bottle of green hot sauce. I could already feel my stomach rumbling. "Try this," she said.

I took a sip of wine, and sprinkled my food with some of the sauce, smiling confidently as I swallowed a large forkful of rice. "Delicious, with or without the sauce."

She uncrossed her legs and leaned back in her chair. "What do you do when you're not fixing—*como se dice*—fan belts?"

My eyes began watering, and I took a swig of wine. What I thought was a slow burn had my tongue on fire, my pores wide open and filling with liquid heat. She laughed and handed me a glass of water that I gulped before handing it to her for more.

"The hotter the better, *querida*?"

As the burning subsided, I cleared my throat and boldly took another bite of the food. "I guess there are limits to how spicy I like it."

"We'll see."

I concentrated on my chewing, staring directly into her eyes, eyes that I couldn't begin to read.

"You make eye contact. I like that."

I swallowed. "My mother always told me that you can't trust someone who won't look you in the eyes."

"More of how you were raised?"

I grinned. "Yes ma'am."

"Can I trust you?"

"I'd like to think so," I said, carefully.

She stretched her right leg out, resting her foot between my thighs, lightly rocking her foot from side to side, before extending her leg a little farther, the stiletto heel I had admired earlier pressing through my slacks and dangerously close to my cunt. "That's good to know," she said huskily.

I smiled weakly, softly squeezing my thighs around her foot, nervously tapping my hands against the table. "You are a very good cook."

"Something I learned from *mi madre*—my mother."

She pressed her foot a little harder, a strange smile on her face. "Where are you from?"

I cracked my jaw, trying to make sense of a normal conversation mixed with the goings-on beneath the table. I inched forward, urging her on. "Around here, born and raised. You?"

"*Soy de Méjico.*"

"I was wondering. The accent, you know?"

She nodded, and we began an easy rhythm, her heel into my cunt, toe tapping against my clit, me inching closer and closer to the edge of my seat, my hands tapping furiously as we gave each other the digest versions of our lives. After explaining why she was in town, we became silent, and I could feel the crotch of my pants soaking, my frustration growing.

"Have I thanked you properly?"

I exhaled loudly. "I'd say so. No customer has ever cooked an entire meal for me."

"*Bueno*," she said, pulling her foot away.

I gripped the edge of the table and quickly crossed my legs, squeezing hard. "I guess I should be going," I said.

Tia stood, slowly walking around the table to where I sat. She leaned down, her hair tickling my face as she softly kissed the back of my neck. "That could be, but we haven't had dessert yet."

"There's more?" I asked, my voice cracking.

She began moving her tongue in tiny circles from the back of my neck to the underside of my earlobe. "There's always more *en mi casa*."

I pushed my barely touched plate away and pulled her onto my lap, my hands resting lightly around her waist. It was a perfect fit and I could feel her body humming against my skin. "Good thing I left room."

She ran her fingers through my hair, clenching them into a fist, roughly pulling my head to the side. Ever so slowly, she began running the tip of her tongue along the soft lines of my ear. I slid one hand to the flat of her stomach, just below her navel and above the waistline of her boxers, dragging my fingernails back and forth. I could feel the warmth of her breath, and I shivered. Then she stopped, and I sat perfectly still, waiting.

She stood and took my hand. "Come."

I couldn't help myself. I giggled, but she turned, shooting me a look that quickly made my laughter disappear. She led me up a small staircase to her bedroom, and standing behind me, she hooked her arms under my armpits, the palms of her hands against my shoulders.

"I don't normally do this on a first date," I stuttered.

"*Silencio*. Neither do I."

Her hands slid down my chest, briefly over my breasts to the hem, then under and back up, as she pulled my shirt over my head and off. She tossed the shirt somewhere behind her, and I felt her teeth grazing across my bare back, softly at first, but then rough, deep biting that made me inhale sharply and hold my breath. I reached back and slid my hands past her thighs to her ass, holding her tightly against me. Again, she kissed the back of my neck and slowly ran her tongue along my spine to just above my ass, kneeling as she unbuttoned my slacks. I quickly kicked off my sandals and stepped out of my pants. I tried to turn around but she forced me forward, slowly standing up, her tongue circling back up my spine.

"I want to see you," I whispered.

Quickly, she slid around me, and placed the tip of her finger beneath my chin, pulling my mouth toward her. Parting my lips softly, I brushed them across hers, running the tip of my tongue along the exquisitely soft surface of her inner lip, as I helped her shrug out of her camisole. Placing the palms of my hands against her cheeks, I pressed my forehead against hers, and closed my eyes. Her hands slid around my waist, pulling me closer to her yet, so close that I could feel no space between our bodies.

"Give me this moment," I pleaded.

The muscles in her shoulders relaxed. I covered her mouth with mine once again, kissing her so slowly and so hard that our lips barely moved. Her tongue darted into my mouth and I could feel it running along the ridges on the roof my mouth. In that instant, I wanted to swallow her into my body; feel her skin become a part of mine. As our bodies started to move as one, I thought, also in that instant, that maybe she wanted the very same thing. Pulling away, just a little bit, I planted my lips against the dark hollow of her throat and started sliding down her body, leaving butterfly kisses between her breasts, around her navel, and along the waistline of her shorts. Carefully, I slid my fingers under the waistband and inched her shorts down, letting them rest around her ankles. I tried to move forward, to rub my cheek against the soft patch of hair between her thighs, but she pushed me away and crawled backward onto her bed. I stood silently, staring at her, trying to memorize every inch of her skin: the fading scar just above her left shoulder, the pattern of freckles on her upper thighs, another scar on her right knee cap, her breasts full, splayed to the sides, the mysterious darkness of her aureoles.

Tia leaned back on her elbows, parting her legs wide, sucking on one finger, before drawing a trail from her lips to her cunt. She nodded her head to the right and I sat on the edge of the bed, massaging her calves. Tia smiled and rolled onto her stomach, and I moved closer to her, kissing across her shoulders, and then lower. My body began trembling as I reached the small of her back, deep and arched. I stopped, letting my tongue memorize the taste of her flesh, clean and salty, almost tart. As I reached her ass, I placed my cheek to her skin, inhaling deeply, rubbing my face down her body to her ankles where I kissed the soft insides tenderly, tasting again clean, salt, and the bitterness of her cologne.

"Stop, *querida*," she said suddenly. "Lie on your back."

I placed a tender kiss on the backside of her left knee, and complied, flexing my toes nervously as I waited. She took her time, looking at every inch of my body. I held her gaze, feeling uncomfortable, yet enjoying this moment of vulnerability. Tia straddled my chest, her warm, damp thighs pressing against my breasts. She leaned down and my face was engulfed between her breasts. One at a time, she lowered her nipples into my mouth and I suckled eagerly, running my tongue over every tiny ridge and crease, enjoying the sensation of them growing harder and harder in my mouth. She pulled away and looked at me again, inching farther up my body, such that her cunt was close, but not close enough to my mouth. Raising my head, I stretched my tongue out, but she planted the palm of her hand against my forehead, pushing me back down to the bed.

"Do you want to smell it?" she asked.

"Yes. Yes."

"Do you want to taste it?"

I groaned softly, trying to pull her to my mouth, but she wrapped her other hand around one wrist, holding it to the bed.

"*Lo quieres?* Do you want to taste it?" she asked. There was a keen edge to her voice that made my back arch.

"Yes. *Si, lo quiero.*"

She thrust her hips forward, letting her cunt hair tickle the tip of my chin. "Stick out your tongue."

I took a deep breath, letting my tongue slide from between my lips. She crawled forward.

"Don't move."

I looked at her quizzically, but did as I was told. Tia lowered her clit to my tongue, slowly rocking her hips back and forth. I could feel my tongue quivering, ready to move, to taste, to please. My jaw muscles tingled, tiny beads of sweat trickling from my forehead and down my face. But I could smell her, and she reminded me of tequila and lime.

"Please," I gasped.

"Please what?"

"Please, let me taste you."

She pressed her cunt against my face, covering my nose and mouth. "Taste me."

I could feel my chest tightening, my cunt throbbing harder. She moved her arms behind her and began squeezing my nipples between her fingers. I thrust my body upward, struggling to breathe—or inhale Tia into me—or both. She raised herself just enough to let some air through.

"Lick me," she ordered.

I exhaled loudly, slowly drawing my tongue from her clit, along her pussy lips, to the well of wetness, sliding my tongue upward. She squeezed my nipples harder and I moaned, in pain, in pleasure. She was still silent, but her body was covered in sweat, her breathing slightly harsh, ragged.

"Stop."

I moaned, more frustrated than ever, the tip of my tongue trembling as I stopped, waiting for her next command. "You're driving me crazy," I muttered under my breath.

She laughed, cruelly. "I heard that. You want I should stop? We could wash the dishes instead, maybe clean the kitchen."

I felt a sharp twinge in my clit and I shook my head, my

cheeks brushing against her warm thighs. "This is where I want to be."

"I know, so hush."

I pressed my lips together and slowly uncurled my fingers, trying to relax.

Tia began moving her hips to a silent rhythm, a languorous circle around my face, letting her cunt barely brush against my skin. "Do you like the way I taste?"

"Yes," I answered, my voice cracking. "I love the way you taste."

Tia leaned back, moved her hand down my body, easily between my thighs, and parting my pussy lips slid the tip of one finger inside me. I gasped, clenching my thighs around her hand, but she pulled it away and sucked on her finger, staring down at me. "I like the way you taste, too," she whispered.

Placing her hands on either side of my forehead, she began grinding against my open mouth. "I want to feel your tongue," she said roughly.

For a moment, I resisted, pursing my lips shut.

"Please, *querida*. Let me feel your tongue."

Giving into the demands of her body, I began flicking my tongue against her clit, her lips, sliding my tongue inside her cunt each time she thrust upward. I felt overwhelmed by her. As she thrust harder, I just knew I would drown. And then she flung herself backward, still riding my mouth as one hand fumbled for my clit, frantically stroking me apace with the strokes of my tongue. I could feel my legs almost convulsing, as if they no longer belonged to my body. The throbbing between my thighs was almost unbearable and too quickly, I saw myself nearing the edge. Unable to control myself, I came, crossing one leg over the other, trapping her hand against me. I grabbed her ass, holding her cunt to my mouth as I flipped our bodies and eased us farther down the bed. She moaned loudly, and didn't bother resisting, spreading her thighs wide, the arches of her feet planted against my shoulders. My cunt still tingling, I began grinding into the bed as I slid one, two, three fingers easily inside her. For a moment, I stilled, enjoying the slick, tight heat of her cunt wrapped around my fingers.

"Don't stop," she panted. "*Por favor*, don't stop."

Very slowly and lightly I ran my tongue over her clit, as my fingers moved deeper and deeper into her pussy with each thrust. I prayed that she wouldn't come. I wanted this to last forever, in case we never made love again. I could feel the muscles of her thighs straining against me, her back arching further, and I begin moving my tongue, my fingers, my entire body, faster and harder, until we became seamless.

"I'm coming!" she shrieked, as a hot spurt of cream slid around my fingers. I kept licking her clit until I felt her hand on my forehead pushing me away. Rolling onto my side, I tried to catch my breath, enjoying the sight of her body tense, quaking. I pulled my fingers from her pussy and ran them up her body, gently sliding them between her lips. She sucked them eagerly, nipping my fingertips with her teeth.

"Come here," she said softly, and I crawled up the bed, lying next to her awkwardly.

"Come closer."

I inched closer, resting my head against her armpit. She kissed my forehead and wrapped one leg around me. She dragged her fingers across my lips, then from my forehead and down my face. "What should we have for breakfast?" she asked.

Staring into the darkness, I smiled.

•

My eyes are closed, the Jeep temporarily forgotten. One hand is squeezing my nipples, as I stroke my clit hard, enjoying the sound of my moans echoing against the garage's cement floor. I don't care who sees or hears. When I get home, I'll have to explain the grease stains on my body. I can't wait because Tia de la Fuera is there, waiting for me.

Mandy

Jolene Hui

I stared at Mandy's skin from across the room. Her wavy reddish black hair was pulled back in a ponytail, a few strands falling across her forehead. She was dressed in a black button-up shirt and gray slacks and smelled sweetly of vanilla. She never wore jewelry, but when she read, she'd put on black-rimmed glasses that made her look like an art dealer. Her father was Mexican, so she had that tinge of bronze to her skin that made her look kissed by the sun, even in the darkest winter.

Half-Chinese, my skin was also tinged with something cinnamon. My hair was straight and silky like my Chinese mother's, but auburn like my white father's. I loved it when women had wavy hair: just enough body to bounce when it's let down. I wasn't born with those genes and in return, I was attracted to women who were.

Mandy and I had been working together for three months now. I had recently been transferred to this particular branch of the company and she had been working here for two years. We sat in the administrative room with three other women in the small office. Luckily, there were no cubicle walls in my way. I could stare at Mandy all day. I loved the way she played with her sleeves when she got in a heated discussion on the phone, or how every so often, another strand would fall from her ponytail. I nearly got lost in her plump lips every day.

I had been alone now for over a year. My girlfriend Clea had decided to leave me for a man. She was twenty-five and had never been with a man and when she met this particular one, a real estate broker with a Rolex, she claimed to have fallen madly in love with him. Clea had been my only girlfriend. I was a late bloomer, unable to open up to anyone until I was in college. Clea, two years my senior, was teaching a course on the New Testament to complete her Master's degree. I took it and fell immediately in love. Her wavy blonde hair mesmerized me, her high heels made her long thin legs look even longer and stronger, and her muscles were defined just enough to leave my heart in constant pitter pat mode. My mother threw a fit when we started seeing each other. "She's blonde," she said, pursing her lips.

"So, you had me with a white guy, Mom. What's the problem?"

My mother, always judgmental like most older traditional Chinese women, just shook her head and walked away.

The long hair, the experience, and those legs—I had idolized Clea. And I hadn't been brave enough to start something new since her. I felt meek in my body and unsure of myself and my own emotions. Did I even want to be with someone again?

"Can I borrow your stapler, Nat?" I snapped back into reality. Mandy was standing in front of me. All thoughts of Clea disintegrated and I was completely immersed in all of Mandy.

"Oh," I stuttered, "of course." I searched around under the piles on my desk. Amongst the chaos, I found it, fished it out, and handed it to Mandy.

I felt like I couldn't breathe. After I handed it to her, she gave me a dimpled smile. "Thanks." Her sexy rough voice floated through the air as she spun around and walked back to her desk.

It was only three o'clock. I had two more hours of torture until I went back to my lonely apartment.

The phone rang at seven that night while I was doing my Pilates video. It was Tammy from work.

"Hey Nat, the girls are planning a happy hour get together tomorrow night." She always sounded perky. "You game?"

My hair was sticking to my back and I didn't feel like going out with a bunch of perky women. "I dunno," I said. "Who's going?"

"Oh, the usual group. Terry, Linda, Pamela, and Mandy."

I sucked in my breath. "Oh, um . . . Okay." My mind blanked.

"Well, you don't have to RSVP or anything," she said. "It's more of a casual get together for the single girls in the office."

"We'll see. I'll see you tomorrow." I hung up as my heart raced.

I'd gone to happy hour with the girls at work before, but not this group of girls. Not this group that included Mandy.

I searched frantically through my closet that night, to find exactly what to wear on such a special day. It was Friday so we were allowed to wear jeans, but I didn't want to look like a slob. I found the perfect pair of dark jeans. I'd wear my sexy black boots and a cute little black sweater I'd wanted to wear for a year since I bought it. I had to remember to do my makeup accordingly. I'd have to remember to use heavy black eyeliner for sexy, sultry eyes. My hair, though, being so straight, was hopeless.

When I walked into work the next day my heart was pounding. Papers were still strewn haphazardly across the top of my desk. I had three sticky notes from my boss stuck to my keyboard and my voice mail light was blinking.

"I'm already ready for Happy Hour," announced Terry from across the room.

"Me too," Linda chimed in.

I was too busy trying to make sense of my mess to even agree or disagree. It was nearly eleven when I looked at my clock after accomplishing my morning tasks. Mandy was sitting quietly at her desk, flipping through an atlas. She must have been making travel plans for her boss. If I wasn't such a frightened child, I would have been able to make some sort of conversation with her.

"Did you want your stapler back?" I jumped as Mandy's voice woke me from my usual work/daydream/zombie-like state.

"Yeah, that would be great."

"Well, do you wanna come get it or what?" She seemed irritated and I felt like an idiot. Or maybe she just sounded tough, like she tended to do sometimes.

Standing up, I walked over to her desk, wobbly in my sexy black heels.

"You could have just asked for it instead of staring over here at me." She plopped it into my hand.

Blood rushed to my cheeks until it felt like my skin was burning off.

I couldn't even say anything. I just turned and walked away. She had to have been kidding. And I didn't realize I was staring severely at her.

Between the phones ringing and my boss constantly paging me, I was busy the rest of the afternoon. When the clock hit five and all of the other girls were digging around in their purses for their keys, I was trying to finish up one last project.

"Girls, it's Friday and it's five!" yelled Tammy. "Abandon

all projects and hurry up and get your asses up and outta here!"

"I have one last thing to finish up." My desk was no longer a disaster.

"I'm coming, I'm coming," said Mandy. "I think I'm going to have to stay an extra few minutes. I'll meet you there."

She was still working? The other girls left and I tried to ignore that Mandy and I were the only ones left in the room. I had spent countless hours over the past few months trying to figure out if she was seeing anyone. I was pretty sure she was a lesbian, but I didn't know for certain.

I turned my computer off and picked up my bag. Mandy was doing the same.

"Long day?" I questioned her.

"Oh god, I don't even want to talk about it." She slung her bag over her shoulder and we made small talk as we went out to our cars.

When we got to the restaurant we immediately spotted the girls.

"Hey, over here!" Tammy waved us over. They were already sipping on some kind of girly drinks. Mandy was at the bar before I could blink.

"There are so many hotties at this bar," said one of the girls. I looked around. It was mostly a male crowd, or middle-aged women with hair styled like my mother's.

Mandy returned and plopped a beer in front of me. "Thanks," I said.

She winked at me.

The next couple of hours were a blur. Shots here. Shots there. Winks here. Winks there. My Asian heritage was showing itself full force. My face was hot and red and my heart was pounding. We'd gone through plates of nachos, potato skins, and everything else you could think of to eat in a bar. We'd even dipped into the peanuts.

While getting a martini, Tammy started talking to a well-groomed guy sitting alone. The other two chicks, well, besides Mandy, went to mingle with a group of men standing in the corner of the bar area. I nibbled on a peanut and sucked on my fifth beer.

"So you're not gonna go talk to those guys?" Mandy was staring at me with her big brown eyes.

"Me?"

"Yeah, you. You're a cute girl. Why not?"

The whole situation was surreal to me. "Not my scene," I said.

"Not mine either," she said.

She sat down on a stool next to me. I could see her soft skin close up and her eyebrows where they needed to be plucked. They looked so seemingly perfect from across our office, but close up, I noticed her small, yet cute flaws.

"This is definitely not my scene," she said. "I hate this whole meeting in bars thing."

"Me, too," I said, making sure she knew that it wasn't the only thing I meant. "And the men. They aren't my scene either."

Slowly, she turned her head to me and tilted it in a question. She scrunched up her nose and asked, "Oh, you mean, the men really aren't your scene?"

"That's what I said." My confidence started to rise in my drunken state of mind.

"What is your scene?" Her large dark eyes moved closer to me.

I decided to play her game and move closer. "Not men."

She laughed her deep laugh that came from her tight stomach.

"What's so funny?"

"Are you trying to be sexy with me?"

"Maybe," I said, backing up and starting to feel silly.

"Well, how about this." She touched my knee "How about we take a cab and go back to my place. Would that be your scene?"

My jaw must have dropped embarrassingly to the floor.

"Sure, let's get out of here." My heart was pounding in my eyes. It was just last night I was picking out clothes to impress this girl, and it was very likely that she'd be taking them off tonight. We left the bar and got into a cab.

"So, Nat, why haven't we ever really gotten to know one another?"

"I've just never thought of work as the place to get to know people in."

"But we're neighbors. I borrowed your stapler. Haven't you ever been curious to meet me?"

Arrogance slightly irritated me. "Weren't you ever interested in getting to know me?"

"I just thought you were a prude little Asian."

"Fuck you." I was sick of people saying that to me all of my life. I turned and faced the window.

"Whoa now." I could feel Mandy scooting up closer to me. "You don't need to get all offended. I apologize. I should have gotten to know you."

I ignored her and looked out the window.

"Oh come on, you're gonna ignore me? I went out on a limb and invited you back to my place and you're gonna ignore me?" She was leaning in even closer. I could feel her breath on my neck. Sense her perfect mouth next to my face. My breath started to steam up the window as she leaned in closer to me. The beers, along with Mandy's creamy vanilla scent, were making my senses go crazy. Her lips were so close I was near fainting. When I felt them on my neck, I gasped. They were so soft, just like I fantasized they would be. She explored the back of my neck as I moaned. I wanted her to tear my clothes off and rub her lips all over my body. But it wasn't going to happen in a cab.

"How far away is your place?" I whispered.

"We're almost there."

Her fingertips were crawling up my back; my flesh tingled from her touch. The cab stopped. Mandy quickly pulled away and dug in her purse to pay the driver. I was too dizzy to know what to do next, but I found the door handle and stumbled out onto the street. Her condo seemed miles away as I followed her up the stairs. She didn't say much, but she hurried in what I hoped was anticipation. I, surprisingly, made it up the stairs without falling. I'd only ever been with Clea and had never been attracted to someone like I was to Mandy. There was something too fragile about Clea and Mandy exerted so much of everything that Clea wasn't.

We reached the door and Mandy smiled and grabbed my hand as she pulled me through the doorway. I couldn't really see her condo as it was pretty dark, but she led me into the living room from the entryway. The living room had leather furniture and a television. I could barely make out art on the walls. My eyes were still trying to adjust. The couch was soft and cold. She had me down on it right after we entered the room. Without saying anything, she pulled my sweater over my head and kissed my stomach and breasts. I pulled the rubber band from her head to loosen her beautiful dark hair. I was so lost in the moment, I didn't even think about what I was doing. I pulled her face up to mine and kissed her. I had no idea that her lips would feel so perfect on mine. So I plunged my tongue into her mouth and sucked on her soft lips until I needed more.

We rolled onto the floor and I frantically unbuttoned her shirt. Our bras were off almost immediately. The rest followed in a flash. I hadn't seen the rug on her floor when we walked in. It was slightly rough but felt good on my skin as we touched each other. She had me on my back almost instantaneously, my legs spread. Starting at my chin, she kissed a line of fire down my body until she got to my pussy. With her moist lips she kissed and sucked until I was moaning so loudly I slapped one of my own hands across my mouth.

I breathed her name, "Mandy," as she licked my clit expertly. Her hands moved under my ass and she kissed my inner thighs. I could feel myself wanting her again.

"Mmmm, please." I pleaded with her to finish what she had started. I was almost at the point of losing control. Her tongue was on the inner folds of my thighs, licking up and down. My toes started to wiggle; I was on the brink of screaming in frustration when she put her lips on me again. It was just enough that my body tightened and released a thousand times, the come pouring out of me and onto her lips. I screamed not in frustration this time, but in release.

I looked down and met her eyes in a tight gaze. Her lips were soaking with my come and turned up in a smile. I could barely breathe or move, but I wanted to touch her. I wanted to feel her wet pussy on my fingers. I wanted to smell her on my fingers and my lips. I wanted to do for her what she had just done to me.

I met her lips with mine and we talked to each other for the first time since the cab.

"How was it?" she asked, and laughed in that throaty laugh of hers.

"I can't even explain it," I replied as she tried to push me back down. "Oh no," I said. "It's your turn."

"But . . ." She tried to protest but I pushed her gently to the ground.

"You don't want more?" she asked, trying to get up.

I wanted to touch her so badly I had to push her down by straddling her chest. "Just be quiet and let me do this."

I had the feeling that she liked to be dominant, but I wanted her to trust me for a minute. I stretched my body out on top of hers and kissed her neck. She relaxed and I continued kissing her face, moving down to her chest and her perfectly shaped breasts, then down her torso and to her thighs. Although I wanted to taste her, I wanted to touch her more. As I parted her, I was thrilled to feel she was already wet. She was silky, with neatly trimmed public hair, so that I could feel every part of her. I stroked her inner lips and then very gently touched her clit with my thumb. A small moan escaped from her and I stroked a little more aggressively. I wanted to feel her so I thrust my middle finger in her tight pussy as I continued to rub her. She was silky. I felt my pussy dripping again, running down my legs as I worked my fingers inside her. She grabbed my hand and rammed all of my fingers hard into her. I bit my lip in ecstasy as I felt her come all over my fingers. Her sweetness flowed over my hand and I reached down to touch myself as Mandy finished coming. A small spray of come squirted out of me and onto Mandy's leg as I pleasured myself. She immediately grabbed me by the hips with her strong arms and put me on top of her mouth. I came into her mouth as she dug her fingertips into my ass. I had never felt such pleasure in my life.

When I rolled off her mouth we were both silent.

My body had felt a release it had never felt before. I didn't know where this was going to lead, but I felt like I was out of my funk, finally. I turned my head to look at Mandy and she had a smile on her face. She said, "We probably shouldn't do this at work, huh?"

I smiled, threw my arm around her body, kissed her on the cheek, and buried my nose in her sweet vanilla-scented neck.

After the Door Closes

Terri Pray

"Gods, I'm glad to see the back of that crowd." Lisabeth locked the shop door and slumped down into the nearby chair. She let out a breath in a sharp puff and sent her carefully tended bangs upward, smiling as they floated back down into place. "They didn't let up, not once today."

"Business is good." Shayla closed out the cash register and turned her attention to her partner. Tall, olive skin, black hair that Shayla had spent many a time holding on to. Even from here she could smell the subtle scent Lisabeth preferred to wear. Nothing over powering, that wasn't the woman's style, just a hint of exotic fragrance that would tease the senses of a customer at the right moment. *Gods, what did I ever do to deserve a woman so beautiful?*

"It should be, with the hours we put into the place. I don't think we've made it home before midnight in the last six months."

"Point taken." Shayla ran her fingers through her close-cropped hair and turned to catch a glimpse of herself in the mirror. Blue-black skin, deep brown eyes, and full lips that Lisabeth loved to nibble on. Even after so many years together Shayla had never grown tired of the way the two women contrasted yet complemented each other so perfectly. "I never thought this place would take off so much."

"Your hair's almost ready to be cut again, love." Lisabeth pushed up from the chair and wrapped her arms about her lover's waist from behind, settling her chin on Shayla's shoulder.

"One of these days I'll let it grow out."

"Why? I love it like this." Lisabeth ran her fingers across Shayla's head, massaging at the scalp beneath. Just that touch was enough—a surge of heat raced through Shayla's body, nipples crinkled and hardened against the short T-shirt, her thighs clenched—and she was left fighting against the growing urge to thrust back into Lisabeth's groin.

"Gods, don't do this to me here."

"Why not, no one can see us. And we've earned a little down time. Once that door is closed what we do is our own affair."

Shayla pulled away. "No, not here. Not now. This is our work. What if someone looks in through the windows?"

"Then they get a free show. Come on, love. What do they expect to see? We sell sex toys for Christ's sake." Lisabeth grinned and followed Shayla back through the shop. "Alright, fine. I'll check the blinds and the doors. Everything is locked up tight but if you're going to be so frightened that someone will see us I'll double check everything. That work for you?"

"I'd still prefer to wait until we're home." She watched as her life mate walked around the shop and even went as far as to check the back door, which was always locked in a way that prevented people from entering through that door without a key, but could be pushed open in an emergency from the inside.

"Well I want you here and now," Lisabeth explained when she walked back into hearing rage. "Besides, there are a few spares in the new arrivals I feel like test driving." The wicked glint in Lisabeth's eyes turned Shayla's inner walls to liquid.

Bold Lisabeth, brazen Lisabeth. A woman with an evil streak a mile wide. Gods how so many people had them wrong. One look at Shayla's short hair and boyish-style clothing normally had them ready to assume that she was the assertive one in the relationship. With the soft skirts and long blouses, combined with her beautiful long hair, Lisabeth gave the impression, to those that did not know her, of a sweet romantic soul. Shit, she even blushed when she had to help a customer find something especially naughty. That Shayla normally took control in the shop added to that assumption, but once the doors were locked the roles reversed.

"I really don't think that we should be doing this." Shayla gave the locked door a long hard look. "I know they can't see us, not unless they peek under the edge of the blinds, but do we really want customers walking in tomorrow morning with the place smelling of sex?"

"That's why we have air fresheners. Besides, there won't be anything left by tomorrow, unless I make you leave some toys around unwashed that still smell of your sweet little cunt." Lisabeth opened one of the new boxes that had been kept behind the main counter. "Well look at this."

Shayla gawked at the monster her partner now held. It had to be at least nine inches long and double the thickness of a normal cock. "Gods, that would be almost like being fisted."

"Fun though. You squirm so prettily when I've got my fist inside your cunt. And the sounds you make. I could eat you alive during that."

"You've tried," Shayla murmured and shifted a little, trying not to let her embarrassment get the better of her. "Why do you do this to me?"

"Make you blush?"

"Yes." Even though the heat was hard to see in her cheeks there were always other signs. The way her mouth didn't want to form words, the fact that she couldn't meet Lisabeth's gaze head on, the pulse that stood out so prominently in her throat. Small signs to a stranger but they were loud blaring ones to the woman she loved.

"Because it makes you squirm and turns you into my sweet pet."

Shayla sucked in her bottom lip.

"Don't do that. You'll only start chewing on it and that's my job."

"Sorry." She lowered her gaze, half-watching Lisabeth through long dark lashes. Was there nothing she wouldn't do for this woman? This other half of her soul. They were so different, yet blended together made almost the perfect couple. Sure, they had their arguments, but once the balance was re-established between them it always worked out. Wasn't that how any good relationship worked?

"Are you going to strip off or do I have to find the box cutters and remove your clothing that way?"

"Oh gods, you wouldn't dare."

"Try me." Lisabeth grinned. "I think the tattered look might just suit you, though of course everyone could then see what a naughty little slut you are."

"Bitch," Shayla hissed and started to tug at her shirt.

"Yes, and you love me for it."

"Never denied that." Her jeans followed the shirt onto the floor.

"No bra, no panties. Oh I should spank you for that."

"Thought you liked me this way?" Shayla frowned and glanced down at the floor.

"I do, but I like spanking you as well."

"You like doing a lot of things to me."

"And with you." Lisabeth set the dildo down on the counter and closed the distance between them. Her soft hands wrapped about Shayla's neck, the long, free flowing folds of her skirt brushed against Shayla's legs in the moment before her lips claimed Shayla's.

Cloth brushed her bare skin; her nipples hardened further, heat built between her thighs leaving her clinging to Lisabeth as though her life depended upon it. With a soft groan she parted her lips, welcoming Lisabeth's probing, demanding tongue. The slender strip of hair that had been left over her mound threatened to soak through as her desire rippled through her inner walls. Her stomach shuddered then hardened, her breath caught in the back of her throat, the urge to rip at the clothing still covering her lover's body grew with each new heartbeat and still she managed to restrain herself.

Lisabeth set the pace, not her.

Never her.

Not something they could tell others about though. Not everyone would understand how someone who could be so strong could then submit. What did they know? Submission wasn't a weakness, it was a need, a part of her makeup, at least when it came to being with Lisabeth.

"Kneel. I want to feel that tongue of yours."

Shayla moved to her knees and lifted her gaze upward. Heat flushed over her lover's olive skin, her eyes widened, lips parted just a little, the shared taste of their kiss coating them.

"Taste me."

Shayla lifted the soft folds of the full gypsy-style skirt and raised it slowly along Lisabeth's toned thighs. No panties here either. Just endless legs and the tantalizing sight of a carefully trimmed patch of dark curls, and there, just where the line of her panties might have hidden it, the tiny scar from an operation long ago. Scars. Marks. Hidden faults. External flaws. They both had them. It didn't matter though, they were just signs of the lives they had lived and had shared for the past ten years.

She disappeared under the skirt, the soft folds closed about her head and the scent of her lover's arousal filled her being. All thoughts of someone else witnessing what they were doing vanished from her mind. Only the treasure that awaited her intimate caress beckoned her attention.

Shayla leaned in and licked softly over Lisabeth's inner thigh, kissing, nibbling, each contact granted her a fresh taste of her partner. She nudged a little closer, wrapping her hand about Lisabeth's thighs. Together they moved, just enough so that Lisabeth could lean back against the counter.

"I want your tongue. I want to feel it in me."

Shayla obliged. With a low moan she slipped between Lisabeth's thighs, licking along the length of the swollen lips, suckling them into her mouth until she could bear it no longer. She had to delve fully into that delicious female offering. Barely able to keep her own lusts under control she still managed to tease her tongue over Lisabeth's clit, circling it, licking as she savored the taste of the woman she loved.

"More." The word was muffled through the cloth, but she still heard it.

With one hand she parted Lisabeth's labia and slid her finger deep into the tight, clenching core. Slowly at first, her lips locked about the tight bud of Lisabeth's clit, she began to ease her finger in and out of the slick heat. She whimpered, her cunt rippled and tried to close on air, desperate to be filled, to know what it was like to squirm under Lisabeth's touch, but it wasn't her turn.

"Gods, more. I need more." Lisabeth groaned and leaned back farther against the counter, parting her thighs that little bit wider.

A second finger joined the first, the heat beneath the skirt almost more than Shayla could stand yet she continued. The taste, the sweet liquid musk urged her onward.

There, that spot, that small hidden place within Lisabeth's body. A shell-like curve within her walls. Just a touch, a brush, is all it needed.

Lisabeth gasped, arching forward into Shayla's mouth.

The trapped clit throbbed between her lips. Lisabeth's groans filled her ears, gasps for breath between each new wave of pleasure. She could control her love from down here—the right touch, a caress just so, and the dominant became the submissive. Shayla tried to shake off the image of how deep that control might run. No, she didn't want to be the one in charge after the door closed.

This was where she belonged. On her knees in front of the woman she loved. Where she could serve her, body, heart, and soul, but especially with her tongue and fingers.

Shayla tapped against that small curved spot, matching the rapid pace of her own heart beat. Each brief contact sent a new jolt through Lisabeth's hips, a fresh gasp or groan. She buried close, lapping at the small nub, pulling into her lips to roll it between them.

Liquid heat wrapped about her fingers, tight inner walls rippled and closed on the probing digits, a scream filled her senses as a pair of olive toned thighs closed about her head. Those sweet hips arched against her mouth. A flood of sheer liquid musk coated her tongue, and still she kept up the mix of pressure from within, combined with the caress from without.

"Mine." Lisabeth voiced a single word, her fingers tight on Shayla's shoulders through the skirt. Her thighs shook, breath coming in short, shuddering gasps. Her body didn't want to stay upright, but between the counter and the grip on Shayla she somehow managed it. "Gods, mine always."

Yours. She didn't want to voice the word, reluctant to lose even a hint of the taste of her lover. But her mind screamed the proclamation with every ounce of passion her heart laid claim to.

Who cared what others thought of their relationship. Once the door closed, once the world outside had been shut out, nothing else mattered but the love and pleasure they shared.

Lick 'Er License

Shanel Odum

I grab the frosted bottle from the crowded shelf behind me and pour a steady stream of Absolut Citron into the ice-filled tin shaker with exaggerated flair. In a single sweeping gesture, I garnish the chilled martini glass with a lime wedge and strain the pink cocktail with practiced precision. No matter how many times I repeat the carefully choreographed routine, I can't help but swallow a satisfied grin as the last drop trickles into the glass, gently kissing the rim. The girls know they can always count on this bartender to quench their thirst . . .

The club is throbbing. It's one in the morning and the party is reaching its climax. The reggaeton bassline erupts from the massive speakers, while the strobe lights slice through artificial fog with a pulsing rhythm that echoes the DJ's renderings. The sweat-slick dance floor is swelling with drenched, half-naked bodies and the Friday night partygoers are still pouring in.

The club may not have an official dress code but the young lesbian community seems to follow an implicit one. Butches and bois sport their usual weekend uniforms—white wifebeater or jersey, do-rag and baseball cap, jeans and sneaks. The ones with a little more dip in their swagger wouldn't be caught out there without a rubber hard-on nestled in the fold of their boxer briefs. The girly girls wear everything from curve-clinging hip huggers to micro minis, but seem to adhere to the basic essentials of femme wear—stilettos, cleavage, and a glossy pout.

All my regulars are here. I'll be the first to admit that my vice has taken its toll on my memory, so it's easier to remember my customers by the drinks they order. There's Henney (straight up)—kind of a gruff-voiced ball player, who always sports a perfectly gel-slicked ponytail. She swims in her oversized Sean Johns and camouflages her C-cups with the same sports bra she wore as a high school point guard. Her sexuality is claustrophobic—she wouldn't dare attempt to lock it in anybody's closet. Every week she parades her porn-star girlfriend, Midori (sour), around the bar with an ironclad grip and a watchful eye. Tonight, the XXX actress is perched on five-inch daggers, habitually flicking her pierced tongue like a python, and wearing the brand new gold sequin J-Lo dress Henney bought from Dr. J's for her earlier that day.

And of course there's 007, the veteran, crew cut lesbian who manages to slither her way into every girl party in New York City. You'll never catch her prowling without her shades and the only girls she manages to conquer are "carne fresca."

Fresh meat. These are the bi-curious or recently pledged lesbabies craving mentorship amongst their new sorority sisters. These are the chicks that flash their older sisters' IDs for admittance into our weekly carnal celebration. They roam in packs, cloaked in their newfound gayness, always overly adorned with rainbow accessories.

Tossing her weave over her glazed, bronze shoulders, Red Devil saunters over to my bar for a quick drink between sets. Her body glitter winks under the glare of the spotlights, and wads of sticky singles peak coyly from the edges of her bikini top and patent leather thong.

"Hola mami! Que linda," she gushes, seductively eying the heave of my breasts as they threaten to spill out of my black lace bustier. She loves how I flirt with masculine and feminine touches in my wardrobe. I usually flaunt my girls for the girls—I like to think it's better for tips—but I'll choose Durangos over Manolos any day. I'm pretty sure that my sheer Mac lip lacquer and the fact that I refuse to leave the house without tracing my eyelids with coal liner qualifies me as a lipstick lesbian, but high femme I am not. I'm more cheerleader than jock, but less sugar than spice.

I can definitely pass for hetero (my ex boy toys can attest to that) but always get a rush when a fellow lesbian gives me a subtle smirk on the train, sniffing out my sexuality like a canine cop. The unspoken recognition that our mouths water for the same female delicacies is like sharing a juicy secret.

Tonight, I offset my delicate lingerie top with army-issued fatigue pants, leather motorcycle gloves, and Chuck Taylor All Stars. My mane of untamed, corkscrew curls is swept into a wild, blonde "frohawk". It's obvious that I like to stand out in a crowd.

"Thanks, sexy," I purr. "You killed that last set. Keep moving like that and I might have to spend all my tips on a lap dance before the night is over." We share a wicked giggle as I instinctively start to mix her usual syrupy, crimson-colored concoction.

"Oh please, mami!" she gripes in a thick Cuban accent. "You know I've wanted to be your private dancer for months now."

Now, Red Devil looks undeniably tasty but I'm pretty sure Esquelita's premier go-go girl lusts after more dicks than dykes. One look at those French-tipped talons wrapped around her bottle of Poland Spring confirms what I already knew. Anyone who hopes to dip into me will have to clip the claws and cancel their weekly appointments with Ling Ling, the manicurist. I've sexed my share of experimental freaks and although I can't say I regret even one frenzied hump or inexperienced grope of my less than pristine past, these days I want someone who craves pussy as much as I do.

The Vitamin "E" that I popped earlier suddenly hit me with a rolling wave. I snatch up a stout bottle of Patron by its stubby neck and chill a shot of silver tequila to balance out my mounting high. I throw back my poison and embark on a mission to the little girls' room. The slimy film that covers the littered floor is a result of hours of bumping and grinding in an unventilated dungeon and makes for a precarious commute to the bathroom.

The cavernous washroom reeks of sex, all the mirrors are completely fogged up, even the walls are perspiring. A bloated security guard points his flashlight at one of the grimy stalls. "Smells like somebody's getting busy in the Champagne Room," he announces with a not-so-subtle wink as he passes me a smoking Dutch Masters. A quick pull is all the stimulus my inner voyeur needs to take over. Without a word, I slip into the next cubicle for a free peep show.

The pleasure-drenched whimpers turn me on immediately. The sounds are barely audible over Daddy Yankee's booming anthem but the desire is tangible. The lustful lullaby strokes me like a lover's tongue and I close my eyes for a second, savoring the aphrodisiac as it pumps through my veins. Then I cautiously step up onto the toilet seat and peer over the partition, trying to remain unnoticed by my naughty neighbors.

"Oi, Oi, Oi." My panties dampen.

I recognize Hypnotiq, the source of the intoxicating moans. She's bent over the toilet, one heel stabbing the tiled floor, the other cocked up on the ceramic bowl. Her head is bowed. I yearn for a glimpse of her expression, hidden by the dampened locks that cling to her cheeks. There she crouches, arms taut, fingers spread against the cold, graffiti-covered wall, dress gathered loosely around her winding hips. Her outstretched digits straddle the words IVETTE Y LETICIA—a lonely scrawling that remains a testament to another couple's long forgotten bliss.

"Ahhh, mami, right there."

Without thinking, I bury my trembling hand in my pants and slip it under my panties. My fingers dip into my wetness and slowly begin to orbit my clit. I can't even blink.

Thug Passion is in full glory standing behind her spread-eagled conquest, her fingers feverishly kneading the fleshy, heart-shaped vessel as it rocks into her. She slides the brim of her Yankee cap to the back and rips aside Hypnotiq's love-soaked thong to accommodate her strap-on. Then she grips her trembling "chichos" (love handles) for leverage and glides herself in deeper.

My breath quickens. My heart thumps. My fingers waltz faster. I begin to match their spastic rhythm.

Their dance is beautiful and organic, not some pseudo simulation of hetero sex. Passion's flexible rubber rod is more than a prosthetic limb; it's an extension of her tiny erection. She moans with such genuine urgency that you'd think her magic stick was covered with a web of nerve endings. If I didn't know from experience that she was actually being aroused by the suction of the rubber base against her clit, I would swear that Tinkerbell had worked some magic and turned it into a real, live dick.

Hypnotiq frantically grabs at the fabric of the Dickies behind her, hungry for deeper thrusts. Her swollen pussy lips devour the silicone dick, greedily sucking on it like it's a Twizzler. When Passion finds that sensitive, spongy nook, it triggers a roaring climax; she abandons her steady rhythm and begins to buck uncontrollably. I watch gap-jawed as the ecstasy seeps from her pores and drips down her face. Hypnotiq sighs deeply as her partner reluctantly withdrawals, leaving the juicy evidence of her orgasm still clinging to the shaft, regretful to say good-bye.

An impatient bang at my stall door interrupts my desperate attempt at self-stimulation and instantly snaps me back to reality. I snatch my hand from between my legs with a jerk and almost slip off the toilet. After avoiding a nasty spill, I try to collect myself and ease the frustration of my sexcapade's abrupt finale. My privates must be bright blue from all the unreleased excitement bubbling down south. I guiltily slink out of the stall and make my way through the crowded bathroom. This feels more like premature evacuation!

Outside, I wade through the sea of dancing bodies, my panties sloshing against my pussy with each step. As much as I want to finish what I started I've got to return to my thirsty customers. Little do they know I'm just as parched as they are—only I'm craving a sip of something that can't be served in a cup.

I'm so distracted that I bump right into my favorite patron, Red Stripe. My hand unintentionally brushes against her chest. My cheeks get warm.

"My bad," she says, looking down at my lingering touch with a wicked grin. "Where you been. You're the only one I want giving me a Screaming Orgasm."

My clit jumps.

She continues to nurse her bottle of Jamaican Lager while I start mixing the shot she just requested. I go a little heavy on the vanilla vodka and add just a few dashes of Kahlua, Amaretto, and Irish Cream. Then I shake the creamy potion a little harder than necessary, teasing my admirer with my milkshake.

"You'd better watch mixing those beers with this creamy shit," I warn her like any self-respecting drink slinger would.

"Don't worry," she jokes. "The one thing I know how to do right is lick 'er!"

I spring a leak.

"You're so corny," I say as I walk away, trying to ignore my sopping-wet panties.

A pretty, caramel dipped honey reaches into her change purse and waves a twenty for my attention.

"What can I get ya, hun?"

"What did you just serve that sexy bitch in the corner?" she demands. "Tell her that her next shot's on me."

"I believe she's got a Buttery Nipple," I answer. Or two.

"Um, um, um," she gushes, glaring at Red. "She looks like a butch Alicia Keys."

I couldn't argue with the aggressive vixen. Red is a Colombian cutie who turns her share of heads. Tonight she's wearing a cutoff T-shirt to show off her toned, tattoo-etched shoulders. Intricately woven cornrows snake over her scalp and down her back. Her tough exterior veils a surprisingly tender heart but she's nowhere near a hardcore butch. That's what I like about her. She doesn't get caught up in role playing or gender bending. She's just being herself—one sexy tomboy.

Her smoldering eyes squint when she smiles and are framed by endless, onyx lashes. Her full, pink mouth is punctuated with a dark beauty mark that sits perfectly between her right nostril and her upper lip. I can't help but imagine her thick, soft lips grazing my . . .

Red catches me staring. I nearly cream myself. Yup, she's definitely hot.

She accepts the drink and winks her appreciation from where she stands, but makes no move to approach her sexy suitor across the bar.

Good girl.

"Last call for alcohol," booms the DJ, sending a surge of people to me for one final libation.

Twenty minutes later, the post-party rubble is illuminated by the glaring house lights. Some of the women, not wanting to be remembered with frizzy hair and smudged makeup, scatter like roaches and run for cover in the darkness outside. Others linger, frantic to make at least one love connection. There's a small scuffle near the exit. It's most likely a feud between a couple of studs turning up the machismo to overcompensate for their lack of testosterone. I spot Thug Passion and Hypnotiq, the unknowing participants in my voyeuristic ménage à trois, walking out hand in hand, glowing with post-orgasmic bliss. My clit screams for attention.

I count my tips and wipe down the bar, absently watching the porno that's playing on the flat screen TV above me. Usually, the ooh's and ahh's of male-directed "lesbian" porn just don't do it for me. There's something about a bunch of silicone-stuffed cum guzzlers posing as dykes that's just not convincing. Reality is that real girl on girl sex is not always pretty. It can be clumsy, animalistic, even voracious but it's usually always sensual.

I can feel her eyes on me as I clean. They turn me on more than the naked women on the screen.

Eventually the club empties. Two hulks stand guard at the front door while my manager counts the night's profits in the office upstairs. A crew of Mexican busboys scurries around, sweeping up the party's aftermath. When they bring the last of the garbage bags out to the dumpster, Red and I are finally left alone.

I can't wait another second. I'm ravenous for her. I need to taste her smile, feel her lips against mine. I'm on her in an instant. Our lips embrace before we do and I swallow her with my kiss. She steals my breath. My eyes flutter shut.

She is delicious.

She pulls away for a moment and time stops. Her hand grabs my chin and steadies my gaze within an inch of hers. My mouth still waters for her tongue but she keeps me firmly where I am, letting my want grow with every shared breath we take until her exhales become my inhales. I try to press my face even closer to hers, but instead she holds strong and caresses the contours of my lips with the tips of her fingers.

My heart truly begins to ache and I don't mean that figuratively. I can actually feel a slow burn invading in my chest. I hurt with need.

When she finally breaks the spell, our kisses turn chaotic, desperate at times. Her hands are all over me and I still hunger for more of her touch. She grabs a handful of my mane and I can hear the tingle of the bobby pins as they hit the floor. I grasp her by the back of the neck to draw her closer and the heat between us blisters until her body fuses with mine.

Something flutters beneath my ribcage.

Red lifts me up onto the bar and tickles my collarbone with her tongue. I trace the lines of her tattoo with the tip of my tongue. She shudders. Then she nestles her head into the warmth of my breasts and reaches behind me to remove my top. Her teeth clink against the cold metal of my pierced nipples, sending a jolt to my groin.

I draw in a sharp breath through clenched teeth.

My pants can't come off fast enough. Frantically, she undoes my buckle, peels off my cargos, and drops my panties in a wet wad on the bar. My eyes snap open when she pauses and I see that she's frozen before me, basking in my nakedness. I'm powerless under her gaze.

"Please . . . don't stop," is all I can manage to choke out.

She's immediately drunk with the power that she has over me. Before I realize what is happening, she is reaching over the bar to grab the soda gun from its holster. She aims her weapon at my chest and squeezes the trigger until a trickle of cool water pours out. It washes down the valley of my breasts, swirls around my bellybutton and disappears where I wish her mouth was buried. Then she uses the soda to stimulate my clit, making my pelvis tilt upward to meet its effervescent rush.

A shiver rakes across my spine.

My seductress can read the impatience that contorts my face and body and takes a moment to savor it before abandoning her water gun and diving into my peach fuzz.

I thrash into her face.

She softly pinches my swollen lips together and slides her tongue between their supple folds. Then she blankets me with it, licking up and down—agonizingly slow at first and then lapping faster like a thirsty dog.

I whisper breathy encouragements.

With just the ball of her finger, she plays at the opening of my slit and then slaps at the wetness she collects there. With one hand she cradles my entire pussy and massages its clean-shaven confines. With the other she forms a tripod. She circles my tender knob with her thumb, fucks me with her middle finger, and grazes my asshole with her ring finger, all at the same time.

Shit . . .

Glistening with a rich glaze, my pussy puckers for her and invites her in deeper. She doesn't just pump in and out with rigid fingers; she massages its walls with fluid strokes, exploring. I feel her gesture for me to come closer while her fingers are still buried inside me—she's fondling my G spot with a familiar intensity, like she's been there before.

Red senses my urgency as the edge of an orgasm tickles my gut. My womb contracts and clamps tightly around her finger, anchoring its heavenly pose.

Fuck!

My cries ricochet through the club as I detonate. I'm left completely limp, quaking in the aftershocks of my orgasm.

My girlfriend scoops me up off the bar and gazes lovingly into my half-closed eyes. I melt into her arms. We've been in love for two years and still act like newlyweds.

"Thanks, baby," I tell her with a peck. She'd played out my bar fantasy perfectly.

"My pleasure," she says with a grin. "Now, come on. It's getting late. We've got to get home and feed our other kitty."

A Special Dessert

Winnie Jerome

"So what are your plans for Christmas, Christine?"

Shit! Is it that time of the year again? I glance at the calendar on my workstation, and yes indeed, it's mid-December. Good one there, Christine. And don't frown at the guy who asked you that question. Jim's new around here, so it's not like he'd know how touchy you are about it.

"I was going to spend it with my partner's mom and dad. We go there every year since I'm not really on speaking terms with my family."

Jim looks stunned. "You aren't?"

I try to avoid rolling my eyes. Why is it so hard for some people to understand that I just don't get along with my parents?

"Yeah," I reply. "My parents are traditional Chinese, so the fact that I'm going out with a Korean woman didn't go over well, to put it mildly."

"I can imagine," he says.

Nice thought, Jim. But you can't imagine it because you're not Asian. I'm sure you never experienced the narrow-minded shit that I did. Did your father rant to you about "racial purity" when you were in kindergarten? Probably not.

And that was only one of the things he did that confused

the hell out of me. Another was to freak whenever I had my friends over. I don't think that I connected the dots until the day I had my friend Cheryl over. My dad took me aside after she left and told me in no uncertain terms that she shouldn't come by again. When I asked him why, he told me that it "wasn't safe to leave her alone near the valuables."

I had just turned eight, so I pressed him for an explanation. He muttered something about how "those people always steal." I was stunned to hear this because Cheryl was African-American. I couldn't believe my ears, so I asked my mom if she liked Cheryl. My jaw almost dropped to the ground when I received a similar answer. It went against everything that I thought was right, and I realized at that moment that my parents were not perfect.

I started talking back to them after that, which didn't go over well. I was supposed to be an obedient daughter, and questioning them was not something they appreciated. I started earning the reputation of being the rebel, which was pretty funny considering that my report card always had a lot of A's.

By the time I hit my teen years, my flippant comments had become loud, daily fights. I probably would have exploded from stress if it hadn't been for my younger brother Steve.

I have five siblings—Steve and I are the middle children, born about two years apart. We wound up becoming the best of friends, since our other brothers and sisters were either much older or much younger than the two of us. We didn't have anyone else to talk to, especially since my parents didn't believe in discussing emotional issues.

And boy, did I have emotional issues. I had been branded as a nerd, so I didn't have much in the way of friends in high school. I was picked on a lot, and some "friends" turned around and made my life hell once it became obvious that their standing in the pecking order was threatened. This made me gun-shy about trusting anyone, and I valued the fact that I could talk about things with Steve.

Then I noticed that I didn't really have an interest in boys, and I went into extreme denial about that fact. Being a nerd was bad enough; if I was a lesbian on top of that, I would be relegated to the bottom of the social heap. I stayed in denial until my sophomore year in college. I had new friends at that point, and they supported and encouraged me when I started questioning my sexuality. I didn't come out of the closet to Steve, though. He had never expressed any anti-lesbian sentiment, but he also didn't have any friends who were queer. I probably would have kept him in the dark if I hadn't met Sarah and fallen in love with her.

My friends certainly didn't expect us to become a couple, because we don't seem to have anything in common. She was an art major; I received a B.S. in computer science. I'm a T-shirt-and-jeans person and couldn't give two shits about what I look like. Sarah is a bit of a clotheshorse and loves shopping. Her shoulder length hair is always fashionably cut; I only visit the hairdresser when my bangs are so overgrown that I can't see.

But that's just on the surface. We could both talk for hours about anything from politics to the latest plot twist on whatever show we're watching on TV. And she has a wicked sense of humor that I never get tired of. But the one thing I love most about her is how compassionate and caring she is.

That compassion was something I needed about six months after I met her. My parents came down to visit me, and decided to belittle me again over my choice of major. After a loud argument, my dad told me that since he was paying the bills, I was going to change my major to pre-med or he'd cut me off. In his mindset, only doctors made money; quality assurance engineers made nothing. There was no way

I was going to medical school. I screamed at him that he could go ahead and cut me the fuck off, because I was tired of his bullshit.

My parents stormed out after that, leaving me sobbing on the couch. And as if my day wasn't bad enough, my landlord called about an hour afterward to tell me that he was selling the house; I had thirty days to get out.

I went to Sarah after that. She held me until I felt like talking, and then we discussed my options. We finally decided to move in together, and I would see about getting a loan. I'm glad that Sarah was a student worker at the financial aid office; she was able to cut through the red tape for me.

Since I needed as much money as possible, I also decided to move ASAP so that I could get my deposit refunded. The next couple of months were hell as I turned my life upside down. I dropped off the face of the planet as far as my family was concerned. I couldn't be reached by phone, and I wasn't answering my e-mail. Steve worked on a hunch and sent a letter to my old address, hoping that it would get forwarded.

He knew about the argument, because my parents had bitched continuously about it after they came back home. But he was getting really worried about me, and wondered if I was all right. I felt a pang of guilt. Steve deserved to know.

I wrote him back, telling him that I was fine, and that I had moved in with my girlfriend. I left him with contact information before I went on for pages about how wonderful Sarah was, how supportive she had been, and our plans for the future. I asked him to not tell my parents, because they wouldn't understand. In retrospect, I probably should have e-mailed him instead, but electronic correspondence is very easy to fake. I wanted Steve to know that it was me and not some hacker. Steve handled all of the postal stuff, so I figured that he could intercept my message without my parents knowing about it.

Was I surprised when I received a piece of blistering hate mail from my parents about a week later. My dad insulted both me and Sarah, told me that I was a disappointment to my family, and demanded that I come home. I think I wilted in my chair after I read his hateful words. Sarah saw me crumpled up, and after she read what was in my hands, she rubbed my back until I had stopped shaking.

We couldn't figure out what had happened, but the mystery was solved about a week later when Steve called me. One of my sisters had spotted him reading my message, and they had told my parents. My parents grilled Steve, demanding to know what had happened to me. He had held out for a bit, but during one heated shouting match with them he "just let it slip out." He apologized profusely, telling me that he couldn't help himself.

I slammed the phone down on the cradle. I couldn't tell him how much it hurt to have him, of all people, betray me. It felt like a part of me had been ripped out and shredded. I guess all of our long talks about sticking together no matter what happened to each other was just lip service on his part.

That wasn't the last of it, though. My parents started sending me notes every month, convinced that Sarah had done something to me. Their outrageous accusations became so upsetting that the notes were tossed into the trash as soon as they arrived. Steve also began writing to me, since I was ignoring his phone calls. Sarah volunteered to screen anything that came in from him, since I couldn't handle his bullshit without getting pissed.

I can't put into words how grateful I was to have Sarah around. She helped me through all of it, being supportive whenever a new letter arrived, letting me cry on her shoulder, and helping me work things out. Steve had lost my trust, but Sarah had more than earned it.

And Sarah's parents were much more reasonable. They

were elated when Sarah first told them about me, and I was welcomed into their home with open arms. I love being around them, but when the holidays roll in, I tend to get a bit morose about how things turned out with my family.

I probably shouldn't go there; I still have a lot of work to do. I can see my manager in the distance, and I just push everything to the back of my mind so that I can concentrate on my work.

Looks like the universe decided that it wanted to shit on my head today. First, one of the developers basically told me I was full of it on a high priority bug. I spent the better part of an hour trying to convince him that he was duplicating it wrong. This thing has to get fixed; otherwise the software will hose the system. Then my manager told my team that our release schedule was shortened again, so I'm going to have to work sixteen-hour days pretty much up until Christmas Eve to make the deadline.

The only sort of good thing that happened this afternoon is that another developer broke the software that we were supposed to test tonight. He's not going to get it solved before tomorrow, so I can at least go home early. Of course, I still have about an hour drive back home. That's one of the things I hate most about commuting; I'll be tuckered out at the end of the day and I'll still have traffic to deal with. I managed to call Sarah before I left, and she promised to have dinner and dessert ready.

At least I'm home now. And the neighbor's dog didn't crap on the front lawn today. Things are looking up. I'm in a pretty good mood when I open up our mailbox, but then I see that I received a letter from Steve. Fuck! Looks like I spoke too soon.

I feel like there's a black cloud over my head when I open

the door. And I'm so out of it that I don't notice the delicious smell wafting out of the kitchen.

"You're home!" Sarah says. Moments later, she comes out and my heart skips a beat. I don't think I'll ever tire of looking at her, especially when she's wearing a nice pair of low-riders and a tight fitting baby tee. I'm enjoying that shirt even more when she hugs me and I don't feel a bra.

"Sorry that today was so shitty," she says. "I poured you a screwdriver to make up for it."

And now things are back on the upswing. Have I mentioned how much I love this woman? "Damn, what did I do to deserve this?" I ask after I kiss her.

"You're completely buff and could snap my skinny body in two?" she replies, trying to look innocent.

I try not to giggle. I had peasant ancestors, so I have football shoulders, a pretty broad chest, and I build muscle easily. On the other hand, my genes also gave me the capability to put on weight like mad, too. "Like you have to worry about that. Try again."

She taps a fingernail against her lips for a few moments before she replies. "Um . . . you're a big, bad engineer pulling down megabucks, and I'm just a freelance, Luddite graphic artist?"

"You're not that bad. You know which end of the computer is up. Try again."

Sarah lets out a loud snort. "I'm not that good."

"Look, when you lose connectivity, you actually bother to check the network cable. You're light years ahead of everyone else," I say as I walk into the kitchen to grab my drink.

Sarah follows me and pauses by the stove to check the food. She makes a satisfied grunt and takes the pans off the burners, letting everything cool before she dishes it out.

Once she's done, I toss the mail from Steve onto the counter. "I got this today."

She glances at the return address and sighs. "Hasn't he gotten the hint yet?"

"I don't really want to find out. Could you do the usual?"

She nods and opens the letter, and I just savor my drink while she reads it. After a few minutes, she makes a rude noise and tosses it into the recycling bin. "Nope. He's still clueless about his 'little slip'."

"Jesus Christ, he still calls it that?"

Sarah reaches over and wraps her arms around my neck. "As far as I can tell, he thinks that his actions were justified because your parents were worried sick about you."

I can feel my blood pressure rising when I hear this. "As if I didn't warn him about that. I wrote it out in black and white in my first letter."

Sarah touches my cheek and says, "And he still doesn't get it. Look, it's not worth the brain power to even think about him anymore." She picks up our dishes and gestures toward the dining room. "Why don't you concentrate on the fact that I slaved away over a hot stove to make you food?"

Her ploy works like a charm. If there's one guaranteed way to distract me, it's by appealing to my stomach. I plop down at the table and dig in, stuffing my face with enthusiasm. After a few bites, I start slowing down. Whenever I have a bad day, I try to burn it out afterward with spicy food. Don't ask me why, it just works for me; which is fine by Sarah, since she prefers food that would scorch the tiles off a space shuttle. And she knew that today was a shitter already, so I'm sure she's turned the intensity level up to ten. That's weird . . . everything's pretty wimpy. Either my tongue grew armor plating, or we ran out of chilies.

"Something the matter?" Sarah asks. "You're making a face."

"Uh . . . I was expecting to be sweating by now. Did you run out of stuff?"

"No. But that's because I was planning on something special for dessert." As she says this, her voice lowers to a sensuous purr, the one that just drips with pure sex.

I feel a rush of heat at her words. It always amazes me that she can look so innocent one minute and wicked as hell the next. I finish up as much as I can without getting too full; having an overstuffed stomach would put a damper on what she has in mind. After I'm done, she comes over and tugs me to my feet. I almost trip over myself, but once I'm upright, she cups my cheek and draws me in for a kiss.

Her lips brush across mine and I open for her, melting as her tongue slides across mine aggressively, telling me who's in control for the evening. I love it when she takes charge like this, knowing that I need to be freed from my responsibilities after a fucked up day.

My head is still spinning when she pulls back from me, and I bite my lip when I see that her eyes are almost black with lust. Her voice has deepened a touch when she speaks to me. "Get undressed while I'm cleaning up and wait for me on the bed."

I think I set records for the time it takes me to strip and lie down. Sarah takes her time before she appears, making me wait for what seems like an eternity. When she makes her entrance, she takes in every detail, letting her gaze linger on me. I shiver when her tongue flicks out and runs over her lips.

"Stay right there," she says before she reaches for the hem of her T-shirt. She pulls the garment off slowly, revealing the smooth planes of her stomach. My mouth waters when I see that her nipples have crinkled into tight points. She starts pinching them, looking right at me, while her other hand drifts down to pop the top button on her jeans. She pulls the zipper down tooth by tooth, smirking when I let out a groan of frustration. Her fingers tease the edge of her panties before she slips them underneath, letting out a soft cry.

Her eyelids flutter closed as she strokes herself, causing me to whimper in frustration. I know the rules—if I move, she'll punish me. And it won't be a punishment that I'll enjoy.

Not that Sarah's making this easy. She looks so decadent as she rubs her cunt, and the throaty sounds coming out of her are driving me insane. I can't figure out anything else to do, so I settle for gripping the sheets. I've almost dragged them off the mattress when she finally stops and peels off the last of her clothing.

"Good girl," she says before she walks over and pulls out our toy box. I watch as she retrieves a pair of leather cuffs. These are my favorites: instead of being joined with a chain, these have a D-ring attached to each side, so that you have more versatility. They can be fastened to each other; or each wrist can be clipped to something else.

Sarah puts the cuffs on me and checks that they're nice and snug, before she attaches one of my wrists to a sash located at the corner of the headboard. She pulls the other wrist to the opposite edge and repeats the process, binding me with arms spread apart.

Sarah admires her handiwork before she bends over and starts nibbling on the tender skin of my neck. I gasp at the contact, squirming as her teeth graze my sensitive spots. "Remember last month? When I worked on you for an hour before I finished you off?" she purrs.

My cheeks flush as I remember that night. She had teased me so much and kept me on the edge until I was ready to explode. She had decided to see how much I could take, and had managed to work in about four fingers.

She pulls open the drawer of the nightstand beside me, and her lips have curled into a smirk "I think you can do better than that," she says, pulling out a latex glove and some lube. "I think that I can put my entire hand into you."

A shiver travels through my body at her throaty words. "Oh, please," I reply, not caring at how needy I sound.

She gives my neck a quick nip before she disappears off into the master bathroom. When she comes back, she has a towel in her hands, and she coaxes me to lift my butt so that she can place it underneath my hips.

A wicked glint is in her eyes as she pulls the glove on, letting it snap loudly. The lube comes next, and she takes her time to smear it on the latex, making me start to vibrate in place.

"You never could wait," she chuckles before she sits down on the mattress at my feet. She nudges my legs apart and pushes her index finger inside. I clamp down in response, and she says, "And you're always so tight, I like that."

I give her a squeeze, whimpering as she pushes in and out. We're so familiar with each other that she knows exactly which spots to touch to reduce me into an incoherent mess. She rotates her hand so that she can rub my G spot, and I gasp as a shock travels through me. She keeps stroking that area until she works me into a frenzy, and I start grinding down on her hand, tugging on my cuffs in a silent plea for more. She notices and adds another finger, twisting both of them around. I arch up and curse, almost biting down on my lip because it feels so damn good.

Sarah slaps my ass and barks out, "You need to relax."

God-fucking-damn it, I'm on the verge of a total meltdown and she wants me to relax? I'm about to protest when she whacks my butt again.

"Do it," she says in a tone of voice that leaves no room for argument. I can still feel her fingers moving inside me, but I swing my focus away. It takes a huge amount of effort, but I manage to slow my breathing down, concentrating on each inhale and exhale.

I'm starting to float as the third finger goes in, and it's the oddest feeling. I can feel myself getting incredibly wet, but it's in the distance, almost like I'm an outside observer. There is some aching as she adds another, but the sensation doesn't really touch me. I let everything go, drifting as my body opens itself to her. Time seems to stand still while she continues to stretch me, twisting and flexing her fingers around with measured patience.

Reality snaps back into sharp focus when I feel a twinge of pain between my legs. "Almost there," Sarah says. "This is my thumb."

Shit, I must have really been out. My next thought disappears when Sarah pushes just the tip of her thumb in, causing me to spasm involuntarily. A tiny part of my brain is telling me that I've reached my limit, but I shut it up. I repeat to myself over and over again that I can do this, and I force myself to relax while she eases her thumb in. There's an almost painful stretch, and then it's over.

"You should see yourself," she says in a low voice. "Your cunt stretched around my knuckles, wet and glistening . . . so hot that it feels like you're scorching me."

I turn into a quivering heap of Jell-O at her filthy words, making a noise that sounds like a choked moan. Sarah laughs and says, "Yeah, you're enjoying this, you little slut."

I bob my head up and down with frantic motions, not speaking because I'm too turned on to say anything meaningful. Sarah is amused by my discomfort. She curls her mouth in an evil smile and growls, "Take it all."

I feel a huge amount of pressure in my cunt as she presses the wide part of her hand in. I try as hard as I can to relax, my nails digging into my palms as I'm being stretched to my breaking point.

Just when I think I can't take it anymore, she gives another push and she's in. I'm about to breathe a sigh of relief when something hits me like a freight train. Every nerve has come alive, and every inch of my skin feels like it's on fire. I scream, pushing down on her hand in a frantic quest for more.

Sarah slowly pumps her fist, and the room fades away. I lose track of everything, the jolts sizzling through my body are the center of my existence, building upon each other until I'm about to combust. I climb higher and higher, going completely light-headed as everything around me shoots upward at a dizzying pace, sending me flying just as the world shatters to pieces.

I'm still drifting while Sarah works her hand out at a snail's pace. It seems like an eternity before she reaches up to unbuckle the cuffs. My arms flop down and I slap my hand over my eyes, too buzzed to do anything other than lie there. There's a shift in weight on the mattress, and my hand is plucked off. Sarah's kneeling above my face, trembling with unfulfilled lust.

"Lick me," she says, before she lowers herself.

My head clears at that moment and I lap at her with enthusiasm, moaning when I feel her wetness against my mouth. She's soaked as hell, and it won't take much for her to lose it. I shift my position so that I can suck on her clit, alternating with rapid flicks of my tongue. I can feel Sarah trembling, so I ease a finger into her and start pumping. Every muscle in Sarah's body suddenly tenses, and then she throws her head back, crying out as she climaxes. I keep licking her as she rides out her orgasm, trying to keep myself from grinning like a madman.

"Ohhh," she groans before she flops over to the side, limp as a jellyfish. A few seconds later, she gets up, disposing of the glove and tossing the towel into the hamper before she returns to bed. I lean over and seal our lips together, letting my actions show her how much I appreciated everything.

She has a lazy grin on her face when we come up for air. "Now wasn't that a better endorphin rush than spicy food?"

"Oh, hell yes," I say as I cuddle up to her side.

"Sorry about not making your usual for dinner. I thought chili oil on my fingers would really hurt."

"I think I'll deal. Anything you decide on to get me out of a shitty-ass mood is fine." I kiss the tip of her nose. "Has anyone ever told you that you're the best thing ever?"

She smirks at me. "Yeah, the postal carrier did."

I growl at her and whap her with a pillow. Sarah rolls over and starts tickling me, keeping up the assault until I yell uncle. "So why do I put up with you again?" I manage to sit up and I try my best to glare at her.

My attempt to look scary is ruined when my bangs flop over my eyes. Sarah giggles before she brushes them out of my face. "Because you're pretty much stuck with me," she replies.

"You're anything but," I say as I kiss her again.

The Sound Inside

Jacqueline Applebee

There's an assumption about black women that Alicia is not comfortable with. There's a persistent stereotype that has travelled around the globe, and Great Britain seems to be no exception. It says she must be constantly sensual and exotic, have natural rhythm, and be able to sing like a pro. Alicia is often too self-conscious to warble out loud, except when she's in the bath. With the lights off.

The stereotype also states that she should only ever listen to "black music", whatever the hell that is this decade. Alicia is not and has never been into gospel, soul, reggae or rhythm and blues; her strict adopted parents would never let that music be played in their house anyway. No, Alicia is a folk junkie and that doesn't mean Old English songs about cider, tractors, and "one-eyed snakes." Alicia loves harmony; guitars without pick-ups that speak to her when played. She likes fiddles and pipes and wishes that someone could touch her the way she manipulates her old Irish tin-whistle, lying on the single bed back home.

She has her back turned when the music starts. It's not music of course; the band is just tuning up, practicing, yet it is the best thing she's heard in a long time. The band knows their stuff; even without trying they are great. She is romanced by a twelve-string, a resonant guitar, and a few interesting percussive instruments played by the talented threesome. Alicia sticks her ass out a little more and closes her eyes. She tries to let the music touch her.

The band is something of a phenomenon. They've only been going for a short while, but are already playing to small, packed out venues up and down the British Isles. That's why Alicia is here in an ancient cramped bar in Central London (replete with a polished wooden plaque on the wall, proudly stating 1634 AD), waiting for the gig to start, awkwardly trying to ignore the red-nosed woman opposite, hunched over a pint of beer, smoking and glancing at Alicia with tipsy lust every time she looks up.

Alicia feels more comfortable looking down for the time being and plays with the wrapper on her bottle of welcomingly cold mineral water. British summertime may traditionally be the shortest of the seasons, but when it comes along for its four weeks of seemingly allotted time, it blisters the entire country with heat waves that make her run for cool cover. It's only the start of June, but already she's roasting.

She notes that the bar is not clean, though the glasses are all spotless, and as they are the most important items in this place, she supposes that it makes sense that they are made sterile by the dishwasher's scalding water. The fragrant lemony steam escapes when a tall barmaid opens it every few minutes, and the vapor rises with clouds of tobacco smoke, blown by the silent woman opposite, over her head and into the non-functioning blades of the still stained fan.

The music catches Alicia again, brings her attention back to her body, to her soft brown earlobes, heavy and stretched with sizeable silver hoops, open and ready for the band.

The three-piece continue to warm up. The amplified acoustic guitars hum, touching a part of her, reverberating off the bones in her large frame, shaking Alicia with a shock of intensity. She would drop to her knees and applaud the band if the floor wasn't sticky, wasn't caked with grime, and if it was in her nature to do that sort of thing.

It isn't. Alicia is upright, poised, and still a little stiff, even though she sneaked away from the late shift to be here. She cannot quite evade the stern British upbringing that lies upon her head like a suffocating blanket; like the hands of her domineering parents, whose old-fashioned rules and views make her feel like she's living in the Victorian era instead of the twenty-first century. It is the thing that says that a woman should not be in a bar on her own—shouldn't, mustn't, cannot.

Tonight, she thinks, she will try to shake free.

Down on the bar, the surface is ragged beneath her smooth elbows. A long black mat obscures most of the etchings in the wood, but Alicia can see a large love heart with the words MOYNI & MANDY inside it. Directly beneath it, someone has carved I LOVE CARRIE although it looks more like CRRRIE to her, but that wouldn't be right.

Not right, not proper, not done.

Alicia is tired of being prim; even in her gauzy blouse, tied tightly beneath her chest, she is held, restricted. She reaches down and tugs at the securing pink ribbon. With a sigh, she exhales, and the barmaid looks up from the dishwasher and grins at Alicia with naughty twinkling eyes and a nod of acknowledgment.

The music plays on in her head, though the band stopped practicing a while ago and is now fixing some of the many cables snaking behind Alicia's shoulders. The silent chords weave and flow though her, from her head, down to her back, which is still turned to the three female band members. They twist further to the skin of her still-outstretched ass and slide surreptitiously around to her front, inward, throbbing aggressively against her sensible white cotton knickers.

More people have arrived and Alicia has to press her

chest against the edge of the bar to let some squeeze by. The poster outside the small establishment had the words SOLD OUT emblazoned across the black-and-white image of the band, and they were not joking. Alicia's breasts are large but her nipples are not, so all she feels is discomfort as a line of rowdy drinkers push past her. The ache in her crotch, conversely, is a constant thrum, echoing their excited voices up into her pussy. Her muscles contract against her will, her shoes stick to the floor, and she is trapped in her own bubble of noise as it envelopes and probes into her growing wetness. She is tormented, aroused by every sound.

She imagines the advancing barmaid going down on her and is shocked by just how hard her pussy tightens at the thought. As a wave of heat sweeps outward, Alicia presses her legs closer together and wonders what she and the barmaid would look like together in bed, or on the tiny stage behind her, splayed out: a slippery tangle of pleasuring bodies, with a cheering, roaring crowd encouraging them on.

The barmaid's lips are vividly red, a striking smear of wild color on her pale powdered face. Alicia imagines kissing those lips; coating her teeth with waxy crimson as she bites greedily on the eager mouth. She wants to look down and see the barmaid's straw-colored head bobbing, sweeping sideways between her spread legs, a long agile tongue stroking, sucking in earnest on her luscious cherry sweet clit, and she can spit out the stone when she's done. She wants to see the barmaid's face, sticky and shiny and smiling up at her, before she lowers her head once more and hungrily licks from her furry mound to her ass. And all the way back again.

A sudden thump from behind jerks her from her fantasy. A throaty female voice apologizes but doesn't move position and Alicia responds by grinding her ass against the stranger, smiling as she hears the anonymous woman take a ragged intake of hot breath and moan deeply with surprised lust. Soon two tanned freckled arms are bracing against the bar, stretched out against her darker ones; this is all that Alicia sees. What she feels however, is much more. The woman presses her hips forward against her, tilting them both against the bar, and Alicia grips the worn wood with the tips of her fingers and rotates in time with the stranger. Friction, heat, and desire make their own sounds low in their throats, with purrs and murmurs that can just about be heard above the din of the other patrons. When the woman reaches round and places a palm flat against Alicia's heated belly, slipping a cool hand under her thin blouse, she feels like she is being played like a resonant cello; she can even hear the melodious low notes swinging to and fro across her chest. Then she hears the band.

The band begins and at last Alicia turns around, sweeping the stranger with her and it is an oddly fluid rotation in the pressing crowd—all limber sweaty young bodies, all of them but hers are white and Alicia stands out and blends in at the same time. She is buoyant in a cool sea of moving people, tight T-shirts and denim legs. They are rough and flowing, dancing slowly as a living mass, celebrating the creation of an orgasm forming above her sticky thighs.

Nobody watches her undulate, or sees a freckled hand free a dark heavy breast from her blouse, squeezing it vigorously. Not even the woman behind is looking at her. Everyone is here for the band.

The stranger presses her hand lower, under the edge of Alicia's skirt and beneath the elastic of her knickers. She rests her head on Alicia's shoulder and pushes with firm motions until she somehow finds her crotch: sizzling, soaking, and pulsing with building need. She pulls, rubs circles, and flutters over Alicia's pussy, making her pant, keeping her on the edge of a climax for only seconds, but to Alicia, it feels like forever.

Without the slightest hint of awkwardness or embarrassment, Alicia moves her whole body to keep in contact with the stranger's skittering fingers, feeling as if she has become the rhythm section of the band; another instrument to be used for their pleasure and hers.

She begins to bloom as the first guitar rings out, opening with the singer's mouth, wide, aching, and pulsing. Her breath hitches, she rises on tiptoes straining with the crowd, and the stranger lets her go, so no one person touches her, but the whole room is behind her, inside her. A sound swells, bubbles up, and shoots over every inch of her skin, pulsing as it travels from her clit right up to her tongue. Alicia screams out.

She sings.

Two Strippers in Love

Rachel Kramer Bussel

Denise swiveled in front of the mirror, watching the ultra-short miniskirt flare up to reveal her taut, toned, fine black ass. She sighed in relief to see it looking just as firm as it had when she'd left the house, full and round—proud, as she liked to say. Sometimes it seemed to fall or change or morph between home and work, as if it could tell it was about to be put to a use it wasn't intended for. She could always tell the girls who tried to sneak by as if they had no asses, or cloak theirs in drab, baggy layers, as if that would make them more invisible to the omnipotent male eyes traveling from near and far, zeroing in on their backsides. But for Denise, her ass was a source of pleasure, pride, and satisfaction.

If there was one thing she'd been taught to feel good about, in addition to her intelligence, it was her full, luscious body, and she had, for her entire life. While other girls at her mostly white school dealt with eating disorders, hiding their pale, often tattooed skin, she'd made sure to wear a full rainbow of colors. If you ever saw a bright green top or a hot pink miniskirt strolling the halls of her suburban Irvine high school, they were as likely as not to belong to Denise. By boldly declaring her love for brightness, she'd hoped to draw attention away from the other way she was different. Unlike everyone else pinning up photos of Charlie Sheen and Kirk

Cameron and Tom Cruise in their lockers, she lusted after those of a different variety altogether, women with curves and smiles and something going on behind their eyes. She'd never gone for just the pretty ones; if she heard them on TV spouting nonsense, it was an instant turn-off. She'd kept those women out of her locker, but couldn't keep them out of her mind, and the minute she was free to go, she raced toward UCLA and never looked back. Finding women to fuck hadn't been a problem. Finding women for more than a quick screw had been more of a challenge.

Denise had always gone for brains over beauty, but when a woman had a combination of the two, she practically creamed herself. It'd been like that all her life, starting with crushes on teachers, including the glamorous Ms. Addington, who seemed to glide around the classroom even though she always wore high heels, albeit fairly sensible ones. She was like an older sister, mentor, and friend all rolled into one, and sometimes, the way the older black woman would look at Denise when she'd stay after for extra credit or just to talk, she could sense a tenderness, and impulse to explore further, but Ms. Addington was too professional to let that happen. Then in college, Denise had joined the soccer team, even though everyone had her pegged for a basketball kind of girl. She'd loved the rush of steamrolling down the field, just her and the ball, the cheering and yells and antics around her falling away as she focused on that singular goal. She'd earned the nickname Scowl because of the fierce look that had covered her face as she made countless goals, becoming the team's most valuable player all four years of high school.

At first, she'd tumbled into bed with any woman who'd have her, but slowly, after finding herself alone the next day trying to figure out where she'd gone wrong, she'd learned to retreat. After college, she'd had her flings, even a few girlfriends, but then things got tough. Real life intervened and cut into her search for the perfect girl. She found herself out of a job and unemployment just wasn't hacking it. She missed sports, missed using her body, missed the company of women. She hadn't really thought all that much about stripping even though her ex had told her she could be a nude model.

But then one day she'd come in to the club that now employed her with some friends, not intending to do anything more than ogle some of the fine female flesh that surrounded them at every turn, a break from seeing only herself in the mirror. It had been over a year, and the more time she spent looking for a job, the less time she had to even contemplate a girlfriend. The minute Denise stepped inside, she could feel the charge in the air. She couldn't help but notice that eyes followed her everywhere she went—male, female—it didn't matter. At first, she thought it was because she was one of the few black girls in the establishment, and certainly the only one not working. She settled into a booth with her three friends, themselves forming a rainbow of colors with Marta, who'd come here from Brazil three years ago and was used to turning heads; Alice, who went out of her way to flaunt the many tattoos along her arms, as if to prove she wasn't just a nerdy, sweet Asian girl; and Marybeth, her whitest, tallest (six feet without the heels she insisted on wearing), and straightest friend, who was along for a lark. The four of them, all women, all here for their own reasons, none of them to catch a man, certainly got plenty of attention that night. One girl, who was introduced on stage as Cinnamon but later told her her name was Genae, had intrigued Denise.

Genae was everything Denise wasn't, except black; they shared that in common, though Genae's skin was lighter, contrasting prettily with her own, Denise thought. But where Denise was tall and lithe, the main padding on her backside, Genae was curvy and plump all over, the kind of girl who made Denise want to sink her teeth into her and emerge with a mouthful of flesh. Now, she always thought of Genae as some sort of food: sometimes she was a thick, juicy hamburger, sometimes a bowlful of the smoothest ice cream, always her favorites, ones she either gobbled quickly or slowly savored, drawing out the meal. She wanted Genae in both ways, from the start—for the fast, against-the-wall fuck, and the long, slow, all-night lovemaking. She wanted her for quickies in the car, and long sessions in their own bed. Mostly, at first, she'd just wanted to taste her, to put her lips against the slithering dancer and find out just how delicious she'd be. Denise felt badly at first, for objectifying her so, for doing to Genae what surely every man in the place did, except that she kept her thoughts to herself rather than hooting and hollering for anyone and everyone to hear.

But then Genae came over, offering a lap dance, her eyes promising something else. Denise proceeded to monopolize the Rubenesque girl's time for most of the night, shelling out twenty after twenty for a few more minutes of those deep brown eyes, those full pink lips, those generous breasts. Her friends were supportive at first, looking on, hamming it up, grateful for the free show. But they all soon figured out there was more going on, and scampered away so Genae could whisper sweet nothings in Denise's ear—when she wasn't sucking on her earlobe—and steal surreptitious pinches of Denise's nipple. Neither woman had ever been so turned on. She was going to ask for Genae's number, but the stripper asked her to wait until she was done.

She shooed her friends away and waited patiently, half-heartedly doling out dollars to girls who were pretty to look at but came nowhere near Genae's power to make her heart pound. Back at her place later that night, Denise found out that Genae tasted like the finest meal imaginable, as she kissed every inch of her skin before ordering the younger woman onto her hands and knees to be treated to the finest pussy-licking. "I hope you're ready, because I've been waiting for this moment all night."

"Girl, I've been waiting my whole life to find a woman who'd look at me like you did out there. Your eyes made me wet," said Genae as she hoisted her sweet ass in the air, giving herself over to Denise completely. Denise squeezed Genae's butt cheeks, grabbing fistfuls of flesh, pulling them apart, watching her new lover's sleek lips moisten even more, until finally she took a lick. She sighed, then went back for more. And more and more, adding a thumb to her tongue's actions as Genae's breasts bounced in a careless way. None of the practiced jiggling of the stage, they just hung down and swayed as Denise slid fingers and tongue inside her until she exploded.

Denise was exhausted afterward, trembling not with exertion but excitement. She knew this was just the start for the two of them, and she was right. She stayed in Genae's bed for the next three days, and they moved in together within the month. When Denise still couldn't find a job, Genae suggested she join her at the club. "Wouldn't you like to see me shaking my ass every night, baby?" Genae teased, as Denise sat on the edge of the bed while Genae cranked up the beat to their favorite radio station and thrust her behind into her lover's lap, slithering, sliding, and colliding with her. When Genae's knee rubbed against Denise's pussy, she leaned close, enveloping her within her breasts, and said, "That move's just for you," before going on to give a highly unprofessional but absolutely perfect lap dance, which culminated in each of them eating the other out.

Denise had always loved to dance and was a shoo-in for the job, easily wowing everyone with her fine butt-shaking and searing gaze, pouty lips fully glossed, the tiniest bikini she owned clinging to her body. On her first night, she simply soaked up the atmosphere. She had to put aside any personal arousal, or revulsion, and just get lost in feeling her body and feeding off the energy of the place. She found that while there was the occasional sleazy, leery guy, most of them simply wanted to ogle her body, much like she'd done with Genae that first night. She couldn't blame them for checking out her girlfriend, but then again, none of the customers knew the two were a couple, though the staff were on to their secret.

In the beginning, Genae and Denise had tried to hide their relationship from the rest of the girls and their bosses at the club. It was one thing to flirt with lesbianism onstage, to titillate the crowds of mostly men into coughing up a few more dollars, to swelling their pants so much the bills practically fell out. But there was a fine line between professionalism and reality, and they were careful never to cross it, until one day backstage when they were caught in a clinch by their boss, the older, harmless yet sarcastic Ray. "You two could make a bundle putting that on tape, you know," he observed wryly, as if he'd never heard of knocking, and wouldn't have cared if he had. They broke apart, a guilty look creeping over Denise's smile, but Genae seemed unperturbed.

"If we ever want to, we'll charge you top dollar, Ray," she said, laughing, her eyes blazing back at Denise with all the furor and desire they'd telegraphed when they first met. Since then, it had become an open secret around the club, but they both knew the situation was temporary. Genae was getting her degree, Denise socking away enough cash so she could start her own vintage lingerie store. Both of them had had boyfriends in the past, and knew how to flirt expertly, so for the first few months, they just watched their bank account grow.

Once in a while, Ray would mess with them, calling out over the loudspeaker: "And now, something you don't see every day, give it up for Cinnamon and Cocoa, two sweet strippers in love," his boomed voice intoned. Denise had gotten over her embarrassment at their over-the-top names, their blackness something to consume, literally, as their candy-coated alter egos strutted onstage. But she didn't mind, knowing it was preferable to the fake make-nice attitude she'd encountered as a secretary at an almost all-white, all-male law firm, big smiles plastered so wide they could only be held in place for moments at a time, eyes greedily grabbing at her no matter how primly she dressed. She'd rather be looked at, stared at, lusted after, as blatantly as she did in her rawest moments, and even thought that maybe she and Genae were teaching the motley crew of "gentlemen" a thing or two about a woman's body; at least, as much as they could in two minutes. When the two of them were on, they were on fire: legs bending and arching and stretching, asses shaking, breasts bobbing, tongues tangling, on display for anyone who had enough cash and interest. Not surprisingly, they were considered somewhat of a novelty act, a secondary attraction behind the Britney Spears look-a-like with the biggest breasts and bluest eyes in the place. They gradually worked out a routine, one that was so exaggerated their dyke friends would've laughed them out of town. Denise would smack Genae's ass, taking the shorter girl under her arm, while Genae made exaggerated gestures of mock horror, then mock pleasure. Denise felt like she was watching someone else, acting the role of horny girl who simply couldn't get enough, which was strange, because it was true—she couldn't get enough, at least when they were alone. Even when they were both completely naked, Denise never had the urge to truly lift her hand and bring it down onto Genae's ass the way she knew her lover could take. She wouldn't give anyone except herself the satisfaction of seeing that.

At home, it was another story. You'd as likely find Genae

in baggy sweats and a tank top as a girlie nightgown, and Denise preferred walking around in the nude, offering up her lingerie fetish to her future company. Being naked at home was totally different from doing so at work, where she always wore a protective layer of "not interested" atop her skin, a veneer of a demure smile masking her inward shriveling. Her nipples perked up in inverse proportion to the palpitations of her heart, even now, so many months in.

At home, though, she was less interested in strutting and more interested in those moments of passion that arose naturally, as if her breasts were a barometer of her desire, leading the way toward Genae at all times. She'd be heading toward the kitchen to make coffee, maybe boil some eggs, when she'd hear Genae in the bathroom, rummaging around or quietly humming to herself. Denise would turn and head toward that private sanctuary, stand there staring at the woman she was still amazed shared a home with her. Unguarded, Genae looked nothing like she did at the club. She was quiet, focused, as she shaved her legs or even scrubbed the tub or rearranged all their bottles and potions. Invariably, Denise would wake up in the morning and find her toothbrush rearranged in some new toilet feng shui system Genae insisted upon.

It was those caught-off-guard moments, the tender ones lacking any kind of artifice, that made Denise swell with desire for the woman who made "girlfriend" feel inadequate every time it tripped across her tongue. She wasn't a girl and she wasn't her friend, but "womanlover" was too much of a mouthful as well. Denise had never felt this way with any of the women before Genae, and she couldn't say precisely what it was about her that did it. But as the sun tickled the sky with its presence, stretching upward much like Denise did as she stood on her tiptoes and pressed her fingertips to the doorframe, Genae looked up at her and made her heart melt. Denise stepped toward her lover, who set aside the razor and welcomed her gardenia, the private nickname she'd thought up for the sweet-smelling woman clambering toward her, into the tub. They didn't both really fit in there; it wasn't some deluxe number suited for whole families. In truth, it barely held one petite person comfortably, never mind two robust women, one tall, one rounded. But they made it work, laughing as the hot water threatened to tip over the edge.

Denise pretended she had no other place to put her leg than between Genae's thighs, even though they both knew better. Laughing, Genae splashed her as Denise ground her knee against her lover. She eased her hand down, down, down, fingering the brief line of hair leading the way toward Genae's silky folds. She shut her eyes and rested her head against Genae's wet, welcoming chest, her large breasts the perfect pillow as she teased her lover with her fingers, tracing her slit with a single digit. She was leaning on her in a way that prevented Genae from moving much, but the sensual goddess managed to make her desires known.

"Baby," Genae said, so grateful to have found a woman who knew just what she needed, who knew when she wanted to be taken, and when she wanted to be seduced. Who could look at her naked body under those garish lights and still want her in the privacy of their home. Who looked so fierce and fabulous when she fucked her, her brow furrowed, her whole body getting in on the act. "You too," Genae said simply, maneuvering along the tub's slippery surface so she could push her short fingers into her lover's sex. The long, press-on nails she sported at the club were gone, leaving only her naturally short, evenly filed nails, "all the better for fucking," as they always said. Denise's fingers stilled as Genae's entered her, making the older woman catch her breath. She was always amazed at how well Genae could read her—better often than she could herself. Denise had to untangle herself from Genae's pussy, opening her legs so they were on either side of her lover's hips, inching closer as the water lapped between them. Denise sank back, back, back, until she was lying down, almost underwater, letting the liquid wash over her as Genae slid her fingers in and out, boldly claiming her prize. Denise's pussy swelled and tightened, crested and crashed, welcoming Genae's twisting, toying, teasing fingers until she simply couldn't stand it any longer.

"Yes," she hissed, using her legs to help push her hips back and forth to meet Genae's thrusts. She didn't know how many fingers the girl was using and she didn't care, as long as she kept going. She took a deep breath and sank underwater, relaxing under the warm bath as she coiled upward, a mermaid dancing gracefully as Genae brought her to orgasm just as her breath ran out. She splashed to the surface, gulping in air, grabbing Genae's hand to kiss it gratefully. "Two strippers in love, huh?" she said, laughing softly as she pulled Genae close for a kiss, their fingers prune-like, neither caring a bit.

"Imagine that," said Genae. They stayed there long after the water had chilled. It took them hours to even notice.

Shopping in New York

Dylynn DeSaint

The big full-body mirrors in each dressing room, illuminated by soft white neon lights, created a sensual ambience in which to disrobe. Most of the gray fitting room stalls were empty, except for the two at the end of the hallway. There two young women, in an almost perfect timed cadence, took turns trying on clothing, each popping out in front of an even larger mirror in the hallway that separated them, disrobing, then throwing the clothes to each other across the hall, oblivious to anyone around them.

I sat on a hard black bench, jamming to the funky music playing overhead, and watched them as I waited for a friend in a nearby dressing room. Both girls were too busy to notice my presence much less care that they had captured my attention.

Answering my friend's questions through the dressing room wall, I made small talk with her as she tried on her clothes. I leaned against the hard surface and stretched my legs out, crossing them to get more comfortable, when a Puerto Rican woman came into the room. She was a brown-skinned Latina beauty with dark eyes and long curly hair.

I immediately started to pull my legs back so that she could get by. She smiled at me and told me not to move, motioning for me to stay where I was. I looked up at her face, not sure what to say, and without thinking, let my eyes travel down the rest of her body as she slowly stepped over my legs. My mouth dropped open as I watched her long shapely legs—in black fishnet stockings and patent leather stiletto heels—pass over the top of my tattered and fashionably faded jeans.

Holy shit.

I watched every rise and fall of her ass in that tight micro miniskirt as she walked slowly into the dressing room, the shiny leather skirt covering only enough of her body to be street legal. It was only when she disappeared into a room that I pulled my gaze away from her.

I shook my head and smiled to myself at how fucking utterly hot she was. Every inch of my body was on red alert, especially my crotch. Damn, the woman had "back." There just wasn't a better word to describe that beautiful, succulent, round piece of perfect female anatomy that passed by me. A woman like that would turn heads everywhere she went and could drive you mad with desire; she was that beautiful.

My mind traveled in the gutter for a few more minutes. I fantasized about what I'd do with a woman like that in my bed. I shook my head and chuckled at the thought.

I never really paid much attention to the nationality of women I dated, but I was mostly attracted to women of my own heritage, the Latinas. Basically, my taste in women tended to be very simple and visceral. They had to be HOT. I had a penchant for the high maintenance femme types who had nuclear-sized fiery tempers. That kind of temperament, I found, was the best and most potent ingredient for the best "make-up" sex ever.

As a young butch woman, I was full of spit and vinegar, untamable and definitely full of myself. Primed and ready to get laid whenever possible and as often as possible; I was a young stud boi on the prowl.

My friend came out of her dressing room and told me that she'd be back with more clothes to try on and for me to stay put. I didn't put up a fuss. I was too busy thinking about the hot woman in the dressing room.

I sat back and made myself comfortable again. As I waited, I looked back in the direction where the Puerto Rican woman had gone. I had been so distracted by what I had seen that I didn't even know which dressing room she might have gone into. The two young women tossing clothes back and forth continued talking and laughing while they took turns popping out of their dressing rooms to look at themselves in the mirror. By now I was completely ignoring them. Their antics no longer fascinated me. My eyes searched the rooms.

I noticed that one room had the door partially open. I caught movement in the room and saw her shoes in the mirror's reflection. She was facing the mirror, her legs spread wide apart, in a defiant and sexy stance. She was looking at herself in a red miniskirt with her hands on her hips. I smiled to myself in approval. Because I was completely obsessed with the sight of those long legs in that skirt, I failed to notice that she was looking at me in the mirror's reflection. I totally missed it; instead I sat there like a dumb ass ogling her legs. I finally looked up and she caught my eye.

Her thick red lips curled into a sexy smile. She was watching me while I was watching her. She slowly undid her blouse, never taking her eyes off me. I watched her drop it to the floor. Without changing her stance, she bent forward to pick it up. As she did this, her skirt rode right up the top of her thighs and over her hips exposing her bare ass and dark pussy lips through the fishnet stockings. Her legs were spread open so that I could take in the whole sight.

I leaned forward, cocking my head to the side to get a

better view, too mesmerized to give a damn if anyone saw me or noticed who I was looking at.

"Excuse me," she said in my direction after straightening up. "Could you help me with a zipper?"

Now *that* was an invitation I was not going to turn down.

She's got to be kidding, I thought. My heart pumped like a jackhammer in my chest. I hopped up from my seat and headed in toward her stall.

As soon as I reached her door, her fierce dark eyes sized me up. She licked her lips slowly. The sexual tension in the room crackled like white hot electricity about to explode. I knew immediately that she'd toss me out the door if I showed any sign of weakness or shyness. I stood there, holding her gaze, my eyes penetrating hers. It was a silent standoff; a mutual signaling of intentions based on pure animal desire that passed between us without words.

I took her face in my hands and kissed her hard, using my body to pin her against the mirror. She brought her hands up to my shoulders as if she were going to push me away. A few seconds later, she did. I stood there in front of her, glaring wildly and breathing heavily. Eyes still locked with hers, I wiped the lipstick away with the back of my hand. Her nostrils flared with defiance and her eyes seared through mine, taunting me to try it again. Without a word, I crushed her body once again against the mirrored wall, kissing her forcefully, my tongue lashing at hers. This time she kissed me back, ravaging my lips, biting them, and nearly drawing blood with her lust. Her teeth scraped hard against mine in our fiery passion.

I kept her body pinned while I used my hands to pull her skirt up above her hips, and thrust my knee between her legs to spread them apart. This time she didn't resist much, in fact she responded by nipping at my neck and running her tongue up along my jawline to my ear. There she teased me with quick flicks of her tongue and hot breath whispering, "Fuck me, boi. Prove to me that you're a stud."

I needed no encouragement and quickly pulled her stockings down just above her knees, low enough to gain access to that luscious, wet, and furry destination: the dark harbor of my voracious and frenzied quest. Her legs were spread as far as her stockings would allow.

In our frenzy, neither one of us had bothered to close the dressing room door. We could hear women talking and laughing, totally oblivious to what was happening next to them. I slammed the door shut with my free hand; the other was still buried in her crotch. The wetness soaked my fingers as I slid them slowly over and over her pussy lips and up and down the inside of her thighs.

She started to moan softly until I reprimanded her by biting her lip hard. Immediately and without warning she delivered a quick stinging slap across my cheek.

I laughed.

She snarled.

I quickly grabbed and held the offending hand away from my face. Rubbing the newly formed welts of her handprint with my wet fingers, I caught a whiff of her female scent and let the cool, slickness of her juices ease the sting.

Before she could deliver another slap, I grabbed her by the shoulders and yanked her around so that her face was jammed up against the mirror, leaving a fuzzy mist with each breath she took. I put my mouth against her ear and demanded that she not make a sound. The wildness in her eyes made me question whether she would comply. I did know one thing for certain; everything that was happening was exactly what she wanted.

I reached around and found my way to her clit, rubbing it slowly and languorously, driving the little nub to hardness. With the other hand, I entered her from behind, both of my fingers sliding easily into her vagina. Her body lurched against mine. She wanted them in deeper.

Smiling, I watched her close her eyes and clench her teeth. Her nostrils flared each time I found a sensitive spot on her clit. She stopped herself from making any sounds by biting her bottom lip.

When I withdrew my fingers and replaced them with my thumb, she opened her eyes. Once inside her again, I probed with my thick digit until I found that delicious and sweet G spot, the mother of all hot buttons. Her reaction was fast. She gasped quietly each time my finger hit home. I watched her long fingernails claw at the sides of the dressing room each time I hit pay dirt. Teasing both her clit and her G spot at the same time, I tested her ability to keep her composure which was slowly, ever so slowly, edging away. She thrust her hips against my hand roughly, undulating in sensuous tandem with my strokes, grinding slowly, gliding closer and closer to reaching a climax.

It was a beautiful dance being played out between two people who couldn't have looked more starkly contrasting, and all within the confines of a public dressing room. She, with her black puta stiletto heels and micro miniskirt hiked above her hips, and me, a young punk boi with a do-rag wrapped around my head, fucking her into silent submission. I bit her neck and urged her to spill her sweet juices onto my hand.

Her sighs were becoming shorter and jagged with each thrust. I rubbed my body against her, emulating the same motion I would have used if I had been fucking her with a dildo. My fingers, wet and slick, continued to work their magic. I could feel her pussy contracting and the wetness seep onto my hand. It turned me on to watch her lose control.

Finally, she shuddered as an orgasm exploded inside her. My body and the mirror that she was pinned against was all that kept her from collapsing as she ground herself uncontrollably against my body. I thought she might scream but instead she bit into my forearm!

I screamed silently.

I gasped in pain and gritted my teeth as she growled, moaned, and bit harder. Her teeth sunk in deeper as she continued to come incredibly hard. She wasn't having just one orgasm; she was gushing all over my hand and experiencing wave after wave of violent spasms.

I thought we were both going to lose it. She was out of control and I felt like I was going to faint from the pain. It took everything we had to keep quiet but somehow we managed.

Slowly she regained her composure and I was able to catch my breath. I moved away from her and leaned against the wall, holding my arm.

"Lo siento baby!" she whispered, suddenly realizing what she had done. She took my arm and kissed the angry red bite mark gently. I cringed. Slowly her kisses turned into soft licks over my tender flesh. I watched her as she flicked her tongue over and over the area and alternately blew on my skin. I enjoyed the cool sensation and liked watching her lick my skin in a sensuous way. Soon I wasn't focused on the pain anymore.

There was something about the way she used her tongue that was starting to turn me on again. She saw me smile at her. With raised eyebrows, she looked at me in disbelief, shaking her head.

"Uh uh, no way muñeca," she smirked. "We're gonna get busted."

She moved away from me, pulled her dress down, and fixed her hair in the mirror.

"I'll see you at home tonight baby . . ." she said as she walked out of the dressing room.

I poked my head out of the door and watched her go.

She turned around, blew me a kiss, and smiled, "... when you're through shopping!"

My friend emerged from her dressing room and looked at me standing there.

"I was wondering where you went. What did you try on?"

"A miniskirt," I said, laughing.

She rolled her eyes and shook her head.

Water Gatherer

JT Langdon

Sun caressed Sparrow's face as she followed the narrow, well-worn path between her village and the river. She could have closed her eyes and walked the path from memory, so familiar was it to her, but Sparrow kept her dark eyes open wide, taking in the beauty all around her. The excited twitter of her namesakes and the buzz of crickets rose and fell in the air, as if their harmonious songs were a celebration that spring had arrived at last. Sparrow shared in their jubilation. Winter had been long and hard, wearing out its welcome. It had been the worst winter she could remember, and Sparrow had been through more than twenty of them now so she had something by which to compare. But spring finally managed to chase the Winter Spirit away. And no one, not the crickets nor the birds nor her people, could have been happier about it than Sparrow. Spring gave her back the purpose winter stole from her, filling her with an almost overwhelming sense of pride.

Sparrow remembered well the morning Father made her the water gatherer for her family. It was a tremendous responsibility, and when Father first spoke of it Sparrow could not believe what she had heard. But it was no dream. Father really had made her the water gatherer. Even now Sparrow beamed at the memory of that day. To place such a task in her hands told her and everyone in the village that Father no longer considered her a child. It had been the greatest moment in her life. Nothing could match it, nothing. That morning, with a touch of sadness in his eyes Sparrow still didn't quite understand, Father handed her two water bags, new ones made just for her from the stomach of the *tatanka* killed in the most recent hunt, and sent her on her way. Sparrow left the tipi that morning a woman.

Those same two water bags Sparrow clutched to her chest now, the bags a little weathered after many seasons of use, perhaps, but still in very good condition. She would not have to replace them for some time. Maybe not ever. The path had also changed little since she first walked it, the bare ground still firm under her moccasins. How many times had she been down this path? Sparrow wondered. She could not even begin to imagine but it seemed like she had carried the entire river back to her village.

Sparrow sensed the power of the river as she approached. It was a living, breathing thing, and she respected its strength. The river existed long before she had, and would still be there long after her body perished. The river could wash away the earth, sweep the mightiest warrior downstream yet there was nothing more delicate than a single drop on the tip of her tongue. Sparrow felt humbled in its presence. She listened to the sound of flowing water, smelled the musk of damp earth in the air, let the sensations wash over her.

Kneeling at the bank of the river, Sparrow gazed down at her reflection in the water. She chose not to braid her dark hair that morning, instead letting it flow over her shoulders in a long, straight line. The water made her eyes seem green though Sparrow knew them to be the color of *tatanka* fur. She did not find herself repulsive.

Something stirred across the river. Sparrow looked up. The breath caught in her throat. She had the urge to flee but made no movement, keeping perfectly still, like a deer that hoped it would not be seen by hiding in plain sight. Panic filled her. She wanted to cry out, call for Father. But Sparrow knew better than to make a sound, knew better than to do anything that would draw attention to her.

Standing on the opposite shore was the palest woman Sparrow had ever seen. She was not very tall, but slender, with hair like the fur of a fox, not quite as long as hers. The dress she had on billowed around her, but the curves of a woman were unmistakable. Sparrow had heard stories but never had she laid eyes on a white man . . . or woman. This woman looked harmless enough, but Sparrow knew that where there was a white woman there had to be a white man, and where there was one white man there were others.

The white woman on the other side of the river crouched down and dipped a wooden bucket into the water. Sparrow watched her intently, torn between fear and curiosity. The woman must have been a water gatherer like her, and from what Sparrow could see not much older than she. Sparrow held her breath, desperately hoping the white woman didn't see her.

But something made the white woman glance up, made her glance up and look right at Sparrow, meeting her eyes, staring at her. Even with the river between them Sparrow heard the other woman gasp. The two of them gazed at each other across the river for the longest time, neither of them making a move, a sound. Even the birds and crickets seemed to have fallen silent. Sparrow could hear the drumbeat in her chest getting faster and faster. She could not sit there forever.

Sparrow blinked away her fear. She was a water gatherer. And that was what she would do. Keeping an eye on the white woman on the other shore, Sparrow dipped her water bags into the river and let them fill. She could feel the white woman watching her but didn't let that distract her from her task, filling each water bag with as much as they could hold. When both bags were filled Sparrow got to her feet, and with one last look at the woman on the other side of the river turned and calmly started back down the path that had brought her there.

When she returned to the village, Sparrow looked for Father and told him about the white woman across the river. His face was thoughtful while he listened.

"The white men will come," Father told her softly. "Just as summer will follow spring. It cannot be stopped. The river sustains us all, so it must be neutral territory. But we will stay on our side. And as long as the white men stay on theirs, we have no quarrel with them."

Sparrow hoped that was so.

The white woman was not at the river the next morning when Sparrow went to gather water. Nor the morning after. Nor the morning after that. When several more days had passed without any sign of the white woman, Sparrow began to wonder if her mind had just been playing tricks on her. She found that hard to accept. The white woman seemed real. When Sparrow closed her eyes she could picture the white woman standing on the other side of the river, her pale skin glowing in the morning sun, red hair moving with every breath of the wind. No vision ever seemed that real or lingered for so long afterward, but the more days that passed when Sparrow went without seeing the woman again the more she was convinced she must have invented the entire thing. Yes. That was it. What other explanation was there? The white woman at the river had just been a creation of her own making, a waking dream.

Sparrow thought no more of it until many days later. She followed the path down to the river with her two water bags, just as she had every morning from spring to autumn since Father made her water gatherer.

The white woman was there.

This was no dream, Sparrow knew. The woman *was* real. She was sitting on the bank of the opposite shore, leaning back with her eyes closed, her feet dangling in the water. She looked very content. Sparrow was again afraid to make a sound. But unlike before, it wasn't fear of discovery that kept her silent. The woman just looked so at peace Sparrow didn't want to disturb her. Working as quietly as she could, Sparrow bent down and dipped the water bags into the river, quickly filling them, pleased with herself, thinking she could slip back down the path unnoticed.

Before leaving Sparrow thought she would steal another glance across the river. The white woman was looking back at her now. But there was no fear in the other woman's eyes this time, no surprise. Once again the two of them stared at each other across the river for a long time then the white woman smiled, raised one arm, and waved at her.

Sparrow wasn't sure what that meant to the white people, but it seemed a friendly enough gesture. She waved back.

Sparrow saw the white woman again the next morning. She was washing clothes in the river, scrubbing them against a rock while softly humming an unfamiliar tune. From her bank Sparrow listened to the white woman's sweet song, kneeling beside the river long after she had filled her two water bags. The white woman would look over at her now and then as if to see if she was still there, and, finding she was, would smile at her. Sparrow always returned the smile. It gave her a pleasant feeling to smile at the white woman on the other side of the river.

More days came and went. Sparrow saw the white woman at the river each morning. Sometimes she gathered water, other times she just sat on the bank. When Sparrow arrived the white woman would smile and wave at her, to which Sparrow always smiled and waved back. Though she couldn't have explained why, not even to herself, Sparrow liked to think the white woman was waiting for her. It made her belly feel light. She liked that feeling. Sparrow found herself looking forward to gathering water more than she ever had before, not because of the pride it gave her to know that Father thought she was a woman but because she wanted to see the white woman again. She took her time filling the water bags just so she could be with the white woman a little longer, hear the sweet song she hummed, admire the way sunlight danced in her fox-red hair.

One morning as she walked to the river Sparrow noticed a flower in bloom along the path. For no reason she could point to it made her think of the white woman. Sparrow picked the flower and took it with her down to the river. The white woman was waiting for her and smiled when Sparrow arrived. She smiled back like she always did and held up the flower she had picked. The white woman looked pleased. Sparrow wanted desperately to give her the flower. Looking around the bank of the river Sparrow found a fallen tree branch wide enough that it might work. She put the branch in the water and set the flower on top of it, gave the branch a gentle push then watched it float across the river to the opposite shore. The white woman knelt down on the bank and stretched her arm out to grab the branch. For a nervous moment Sparrow feared the branch would escape her but the white woman grabbed it before it could float downstream. Relief flooded through Sparrow when she saw the flower in the other woman's pale hand. The white woman held the flower up, looking at it intently, and when she turned and smiled Sparrow felt that lightness in her belly again.

•

The white woman constantly filled Sparrow's thoughts. She wondered what the white woman did when she wasn't down by the river, what name she was called by the white man. Did the white woman even think about her at all when they were apart? These questions filled her mind with a noise like the hooves of a charging herd. Sparrow went to sleep eager for morning to come so she could hurry down to the river and see the white woman again, softly humming the white woman's song to herself until the world of dreams claimed her for the night.

Sparrow awoke one morning earlier than usual filled with an overwhelming need to be with the white woman again. She gathered the water bags and hurried down the path that led from the village to the river, the drumbeat in her chest pounding faster than ever. It didn't matter that the white woman probably wasn't there yet. She would happily wait for her for once.

But the white woman *was* there.

Sparrow stood silently on the bank, clutching the water bags tight in her arms, breathing hard, her belly the lightest it had ever felt. The white woman was standing in the river, up to her waist in water, her dress in a pile on the opposite shore. Her pale skin looked like mother's milk in the early morning sunlight. Sparrow allowed her gaze to follow the curves of the white woman's naked body as she bathed in the river, from her creamy hips to the swell of her bosom. Though she was turned slightly away from her, Sparrow could see that the white woman's ample breasts were capped with dark rings. Sparrow felt the lightness in her belly travel lower down her body, to that soft place between her legs, and before she knew it a heavy sigh escaped her lips.

The white woman turned suddenly, her face turning pink when she saw Sparrow standing there. She lowered her body into the river, covering herself, the water now just over her breasts. Sparrow stood there, unable to move, unable to breathe. She filled her water bags and returned to the village as quickly as she could.

Sleep just did not want to come for her that night. Sparrow tossed and turned on the floor of the tipi, her mind racing frantically. The image of the white woman standing in the river, naked, haunted her like a restless spirit that would not let her be. And the more that image danced in her mind the more her womanflesh ached with need. Sparrow found herself wanting to run her hands over the white woman's body, wanting to know if her skin was as soft as she imagined. When Sparrow closed her eyes she could see the white woman standing in the river, the beads of water on her breasts glistening in the sun. What would it be like, Sparrow wondered, to lick those drops of water off her skin?

Sparrow was still wondering about that when she walked the path to the river the next morning with her water bags. The white woman wasn't waiting for her when she got there. Disappointed, Sparrow filled her water bags then sat down at the river's edge to wait. The white woman did not come. The sun moved farther and farther across the sky and still Sparrow sat there, waiting, hoping. And still the white woman did not come. Fear made her insides clench like a fist. What if something had happened to the white woman, Sparrow wondered, something horrible? Or worse. What if the white woman did not *want* to come anymore, did not want to see her anymore, did not want to smile at her across the river anymore. Tears filled Sparrow's eyes. She could not bear to think that. But where was she?

Father came looking for her.

"Why have you not returned to the village?" he asked her. There was grave concern in his voice.

Sparrow looked across the river but saw no sign of the white woman, saw no reason for her to keep waiting. She gathered her water bags and walked back to the village with Father.

The white woman was not at the river the next morning, or the morning after. Sparrow stopped expecting to see her. For whatever reason, the white woman was gone.

Sparrow did not want to gather water anymore. She did not want to walk the path from the village to the river and fill the two water bags Father had given her that morning years ago. She had to, though, and she did it for no other reason than that. But she took no joy in it, felt no sense of purpose in doing so. Though she wished Father had never given her the task, she was still the water gatherer and she would do what she must for her family. But it didn't matter to her. Nothing mattered to her.

With her water bags in hand, Sparrow once again walked the path to the river. Sparrow could not believe her eyes when she reached the river and found the white woman standing on the opposite shore. She was holding a flower much like the one Sparrow had picked those many, many days ago. This time her mind *had* to be playing tricks on her, Sparrow thought. She was only seeing what her heart wanted to see. It could not be real. Could it? Sparrow again felt a lightness in her belly.

Sparrow dropped the water bags to the ground and slipped off her moccasins, letting her dress slide off her shoulders to pool around her now bare feet. The sun felt good against her skin, but not nearly as good as the feel of the white woman's gaze on her naked body. She stood there for a moment longer, letting the white woman look at her, then stepped down into the river, wading through the water until she reached the midpoint between the two shores. There she waited. With a nod, the white woman began to undress, revealing more and more of herself until she too was naked, then she joined Sparrow in the river.

The two of them stood face to face at last, the only movement that of the water flowing around them. Sparrow glanced down at the flower the white woman was still holding in her hand. The white woman smiled and handed it to her. Taking it, Sparrow brought it to her lips and inhaled the sweet smell of it before pushing the stem into her hair. The white woman's face seemed to express approval at that. Her hand trembling, Sparrow reached out to the white woman. Part of her was still expecting her to be an illusion and when her hand touched solid flesh she gasped in pleasant surprise. The white woman moved closer, close enough that their breasts were touching. Sparrow ran both hands over the other woman's body. The white woman's skin was even softer than she imagined. Sparrow delighted in exploring her curves, easing her hands over the other woman's hips. The white woman answered in kind. Sparrow moaned softly as the other woman's hands slid across her waist then moved upward to cup her breast. The white woman used her thumb to caress Sparrow's nipple, the wrinkled nub growing firm under the other woman's touch. Sparrow moaned again, the strain in her voice echoing the deep ache between her legs.

Sparrow dipped her hand into the river then poured a handful of water over the white woman's breasts, the coolness of the water making the other woman's plump nipples stiffen. Pleased with that, Sparrow bent down and licked off the beads of water that remained, just as she had imagined doing. The white woman sighed, running impatient fingers through her hair as Sparrow licked up every drop of spilled water. But she didn't stop when it was gone. Sparrow kept licking the white woman's breasts, dragging her tongue over a nipple then taking it into her mouth and suckling like an infant at the bosom of her mother. The white woman moaned, tangling eager fingers in her dark hair. Sparrow hungrily sucked on the white woman's breast, taking as much as she could into her mouth. The more she sucked, the tighter the grip in her hair became until Sparrow thought the white woman would pull it out completely. Sparrow slid her mouth from the white woman's breast and stood up straight, gazing into the other woman's eyes. She kept looking into them as she dipped her hand into the river again, but instead of bringing up a handful of water to pour over the other woman's breast, Sparrow moved her hand under the water until she found her way between the other woman's thighs. The white woman's eyelids fluttered and she moaned softly. Sparrow caressed the woman's folds, rubbing them with just the tips of her fingers. Each stroke brought another moan across the other woman's lips. Sparrow rubbed even harder, faster. The white woman grunted and lost her footing, landing in the water with a splash. Sparrow laughed.

The white woman turned around in the water, wading closer, until she was facing Sparrow's belly. Sparrow looked down at her, breathing heavy, watching as the white woman leaned into her then pressed soft lips to her belly. She whimpered for more and the white woman gave it, kneeling in the water, pressing her lips to her belly again and again, creeping lower and lower until her chin was in the water. Then the white woman pressed her lips to the throbbing flesh between Sparrow's legs and Sparrow moaned low in her throat. She closed her eyes and felt the warmth of the sun on her face as the white woman's mouth covered her folds and warmed her from within. Her insides swelled with pleasure when the white woman began to lick her down there, the drumbeat in her chest pounding faster and faster, her breath uneven and shallow. Sparrow could feel the other woman's tongue swirling around inside her and thought nothing could possibly bring her more pleasure. Then the white woman found the hard button at her very center. Light brighter than the sun beating down on them from the sky above filled her head and Sparrow cried out, the world spinning around her, leaving her dizzy, making her feel like she was falling even though she hadn't moved.

When she could breathe again Sparrow opened her eyes. The white woman was still in the water, looking up at her. Sparrow smiled. She put out her hand and when the white woman took it, pulled her to her feet. The two women shared a look then both of them headed to their own shores.

As Sparrow followed the path back to her village, the two water bags she carried under her arms filled to bursting, flower in her hair, she thought about the wetness she had felt on her fingers and smiled. She was a true water gatherer.

Glory B.

Cheyenne Blue

When I was young I had an imaginary friend and her name was Glory B.

"Gloria?" said my mother, indulgently. "That's a pretty name."

"No. Her name is Glory Brown, but she calls herself Glory B. She's prettier than I am, and her hair is in cornrows, but they're too tight and her head hurts. She lives where it's hot, and sometimes she can't sleep at night because she hurts, and because of the yelling, and that's when she comes to see me. She has a gap in her front teeth, where they pulled a tooth out when it ached, and her skin is black. She's blacker than the space under my bed, and she tastes of guava juice."

"Oh," said my mother, faintly. "Oh."

Glory B. was there during my teen years, and she told me it didn't matter that I could run faster than the boys, that it was a good thing to do, that she wished she could.

"I think I'm different," I whispered to her at night, into the pillow.

"I know," came back the answer, weaving through the fantasies in my head. "So am I."

"I can't get a prom date," I told her, when I was seventeen. "The boys think I'm strange, and I don't like them. And no girl will go with me."

"Sssssh," she whispered soothingly. "It will be all right in the end."

If I opened my eyes, I could sometimes see her outline on my bed. Lying on her stomach, her round rump enticing, and her hair still in the cornrows. She would always fade, but like Alice's Cheshire cat, her grin would be the last to leave.

When my mother pressured her oldest friend so that her son took me to the Prom, Glory B. told me to relax and enjoy the night. "I'll be here when you come home," she said. "You can tell me all about it."

So she was the one who heard how Danny covered my mouth with his meaty paw, and forced my compliance with his solid thighs. Glory B. soothed my tears and gently wiped me down.

"It hurts," I whimpered.

"I know," she soothed, and then she kissed me.

I looked for her, the real Glory B. She had to be somewhere, not just on the edge of my dreaming. Maybe she was down in the south with her braided hair and bright colors. With a scarf around her head, and long, plump legs, and skin that tasted of the heat between us.

I moved to Baltimore and looked for her there, among the bars and along the waterfront at Fell's Point. She wasn't among the college girls in shorts working at the aquarium, nor one of the people running the water taxis around the inner harbor.

My brother and his friend came to visit me, and slept in sleeping bags on the floor in my tiny living room. His friend didn't come home one night, but he reappeared early the next morning and his grin stretched to Annapolis.

"Met a girl," he said. "Works at the biker's bar. She was hot. Called herself Glory."

My hand stilled on the coffee jug. No, I wanted to shout. She's mine.

I went looking for his Glory, and found a redhead with watered milk skin. She was tired, and her eyes strayed constantly to the door.

"He's not coming back," I said. "He returned to New York."

Her nametag said Gloria, but I had to try, and for a month or so I was her rebound girl. Sworn off men, she said, even as her eyes searched over my shoulder. I held her close and kissed her, loved her, as she waited for the call that never came.

With my head between her legs, her taste coating my tongue, and her cry in my ears, I could believe she was my Glory B. But after she'd come, when she'd made another half-hearted attempt to please me, when she'd abruptly dropped my hand in public because she'd seen a friend—those were the times I knew she wasn't what I sought. And so she went.

Departed Glory.

There were women, of course. Relationships that unfurled in an evening, peaked through the night, and withered over coffee the next morning. Some that lasted longer, one that I thought might be more. But Evienne was a foreign exchange student, and it was simply a year out of her normal life.

"Stay," I whispered to her in the night. "You can make a life here. We can make a life."

"I can't," she said. "*Je ne peux pas.*" And in her native language the words had a finality that they lacked in English.

Glory B. faded in those years, and I put her aside. She was my girlhood imaginary friend, nothing more. In rare wistful moments, I'd bring her memory out of my mind, unfold it, hold it to my cheek and wish that she were real, and somehow we would meet. But time was passing, and if this were to happen, it must be soon.

Faded Glory.

My mother called. "I know what you hide," she said. "Your brother told me. It will be your undoing."

I hung up.

My company loved me, the career woman with no entanglements, no kids to pick up from daycare, and a flawless executive style. I could golf with the boys, accompany their wives to day spas where the real decisions were made, host a dinner party for twelve, cocktail hour for fifty, and still slice and dice in the boardroom.

One day, the president took me aside. "I need a successor," he said. "And you need a husband."

"What about a wife?" I shot back, and the next month I was transferred to Phoenix.

I lay under ceiling fans, swamp coolers, air conditioning, and in backyard swimming pools. My skin hardened, my hair gilded with gray. Phoenix does that to you. It leeches the life from you, drains it through your feet into the burning sidewalks, evaporates your essence into its blue, blue skies.

On a whim, I took a trip. Ostensibly, a golfing trip to the Deep South. To New Orleans, Charleston, and Baton Rouge. I golfed, improved my handicap by three points, and, even as I mocked my own whimsy, I looked for Glory B. in the streets, on the golf course, at the overpriced hotel, and in the under priced diner.

After that trip, there was another woman. Young, ambitious, determined. She courted me and what I could give her. So I took what she offered, and flaunted her on my arm. My trophy wife. When she moved in with me, she unpacked her cases, and set a small rag doll on the bedroom shelf. The doll had chocolate corduroy skin and hair in wispy cornrows, and her gingham dress was faded from years of handling.

I picked her up, arched an eyebrow in superior question, even as my hands caressed the doll.

Emmaline flushed. "My comforter," she said defensively. "I was only a kid."

"Does she have a name?"

"Susie." She hesitated. "Yeah, Susie."

The name was bitter on my lips, and I hurled the doll into a corner. She sprawled, legs akimbo, something fragile and broken.

I stalked over to Emmaline and ran my hands firmly down her shoulders to her breasts. I pinched a nipple, a sharp move, a heartbeat away from pain. "I don't want to see that doll again. Do you understand me?"

Emmaline's eyes widened. "Yes," she breathed, and her voice fluttered like a captive moth, beating against the hand that restrained.

I took her roughly that night, fucking her with fingers, then fist. Stabbing her sex with my tongue, then—in guilt—laving and gentling her, soothing away the rawness I'd caused. And I took what she offered, forcing her head between my thighs, and keeping her there, even when she cried out that she was hurting. Then I pulled her to my breast, whispering words of tenderness, stroking her hair, arranging it in patterns on her skin.

In the end, I couldn't love her; neither her eagerness nor her compliance was enough. I began to hate what she had made me. In the heavy night, when the air was redolent with our sex, I wondered why my Glory had left me.

I retired at fifty-five. I made COO, but that was all, and it got old quickly. My farewell was at an exclusive restaurant in Scottsdale. My successor was there, and so were many contacts, old and new, in the business world.

There was a woman across the room. She was tall, and her skin was the bitterest chocolate. Her cropped hair clung to her head, and she wore the power suit with confidence.

When she moved toward me, I saw she had a limp. She crossed the room to me, while I stared, and wondered.

Her handshake was firm. "I'm Gloriana Brown," she said, "but my friends call me Glory B. and I already know we're friends."

We left together, and went home to my sun-browned adobe on the edge of the desert. We lay on my bed under the ceiling fan and drank the champagne they would have been toasting me with at my retirement, had I not left so precipitously.

Later, much later, when the talking was finished, and the loving was about to start, we lay together watching a small printed gecko climb the adobe wall. I saw the scar on her back and the tiny twist of her spine, all that was left after they straightened the curve when she was eight.

"Pain does strange things," said Glory B.

"I know it does."

I smoothed her beautiful skin with my palm, imprinting the feel of her on my heart. And the smoothing became a stroking, and the slow, soft, slide into love.

Glory Be.

The Window of the Soul

Michelle Houston

As I patiently waited for the Morrisons' baby to toss me an "I just farted" grin so I could take his picture, I reflected on just how much my day job sucked. If taking portraits of smiling, chubby babies was all my life had become, I seriously needed to reevaluate my career choice. Although, my sideline of taking boudoir photos was slowly taking off, it wasn't bringing in enough to pay the bills yet.

Finally, Morrison junior decided to give a toothless grin, and somehow, I caught it on film. As the happy parents looked over the twenty-some shots they needed to narrow down to six, I skimmed through my schedule. Only two more sittings and I would be able to close shop for the day. Oh the joy of my life.

Several hours later, as the Brocks headed out the door, I breathed a sigh of relief. It was Friday night, and I planned to enjoy my two days off. Leaning back in my chair, I closed my eyes and drifted, listening to the soft sounds of Mozart playing on the sound system.

A gust of wind preceded her, as she thrust open the door to my studio. I bolted upright, slamming my feet down on the floor so hard my teeth snapped together. Damn, she was hot. A real looker. Although what she was doing in the old maid get up, I would never understand. Women who had long, regal necks and sultry facial features with a curvy body to match should never be allowed to wear their hair pulled up and in a bun. Nor should they be allowed to dress like a dowdy librarian.

"I'm sorry for coming by so late, but I just got off work. I was wondering if you could help me. A friend gave me your address and told me you sometimes take intimate photos. Is that correct?"

I admit, I wasn't paying as much attention to her words as I was to her lips. Full and lush, they were perfect, without enhancement. I could only imagine what they'd look like with a rich red lipstick. As it was, I struggled to stay focused on her words as several illicit images raced through my mind.

She had a job for me. If I was reading her body language and her subtle language correctly, I was about to see this lady in her underwear.

"Boudoir photos? Yes, I take them. Are you wanting to set one up for yourself?" I wanted to cross my fingers, I was hoping so badly it wasn't a gift she was purchasing for someone else, but clients had done that before.

As she shyly licked her lips and nodded, I felt my panties grow damp. Hot damn she was fine. I couldn't wait to see her in the altogether, and answer for myself the questions of what she wore under her clothes. If I had to select for her, I would go with a light cream to draw out the subtle color shifts in her gorgeous coffee-colored skin.

"When would you like to do the sitting?" I felt like the big bad wolf, waiting for Little Red to get just a bit closer so I could eat her up. Oh yeah, I was so bad.

"Do you have any openings tonight?"

"Sorry. I'm about to . . . well, come to think of it, yeah I could fit you in tonight." I was thinking I could fit her in, right between my legs while her tongue danced on my clit. I internally yelled at my inner whore to be quiet and remember she was a client. “Do you have whatever you want to be photographed in?”

As she nodded, I felt my pulse flutter. Oh I hope it’s leather. She had a body for a leather corset and thong. Maybe even a collar and leash.

“I just have to run out to my car and get it.”

“First, if you’d fill out some quick forms, and then I’ll get the camera ready and set up some of the lights while you get whatever you want to be photographed in.”

Her handwriting matched her appearance, delicate but with broad swoops and curls. I had always wished for handwriting like that, but had long ago settled for chicken scratch. I flipped the paperwork around to face me. “Ok Diana, I’ll meet you down the hall, second door to the left, and we’ll get started.”

As she turned and walked away, I allowed myself to picture just what she was wearing under that prim and proper outfit. It was one of my more perverse hobbies. I loved picturing what my clients were wearing. Frankly, I love lingerie of any kind, satin or lace, leather or the softest of silks. Seeing it stretch tight between a woman’s legs, her lush lips pressed against damp cloth, always made me wet.

Forcing myself back to my job, which, given the promise of the luscious body of my new client, I knew was going to only get tougher, I unlocked the door to my boudoir studio and flipped on the first set of lights. In one corner, around a big four-poster bed, I had positioned candles for effect, if my client wanted a romantic atmosphere. Across the room, a floor-to-ceiling mirror stood, with metal and chrome bars and a padded bench, for those into more of a kinky look.

“Ok, I’m back.”

I turned as she called out and got the full effect of her walking into the room. The dress revealed a hidden slit that teasingly opened as she moved toward me. The little librarian was wearing a garter and hose. Maybe she wasn't as reserved as her manner of dress and hair indicated.

"Where do I go to change?"

As much as I wanted to tell her "right here" I knew I might possibly lose the work she was offering. "There's a bathroom right through that door." I nodded my head and watched as she walked away. Playing my little game, I imagined her slowly stripping off her peach dress to reveal a demi-cup lace bra and matching panty set. Maybe the garter was even peach, with tiny roses along the band, the perfect foil for her vibrant flesh.

Before she was back out, I had the candles lit, turned on some soft mood music, and was crouched on the floor setting up my tripod. I found my mind wandering, imagining the rich color of her pussy lips, parting to squeeze around a dildo. Her nipples would be a deep rosy brown, standing proud on firm breasts. The door opened behind me, drawing me out of my fantasies and back to reality.

As I watched her step into the room, I almost swallowed my tongue.

Gone was the god-awful bun and dress. Her hair was a vibrant cascade of browns and blacks. Long enough to brush against the tops of her breasts, her hair did nothing to cover them. For that, I was grateful.

She had kept the hose, but must have changed the garter. Because she was sporting a naughty red peek-a-boo lace bra, and a red garter belt and thong, I knew there was no way such a rich red wouldn't have been visible through her light peach dress. Even her shoes had changed, from a modest low heel to what I affectionately termed fuck-me heels.

"Where do you want me?" As she neared I could see the lightly applied makeup, which subtly accented her features. Her eyes had gone from flirty to downright sinful. From prim and proper to sex kitten, in under five minutes; hot damn, a new world record. Someone call Guinness.

I shook my head slightly and forced myself to turn back to the tripod. "Let's start over by the bed for starters. I thought maybe you could stand next to it, with your foot propped on it, and slowly pull off one of your heels."

I tightened in the focus and knelt behind the camera. Although I could have done it differently, I always preferred to get the first few shots from waist height, then switch cameras and positions as I went along, generally with fantastic results.

"Ready when you are, Diana." I looked through the lens and got an eyeful. She had seated herself on the edge of the bed, her legs crossed and arms wrapped around her waist, succeeding in pushing the mounds of her breasts half out of her demi-cups. Before she had a chance to move, I snapped a picture, catching just the briefest edge of her nipple peeking over the lace.

Startled, her dark eyes widened. "Ready?"

As I nodded, she took a deep breath and stood. If anyone ever says that I don't have a fetish for lingerie, they don't know me. Nothing, and I mean nothing, beats a man or woman in a fine piece of silk or satin. I don't care what color their skin, or even their age. As long as they felt sexy, truly felt it deep down, there is nothing that compares to the way they moved in lingerie—okay, maybe if they're in leather too.

As she turned away and set her foot on the bed, I captured a shot of her heart-shaped ass, then another of just the hint of mound when she bent over. My tongue longed to slip between her lips and sample the dew already darkening the crotch of her thong.

"Ok, look at me. No, no, don't turn your body. Just kind of lean down a bit and look back over your shoulder. Yeah, just like that." Definite sex kitten material, I thought. The woman positively oozed sex appeal.

Whoever was getting these pictures had better damn well appreciate not only her, but the effort it was taking me to concentrate on taking them. Normally, I was only partially interested in my subjects, just enough to get the best possible shot. But Diana had gotten to me.

"Now, take off your shoe. That's right, slow and easy. Now, look at me again, purse your lips a bit more. Perfect." The camera whirled as I struggled to capture all the shots in rapid succession.

"Now, the other one. Let's have you sit down. All right, lean down, pressing your breasts against your legs. Good, good. Now, unbuckle it slowly." She was starting to move more naturally, less stiffly. I zoomed in quickly as she licked her lips, and then tossed the shoe aside.

"Let me change cameras." I reached down and grabbed my alternate camera, quickly checking the memory, and moved closer to her.

"Close your eyes. Just relax and lose yourself in the moment. Pretend your lover's here, watching you as you strip." Almost unconsciously her hands lifted to her breasts. Cupping their weight as I'd ached to do, she gently rolled her thumbs past her cloth-covered nipples. "That's right, let yourself go."

Keeping my movements whisper soft, I moved closer and took a few good shots. As she leaned back against the sheets, I captured a full shot of her lying there, her body dark against the light sheets, the red of her outfit stark against her flesh. I wanted to run my fingers through her rich tresses and spread them out around her head, fanning her delicate face.

Her eyes snapped open as I kneeled on the bed, but rather than stop, she slowly slid her hands down, as she arched her back. The clasp of her bra sprang open and her glorious breasts were free. Catching my breath, I snapped the shot as mentally I acknowledged I was right, her nipples were a deep rosy-brown, and almost as big as half-dollars. My mouth watered just looking at them, imaging the feel of them hard against my tongue, as I rolled them around, creating a light sting as I bit gently down.

Her hands traced over her stomach, light as a butterfly's wings, fluttering here and there, as she slowly worked her way down, down into the band of her panties. Some women hook their garters over their panties, making it so they have to unsnap them to remove their panties. Diana had hooked hers under her panties, so all she had to do was arch her back and slide them down her long legs. Which she did, slowly, and with a hip twist that I knew I would have to see over and over again to figure out how she did it.

She kicked her panties free, right into my face. As I removed them from the camera, I caught the mischievous look on her face. "How far can I go?" Her husky voice sent shivers down my spine.

I cleared my throat. "As far as you feel comfortable. This is your shoot."

She smiled and started tracing those hypnotic circles again on her stomach. Her skin glistened with a soft sheen of sweat, which added to her wanton look. I watched the muscles ripple under her skin, trying to capture the subtle movements on film even as I tried to figure out just what color her skin would be if I could paint. Not straight coffee; there was a richness there that coffee just didn't match. Maybe a half creamer mixed in. No, not cream, milk. A full teaspoon of milk.

And her eyes, they were deep dark caverns of passion, daring those around her to go exploring. How I wanted to explore, but it wasn't caverns of her eyes that truly tempted me. It was the lush hair above her mound trimmed in a neat patch, which sharply ended at the tip of her pussy lips.

My inner slut beat at my pussy, demanding I quench her

thirst. But I pushed her away, and continued to take photos as Diana slipped a finger past her pouting nether lips, dipping it into the moist depths of her pussy. I shuddered as I took the picture, then quickly hopped off the bed.

Moving around to the foot of the bed, I kept the camera locked on her body as I tried to get the best angle to catch the motions of her fingers, as a second one slipped into her pussy, joining the first.

Her legs parted and I stepped between them, her silky skin brushing against my legs as she withered in the bed, one hand cupping her breast and punishing her nipple with light pinches while the other manipulated her pussy and clit.

The camera beeped at me, and with a whispered curse as I quickly changed out the disk, hoping not to miss anything. Her gaze locked onto the lens when I zoomed in on her face.

I angled my view back down, capturing the breathtaking sight of her fingers pulling out of her moist red pussy, shining with her essence. The musky smell of her sex floated up, teasing me, tempting me to drop to my knees and bury my face between her legs.

She thrust her fingers back in, arching her back, softly moaning as a third joined the other two. And I somehow managed to capture it on the camera, her pussy widening to accept the offering, sucking the third into her depths. Her other hand slipped down her body, and with an elegantly long finger she manipulated her clit, rolling the tiny bud around.

I moved back to her side, my pussy clenching with need, as I continued taking shots. I know some of the shots were slightly out of focus, but the rest—the rest would be some of my best work. Forget farting babies, this was what I worked and slaved all day long for. To see beautiful women come apart, and to capture that moment, that intimate moment on film.

Her whimpered moans drowned out the softly playing music and the whirr of the camera, as I struggled to keep up with her rapid pace. She was on fire, and I knew whoever was lucky enough to share her bed had a truly sensual being on their hands. She was sex incarnate, a living breathing Aphrodite, tempting us mere mortals with her wicked ways.

I snapped a shot of her inner thighs, glistening with her juices. I zoomed in on her breasts, shooting their rapid rise and fall, as she gasped for breath. And as she screamed out her ecstasy, I captured the look on her face on film. Her eyes closed, her lips slightly parted, her nostrils flaring. In that moment, she could have been eighteen or eighty, as her facial features smoothed out, her face completely and totally relaxed.

Some people think when you're sleeping is when you truly have the face of an angel, but I disagree. It's when you come that your inner radiance shines the most. There's no artifice, no hidden emotions; it's all there for your partner to see.

The camera beeped again, and I stepped back from the bed. The memory was full, and there was no need to change it. Every moment from now, Diana would begin to regain some of her layers of inhibition. But in that last moment, with my last picture of her, I had captured the true essence of her being. I had seen her core, and it was perfection.

I turned away to give her some privacy, and knelt down to gather up my equipment. A soft touch against my shoulder startled me, and as my head came up I brushed against her breasts. Less than an inch away her nipple beckoned me.

Forcing myself to move my gaze up, I locked on her eyes as she took a step back and held out her hand. I allowed her to pull me up, until I was standing before her, fully clothed while she only had on her stockings and garter.

"Thank you," she whispered, then pressed a soft kiss against my lips, a brief flutter, and then it was gone. "I was worried it would feel uncomfortable to take these photos, but you made it enjoyable."

I nodded, unsure what to say. "Um, I'll have them ready for you in about three days, if you want to stop back by then."

Almost shyly she nodded, her hair swirling about her face in disarray. "I'll be here just before closing time."

I nodded again and she turned and walked away. As I watched her heart-shaped ass move away from me, I clenched my legs together, generating a delicious friction against my pussy. Although I didn't want to see her leave, I was in a hurry for her to go so I could be alone. The ache in my pussy was not going to be denied much longer.

Turning away from the sight of the door closing behind her, I caught a glimpse of myself in the mirror and for a moment, I didn't recognize myself. Gone was the cynical glint in my brown eyes, replaced by a subtle "come hither" rather than a "go the fuck away" look. My skin glistened with its own light coating of sweat, darkening from a soft caramel to almost a toffee hue.

Damn she was good.

When she stepped back into the room, I bit my tongue to keep from asking if she was available, and let her walk out into the night.

The Portrait

Nan Andrews

The woman wasn't conventionally beautiful but she held Rachelle's attention. Dark eyebrows nearly met in the middle of her somber face. She was holding a monkey. Rachelle stood for a long time, studying the way the light illuminated her face. She wanted to learn how to paint as well as this.

The painting was one of a series of self-portraits. Rachelle had been waiting for the new Frida Kahlo show to open at the George Belcher Gallery for weeks. The gallery was one of the few places she could see original paintings by her idol, as well as those by Kahlo's husband, Diego Rivera.

Kahlo had lived a vivid and difficult life, scarred by a traumatic streetcar accident when she was a teenager. Rachelle felt an affinity with her; early years in a rough part of San Francisco had been marked by gang shootings and poverty, but her mother had moved them to a safer neighborhood when she was twelve. The sound of gunfire still disturbed her dreams, but she tried to work through her fears by painting. She'd discovered one of Rivera's murals during a class field trip and later sought out his work all over town. From there, she learned about Frida; soon she began dressing in bright Mexican colors and styling her early drawings after Kahlo's vision of herself.

Today, Rachelle was focusing on the color of Frida's skin.

It varied in the paintings from a pale ivory to a warm blush of red. Rachelle had been stymied by her attempts to recreate it. Looking in the mirror, she saw only the reflection of her own dark ebony skin. She needed someone pale to paint, a model to look at.

Turning the corner, Rachelle almost walked into a young woman standing in front of another Kahlo self-portrait, entitled "My Birth." The painting showed an intensely intimate view of the lower half of a woman's body. The upper half was covered in a white sheet, as if dead, and the legs were spread wide to reveal the infant.

"Excuse me." Rachelle reached out to steady the smaller woman as she tried not to knock her down. "I'm so sorry."

"That's okay. No harm done."

The other woman was Asian, possibly Japanese, and only came up to Rachelle's shoulder. Rachelle had the build of a basketball player, long and rangy, although she'd never been good at sports. This woman was petite and delicate. Rachelle stepped back and looked at her. She felt a sudden desire to touch the woman's skin. It was such a beautiful color.

The other woman turned back to study the painting and Rachelle felt a pang. She didn't want to walk away.

"My name's Rachelle." She held out her hand toward the other woman's back.

"Oh, hi." The young woman turned and looked from Rachelle's face down to her hand and back up. "Gina, Gina Nakamura."

She took Rachelle's hand and squeezed it once. Rachelle looked down at the tiny, ivory hand held in her own larger, dark one and felt a shiver run across the back of her neck.

I wonder if she would let me paint her? Rachelle thought.

"Do you like Frida Kahlo's work?" she asked, trying to start a conversation.

"Well, some of it. She's pretty intense."

"Yes, she was a bit of a revolutionary in everything."

There was a pause. Rachelle decided to be bold.

"Can I buy you a cup of coffee?"

"Um . . . well. I wanted to look at the rest of the exhibit." Gina gestured at the other paintings.

"I don't mind waiting."

"Okay. I'll meet you at the front in twenty minutes?"

"Great."

Rachelle turned to find a seat. She wanted to watch Gina, see how the light played on her long, black hair, watch the way she moved. She pulled a tiny sketchbook from her bag and sat doodling line drawings of Gina as she examined the paintings. When Gina went into the other room, Rachelle considered getting up to follow her but didn't want to seem like a stalker, so she sat and looked at the paintings around her.

Gina quietly sipped her cafe au lait. Rachelle drank in the planes of her face, the shaded cheekbones, the dark eyes and delicate eyebrows, her creamy skin. Having Gina so close, to study openly, was a wonderful opportunity for Rachelle. Her fingers itched to be painting.

"Would you be willing to sit for me?"

"What do you mean?"

"I'm a painter. Well, a student, actually. I'd like to paint you."

"Me?" Gina seemed amazed, as if Rachelle had asked her something totally foreign.

"Yes. I love the way the light plays across your skin. I'd like to paint your portrait."

Gina looked down and a blush rose slowly over her cheeks. Rachelle wondered if she'd be able to see that blush again and capture it somehow. It was beautiful.

"I don't know. I've never done anything like that before. I don't think I could."

The blush came back again. Suddenly Rachelle realized what she must be thinking.

"You don't have to be nude. I don't mean that kind of picture," she said in a rush. "I just want to paint your portrait."

They both laughed, breaking the tension.

"Good. I thought you wanted me to pose without any clothes on."

"No, no. Just like this is fine." Rachelle looked at her feminine T-shirt with the small flowers on it and the slim pants, the sandals. Yes, she'd like to paint her just like this.

"Um, one other thing. I can't pay you right now, but if I finish the painting and sell it, I could pay you then."

Gina brushed her hair over her shoulder and looked into Rachelle's eyes. Her face was unreadable. Rachelle didn't know if she was going to agree or not. The moment of silence stretched.

"Okay."

Rachelle realized she'd been holding her breath and she let it out.

"When do you want to start?"

"How about tomorrow afternoon? The light is good in my room after two o'clock. Let me give you the address." Rachelle scrawled her address onto a napkin and pushed it across the table.

She fussed with the brushes for the tenth time, plumped the pillows on the day bed, adjusted the curtains, and still worried that Gina wouldn't come. In her nervousness, she'd forgotten to exchange phone numbers and she worried that Gina had changed her mind or something had happened, but she couldn't call.

At twenty past two, the bell rang in the lobby and Rachelle raced to press the buzzer. She waited by the door until she heard footsteps on the stairs and then pulled it open. Gina climbed into view. She was wearing a fancy cocktail dress and heels, which made her taller but somehow younger, like a young girl playing dress up.

"Hi. Come in." Rachelle opened the door widely to invite Gina in. "I'm glad you came."

"Sorry I'm late. My last lecture ran long and I had to run home to change. I hope this is alright."

"You didn't have to get dressed up, you know. What you had on at the gallery yesterday was fine."

"I know you said that, but I wanted to look nice for the portrait."

"You look beautiful."

Gina blushed again. Seeing the warm glow on her cheeks made Rachelle smile.

"Can I get you something to drink?"

"A glass of water would be nice."

Gina walked around the living room. The walls were covered with prints of Frida Kahlo's paintings.

"So, you really like her work." Gina called out to Rachelle, who was in the kitchen.

"Yes, I've loved her style since I first saw it."

"Well, I don't look anything like her." Gina seemed self-conscious.

"No, I'm not trying to copy her work. But I need to work with lighter skin and when I saw you at the gallery, I just really wanted to try and paint your picture."

Gina took the glass of water and sipped it. An awkward quiet descended. Finally, Gina broke the silence.

"Where do you want me to sit?"

"Oh, over here by the window, on this day bed." Rachelle showed her to the bed covered in a dark red comforter, the back edge filled with brightly colored pillows. Gina handed the glass back to her and sat down on the edge of the mattress.

Rachelle stepped back and looked at her, now that she was finally here. She'd lain awake the night before imagining Gina there, positioning her this way and that like a giant porcelain doll. But now, she was almost afraid to touch her.

"Do you mind scooting back against the pillows? I'd like you to lean back a bit."

"Shoes on or off?"

"Off?" Rachelle didn't want her to think she needed to disrobe.

Gina kicked off her shoes and then shifted back and crossed one slender ankle over the other at the edge of the bed. She pulled her hair over her shoulder and leaned back against the pillows.

"Like this?"

"Yes, thanks. That's great."

Rachelle walked across the room and repositioned her easel and a table for her paint. She turned to look at Gina. The light coming through the window wasn't shining directly on her, but her hair glowed like every color of the rainbow mixed together, like something alive. Her face was still, an expectant look turned in Rachelle's direction.

Rachelle pulled up a stool in front of her easel. She needed to do a few sketches first.

"I hope that this doesn't make you uncomfortable, but I need to look at you for a little while so that I can figure out how to start the painting."

"No, that's okay. Do you want to talk or should I be quiet?"

"Quiet now, if you don't mind. After I start, we can talk."

The two of them sat quietly. The room filled with glowing afternoon light, the only sounds were the buzzing of a fly against the windowsill and Rachelle's graphite pencil on the paper. She sketched Gina's shape as she lay against the pillows, and made a few studies of her face and hair. She couldn't decide where Gina should put her hands.

"Could you move your left arm to the side?"

"Like this?" Gina laid her hand on the pillow next to her thigh.

"No, just lay your hand on the side of your leg." Gina moved it again. "Yes, just like that."

She made another full-length study, working quickly to shade in the lights and shadows. Finally, she stood up and went to work at the easel.

"I need you to hold still for another couple of minutes while I transfer this pose to the canvas, and then you can get up and stretch."

"No problem. This is quite comfortable. It's nice to just sit here and watch you work."

Rachelle's first few strokes were tentative, but then she began to sketch out the body of a woman on the canvas. At several points, she stood back and watched Gina again.

"Have you been painting long?" Gina asked.

"Since I was in high school. I went to a school that had a big art department and I really liked my teacher, Mr. Johnson. He encouraged me to see the world with paint."

Gina fell silent and Rachelle went on with creating the outline of the portrait. She worked in shades of gray to create the shapes before she could begin adding the color. The portrait slowly began to take form.

"I think that's enough for today. You can move now."

Gina got up off the day bed and stretched.

"Can you come back tomorrow? This will take a few more sessions."

"Sure. At the same time?"

"That would be great."

After Gina left, Rachelle sat and looked at the sketches.

She'd made a good start, but getting the picture she saw in her mind's eye onto the canvas would be the challenge.

Gina was beautiful and her skin was a delicate shade of ivory porcelain, from a distance. Up close, though, her skin was a riot of different colors; linen and bisque, coral, salmon, rose, even orchid and lavender. Blue veins throbbed beneath translucent layers of almond and shell. Rachelle wanted to capture it on the canvas, but each color she added to the composition seemed to conflict with the last one. It just got muddier and muddier.

"Damn," Rachelle muttered in a low voice as she reached for the turpentine and a rag. She wiped the paint off the canvas and scrubbed the spot clean where she'd been working on Gina's face.

"Is something wrong?" Gina asked softly.

"I'm just having some trouble making it look the way I want it to."

"I'm sorry. Is there anything I can do? Would you like me to move or sit somewhere else?"

"No, no. You're fine and the light is fine. I'm the problem." Rachelle stood with a paintbrush gripped tightly in her fingers, her fist pressed against her chin. She took a few more swipes at the canvas and then set down the paintbrush.

"This just isn't happening today. Would you be able to come back another time?"

Gina looked pensive for a moment, then smiled.

"I'm really busy for a few days, but I can come on Sunday. Would that work?"

"That would be great."

Rachelle felt a mix of disappointment and relief as she walked Gina to the door. They agreed on a time for Sunday and then Gina left. Rachelle stood looking at the canvas for a long moment and then thrust her brushes into a jar of turpentine. There would be no productive work done today.

Several days of restless sleep and two more sessions trying unsuccessfully to capture the images she wanted on the canvas were making Rachelle a wreck. She drank cup after cup of coffee, until her hands shook when she picked up a brush. Gina loomed in her dreams and they began to take bizarre turns.

One night she dreamed of searching for Gina through the halls of the subway stations, finding her and then losing her again in the crowds. In another dream, she was flying above the city, searching the heads of people on the streets until she found her. When she landed on the sidewalk, she wasn't a person, but a black crow and Gina walked right past her. As she tried to follow her, Gina began taking off her clothes, leaving them like a trail on the sidewalk. Rachelle caught glimpses of more and more perfect ivory skin but couldn't catch up with Gina in between the buildings.

She was afraid to confess any of this to Gina, worried that she would leave and then Rachelle would never be able to finish the painting.

For their most recent session, Gina arrived wearing all black: black Capri pants, a black ruffled shirt and shiny patent leather flats on her tiny feet. The contrast in color only made her face stand out more. Rachelle found herself frozen when she tried to paint Gina's face, and worked on her body instead. Legs and arms encased in black fabric only served to disappear against the canvas. Rachelle sat down on her stool and dropped her head. This wasn't working at all.

"Can I see what you've done?" Gina got up from the day bed and walked toward the easel. She'd politely refrained from looking at Rachelle's efforts on earlier visits.

"Not much to see."

Rachelle was beginning to think it was hopeless. What was it about this woman that defied her ability to capture her on canvas? It wasn't for lack of thinking about her. Rachelle could picture her in her mind's eye at any time of day or night. She'd watched her move and watched her sit silently still until she wanted to scream.

"You know, it looks like me, but I don't feel like I'm there."

"You could say that again. I've been trying to capture you and just can't."

"Hmm." Gina walked back over to the day bed and sat down on the edge. "You know, I've been watching you work, watching you struggle with this, and it feels like there's some kind of barrier between us."

Rachelle didn't know what to say.

Looking as if she'd made up her mind about something, Gina stood up. She caught Rachelle's eye and held it. Slowly, without looking down, she began to unbutton her shirt. Delicate pearl-tipped fingers worked the buttons until the black was released to reveal more pale skin. She dropped the shirt on the ground and reached around to unhook her bra. It followed the shirt.

Next, Gina unhooked and unzipped her pants. She slid off her shoes before stepping out of the pants. The pile of black on the floor grew. Finally, she edged the black cotton bikini briefs down off her hips and on top of the pile.

Rachelle didn't know where to look first. Whale-bone clavicles stood out above delicate rose-tipped breasts. The soft rise of her stomach fell gently down to the arch of her pelvis, a triangle of black hair disappearing into the Y of her thighs. The ivory skin descended over kneecaps and fragile arched feet to end at the pink tips of her toes.

Letting out a deep breath, Rachelle stood up and walked toward the bed. She didn't know how Gina would react if she touched her, but she couldn't resist. She placed her dark rose fingertips on the backs of Gina's hands and then drew them up her arms, across her shoulders and then down her front. Her skin was so soft, like silk under her fingers.

Gina's nipples hardened and a soft sigh escaped her as Rachelle traced small circles around her breasts. Rachelle was mesmerized by the glow of her skin, the luminous quality of it, so different from her own mahogany color. She leaned closer and looked at the underlying colors. She could see so many shades, of sienna and golden ochre, cerulean blue and auroelin yellow. Rachelle saw the world of paint colors in Gina's skin.

Her hands twisted as she reached Gina's hipbones, cupping the sharp points and then sliding around to cup the softness of her buttocks. Rachelle held two warm handfuls and closed her eyes, imagining for a moment squeezing out curls of paint directly onto Gina's skin and dabbing into them with a brush. The thought became a shiver down the back of her neck and curled into a ball of warmth in her stomach.

With the sound of her blood rushing in her ears, Rachelle crouched down and ran her palms down the backs of Gina's thighs. She felt the muscles under the skin, the strength of them. The contours and shadows formed in her mind as she felt the smooth skin and long muscle fibers. She continued down, caressing calves, feeling the shape of her ankles, and then finally tracing the spaces between her toes.

Head level with Gina's waist, Rachelle could smell her warm, spicy scent. It touched a primal place inside her. She wanted to dissolve into Gina's skin. She leaned close and touched her lips to the shell of her navel. The warmth of the skin under Rachelle's mouth sent further spirals of heat into her center.

Gina rested her hands gently on the top of Rachelle's head, as if giving her permission for this exploration.

Standing, Rachelle ran her hands up Gina's sides, until she almost lifted Gina off the ground by her armpits. She guided her onto the day bed, helping her shift back until she was lying back against the pillows. For a moment, Rachelle stroked the expanse of ivory skin again from shoulder to knee, as if memorizing it, and then she turned away. Stepping back to the easel, she picked up a brush, and with a wide smile, she began to paint.

Waiting

Tenille Brown

I wait for Lucinda in the living room, my restless limbs shaking and tapping against the bottom of the couch. I have been waiting this time for two hours—she had arrived last time at four—and now almost a quarter after six, the cars only continue to pass, horns honking, brakes screeching on these rainy Brazilian streets.

I have a mantra that I always practice in my head while I wait for her: *Let her knock twice. Count to five. Walk slowly. Be sure to look surprised. Don't look as though you've been waiting—never let her know how long you've been waiting.*

I've never stuck to that mantra, though, and today is no different. And at five 'til seven, when, finally, one of the vehicles slows and stops, I spring from my seat as though I've been pushed.

I hurry to the window and see Lucinda let herself out of the backseat—she'll take no help from the driver—and bend over for her bags. From behind the curtain, she looks as though she is loaded with energy, like she could run the hundred feet to the door, her heavy bags in tow, without even getting out of breath.

Lucinda pays quickly before I can even get outside to offer and brings her own bags to the door. She drops them on the mat before she brings up her fist to knock softly and swiftly.

When I hear her knock, the goofiest and most ridiculous smile you've ever seen plasters itself across my face. I snatch open the door, and if she had the energy, I'm sure she would laugh and tell me how silly I look, but she just cocks her head and lets her arms fall at her sides.

I reach out as if to catch a collapsing body. With my hands around her shoulders, I guide her inside the door. She barely makes it into the living room before her body gives in and she falls onto the couch. I step outside and gather her bags and carry them into my bedroom.

We don't make plans or even speak outside these few days. Before she arrives and after she leaves, she does not exist for me and I do not exist for her. But, when she is here, we become what we are for this time, and for this reason alone, every summer, I wait.

I used to make a big fuss about the day of Lucinda's arrival, making sure the house was cleaned up real nice and my best bottle of wine was chilling. I always had something good simmering on the stove, and a long, romantic movie to watch in bed. But I learned two years ago that it was a waste, all of it, as Lucinda always sleeps the first twenty-four hours like she's been drugged.

So, now I do other things.

I leave her sitting on the couch sipping from a bottle of water while I run her bath. She likes the water hot and clean, none of that fizzy, smelly stuff I put in my own bath. She prefers the washcloth to a loofah and a bar of soap as opposed to the stuff that comes in a bottle.

I undress her slowly, slipping the straps of her sundress off her shoulders and pulling it down over her small breasts. It slides freely down her long body and lands in a white heap around her ankles. I resist the urge to kiss her, to press my anxious lips onto her dark berry skin, to whisper in her ear and sweetly suggest that we bypass the bath all together and fall into my bed and get tangled in the sheets.

But I know that will come in time.

Lucinda stretches her arms high above her head. Her breasts rise slightly on her chest like small hills on a dark stretch of land. She pulls her dark locks atop her head and slides in bobby pins to keep it in place. Last year they had barely grazed her ear and she had kept them away from her face with scarves and wooden headbands, now they are past her shoulders.

I place her clothes in a pile to be washed later. We walk slowly into the bathroom and Lucinda steps into the tub, lowering her body into the steaming water. Too tired to move once her body is submerged, she lays back against the bath pillow and I begin to take care of her.

I pull the washcloth down her back, paying close attention to the many small ridges of her spine. I wash her shoulders and her neck. Lucinda shakes with fits of giggles as the washcloth tickles the lobe of her ear.

I reach around in front and gently wash her breasts and belly. I wash her legs, her thighs, and her knees. I pull the cloth between each toe and wash the bottom of her feet.

Then I part her thighs and wash there, too. She relaxes then and closes her eyes. She throws back her head and licks her lips. I know not to go farther than this. I know she is not quite ready.

I tap her on one wet knee and say, "All done."

Lucinda grabs my hand and uses my shoulder for leverage as she steps out of the tub and onto the towel I have stretched out on the floor. With another large towel, I dry Lucinda's body. Then I wrap it around her and she steps back into the bedroom.

She sleeps in a T-shirt and a pair of gym shorts. I opt for a tank top and panties. She crawls into the bed and slides under the covers. I lay down on a pallet of quilts and sheets on the floor beside the bed. I used to climb into bed beside her, cradling her in my arms, but she never slept well that way, not on the first night, so now, this is what we do.

I have long since given up on talking the first night, of catching up on the past year and chatting until we are both asleep because I know that as soon as Lucinda's head hits the pillow, she is transported into a world far, far from here.

She is the only one who sleeps peacefully the first night because I always have to fight to keep myself from reaching up and touching her, have to fight to keep myself in place and not lay down beside her, to not begin to ask the many questions that clutter my mind.

The only thing that calms me is the fact that she is here, that for the next three days we will lay, we will speak, we will love, and this is what warms me, and on the first night, gently rocks me to sleep.

On the second night, I feed her. Lucinda is always hungriest when she is here. At home, she says she eats like a bird, sometimes forgetting to take breakfast or even dinner when she comes in from her studio too tired to cook. But here, in my home and at my little kitchen table, her thin, moist lips are always eager for new tastes. She often jokes that she had planned it that way, that she had decided her next woman would have to be a damn fine cook to keep her interested.

And though I know she is only joking, I cook tons of food when she comes, as if feeding her will keep her here. I make things especially for Lucinda, flavor them with seasonings that I know will make her lips curve and eyebrows arch. I fix things I don't normally care to eat myself or even care to serve customers from my stand at the beach.

The second night, I fill my kitchen with baked codfish

and rice, lettuce salad and fresh mango. I serve Lucinda from dishes rarely touched.

She tastes everything—chewing, nodding, and smiling. She shares her food with me as if she is showing me something I myself haven't experienced before and I take it from her fork, from her palm, from her fingers as if it is the newest and sweetest taste in the world.

After all, it was this food, these tastes, that first bought Lucinda to me five years ago.

She had been coming from America to Sao Luis every year to teach a workshop in the summer. She came to my stand one day and asked for one red fish, whole. She had heard it was good and if it really was that good, to ask for half would have been a waste and frankly, half of a divine tasting red fish would have pissed her off.

I remember how I watched her devour every bite, how she followed each morsel with a piece of white bread, how she ate everything from the napkin before she crumpled it in her palm and wiped at the corners of her mouth.

It *was* as good as they said, Lucinda had told me, turning up her small cup of rum punch. She wondered, then, what other dishes I could make that were half as good as my red fish.

So, that very night I invited her over for breaded beefsteak and fed her with my fingers. She showed me some of her paintings and for three days after, we talked and touched and loved.

Then she was gone. And although I slipped my phone number into her satchel next to her sketchpad and paintbrushes, she never called.

The next summer she arrived on my doorstep, and every summer after, it has been as though she never left.

•

Lucinda's lips taste sweet when she is done eating, and I can't keep mine off them. Her energy has returned in a thunderous roar. We leave the dishes where they are and stumble to the bedroom.

Between kisses we remove each other's clothes and she guides me to the bed. She stretches her long body above mine. Her locks fall against my shoulders and chest. Her nipples graze my own. Her knee is wedged between my thighs and she parts them quickly, roughly.

Lucinda lowers herself on top of me, rubbing her thigh against my cunt. My nipples rise and harden and I am slick between my legs, sensitive to everything. She places her hand there, sliding her palm against the wetness, her thin fingers finding their way inside.

She explores the inside of me as if seeking something and I lay hoping she never exhausts her search. She kisses my neck and shoulders; she licks my nipples. She slides down my body, her lips nipping at my navel while her fingers work their way in and out.

I know Lucinda wishes I would wait. I know she wants to sink between my thighs and put her mouth there first, but I buck and jerk and unleash my orgasm against her hand.

When I can breathe again, I rub my hands across her belly. Hovering above her, I take her small breasts into my mouth, first one then the other. I am finally free to explore her and I part her knees gently with my palms, pulling my hand against the warm skin on her thighs until I find the fuzzy center just below her navel.

Every time I touch her it is as if I'm touching her for the first time. There is always something new to explore, something that has always been there but I've never seen, like a deep curve in her hips or a scar on her legs.

Her eyelids flutter now when my lips touch her. She folds

her lips, terribly close to orgasm; she breathes heavily immediately following.

We are never as close as those few moments after we make love. When we lay where we've collapsed as if moving would disturb the calm.

"I like your hair like this," she says, reaching over to touch it. "It's sassy. It's you."

"Really? You like it?" I reach up and pull my fingers through the slick waves, shy, self-conscious.

"I love it, Gabriela," she says.

I am sure my cheeks are flushed.

I say, "It's been a hot summer and I needed a change. Yours has grown a lot since last year."

I reach for it, twirl the rough tendrils between my fingers. A smile spreads across her face as she places her hand on top of mine and guides it from her hair to below her waist, where it is wet and warm and waiting for me.

On the third night, Lucinda and I sit together in a tub of warm, soapy water, my legs wrapped around her. My hands slide over her long, lean body, washing and massaging her soft, dark skin. I rub my lips across the slick places on her neck and shoulders. I slip my arms underneath hers and clasp my hands across the slight curve of her belly, pulling her body back against mine. I inhale her scent and enjoy her warmth.

When the water goes cold, she sits straight up. With her back still turned to me, she speaks.

"I've been offered a fellowship back home," she says.

I smile because I like when Lucinda speaks of home, when she lets me into her world for brief moments like this, I am happy. I am proud.

"Oh really?" I say. "When did you find out?" I never ask her questions, but she makes me feel that this time it's all right.

"I found out a few months ago, right before I left to come here." She hesitates for a moment, and then she adds, "It starts next summer."

I try not to be alarmed at the words. "Oh. Early summer, then, or later when you're done here?"

Lucinda turns to look at me. Her smile is slight. She reaches for my hand.

"No, it's mid-summer, actually. And no, there won't be any here next year."

The washcloth falls from my hand into the water. I hold on to the tub for balance. I don't look at her when I say, "No here?"

Lucinda immediately begins speaking again. "I know what you're thinking, Gabriela, and I want you to know it wasn't easy for me at all, but this is such a great opportunity for me. It offers a lot of money, more than I ever made coming here all these summers, and it would mean a lot more chances to show my work."

She pauses, licking her lips. "I thought about not telling you at all. I thought about just leaving here and not looking back, but next year this time . . . knowing you're expecting me, looking for me, waiting for me . . . It wouldn't have been right and I wouldn't have been able to live with myself."

"It *isn't* right," I say and step out of the tub. I pull a towel from the rack and wrap it around me. "It isn't right for you to do me this way, for you to come here this time like it's no different from any other time. You might as well have said it as soon as you hit the door, Lucinda, or better yet, not come at all."

"Would you have wanted that?" She steps out of the tub and takes the extra towel. She brushes her hand against my arm.

I shrug. I feel a tightness in my chest that is uncomfortable and unfamiliar.

Lucinda is speaking again. "Look, we never made plans for the future. We never really said what this would be."

For the first time I want to ask if she loves someone else, if that is the reason. I am careful not to look at her, to walk into the bedroom and busy myself with putting on my nightclothes and brushing my hair.

She approaches me from behind and holds onto my hips. I am angry and I don't welcome her touch. As much as I want to, I don't turn around and fall into her arms.

I crawl into bed and turn my back to her when she climbs in beside me. My eyes remain wide open as night goes to day and I rise when I know it is time for Lucinda to prepare to leave.

We busy ourselves with getting her bags packed and calling the taxi. I send a fish sandwich and a small mango with her. I give her my cheek when she leans forward to kiss me.

When Lucinda takes her bags from the living room to the end of the driveway, I do not offer my help. And when we hug, I beg the tears not to fall.

I close the door behind her. I do not say good-bye.

When I arrive, I am tired and I am hungry. I long for her arms, for her lips. I wait outside her door until she arrives, satchel in hand, stained smock covering her cropped T-shirt and baggy jeans.

I look at her face when I can't keep my eyes away any longer. I want to see it there, what she feels, what she doesn't, what she wants to say and cannot.

Lucinda doesn't speak. She doesn't ask how or why. She only drops her satchel at her feet and crouches in front of me. She cups my chin in her hand, her fingers soft against my cheek. Then she stands and offers her hand. I grab on and struggle to my feet.

She reaches into her pocket and pulls out her keys. "I haven't had a chance to clean up around here, so, you'll have to excuse the mess," she says, as if these are words she speaks to me every day. She pushes open the door and steps aside to let me in first.

"Oh, it's fine," I say, just as casually, and step over a bag of garbage she forgot to put outside.

"I don't know if you're hungry but I usually get in pretty late around here. I end up ordering out all the time. Mostly pizza. You like pizza, right, Gabriela?"

Before I can answer, she pulls a large flat box from the refrigerator and I mumble, "Sure."

"Microwave's in the kitchen. I think I've got some paper plates in the cabinet."

"Okay."

Lucinda rubs her hand across the front of her jeans. "I'm just gonna go grab a quick shower before this paint sets in. You just, uh, make yourself at home."

She disappears into the bathroom and her shower takes longer than it takes for me to eat, clean the kitchen, and take out the trash. When Lucinda emerges, she is dressed in a man's T-shirt and pale blue drawstring pants.

She wipes her hands against her pants and stuffs them in her pockets. "So, you wanna watch a movie or something?"

"Whatever you want to do." I am sitting patiently on the couch, my hands folded in my lap.

"Well, I'm pretty tired. Worked really hard tonight."

"Then we can go to bed." I stand up and look down the hall toward the closed doors.

"Oh, yeah sure," she says. "I didn't even show you to the bedroom, did I?"

I am not sure, but I think her eyes soften a bit and she

smiles, reaching out for me to take her hand. She leads me to her bedroom where she places my bag against the wall below the large window.

Lucinda's eyes dart across the room as if she herself is in a foreign environment.

"I'm gonna let you get changed, then I'll come in and say goodnight," she says.

I stop pulling at the button on my blouse. "Then you . . . you're not . . . staying?"

She folds her lips, pulls at the drawstring on her pants. "Well, it was a long trip and I figure you must be pretty tired. I'm just gonna crash out here on the couch tonight so you can get some rest."

I want to tell Lucinda that I didn't come here for rest, that I could have rested at home if that was what I wanted, but I say nothing. I simply watch her turn and walk away before I pull my nightgown from my bag and slip it on.

I lie down on Lucinda's bed, bury myself beneath the covers, pull her pillow close to my face, and breathe. I listen for her coming through the door. I wait to feel her to crawl into bed beside me, whisper in my ear how happy she is to see me.

I do this all night.

"I've been waiting for you. I've been up since seven."

I sit on the couch, my legs tucked under me. I watch Lucinda as she walks through the front door, purse and plastic bags in hand.

"I swung by the studio. Then I stopped and grabbed some breakfast. I didn't know if you liked your eggs scrambled or sunny side up, so I got one of each and you can just pick."

"You could have said something." I don't mean to snap, but it comes out venomous anyway.

Lucinda exhales loudly. "I didn't want to wake you."

"Then you could have called. I was worried."

Lucinda drops everything in her hand. "You see! That's exactly what I was afraid of. I don't *need* you to worry about me, Gabriela! I don't need you here waiting for me. I'm not used to this."

I hold my head down when I don't know what else to say.

Lucinda continues. "Listen, I don't know how to do this. I'm out of my element here."

"I see." I can barely speak the words.

"We have our thing. Four days once a summer. It's the way it's always been—"

"Except it's not anymore, Lucinda," I say. Then I ask. As much as I don't want to hear the answer, I ask. "By the way, how is your fellowship going?"

"Oh, that . . . well . . ."

"I'm sorry I came here, Lucinda. I'm sorry I've made things difficult for you." I stand and straighten my skirt.

"Gabriela, I tried to be as sensitive as I could about it, but you came here anyway. What were you thinking? What were your intentions, to check up on me or something?"

"I said I was sorry." There is a lump in my throat and quiver in my voice.

"Look, I'm sorry I'm being such a bitch about it, but you gotta know that's how I am most times. All those times when you're not around, I'm stone cold. See, you get the good parts of me, those four days when nothing else matters and everything is perfect," Lucinda says, head cocked.

"Right." I bite my bottom lip.

"So, why don't we just nix this whole thing and I run you to the airport? Life can go on as normal . . . You have yours in Sao Luis and I have mine here. You have things you need to get back to, right? There's your stand and your house . . ."

I only nod. Speaking is too risky. Speaking would surely bring tears and screams and words I'm not ready to hear.

I stand on unsteady feet. I wait while Lucinda brings my still packed bags from the bedroom. She loads them in the backseat of her car and waits for me there.

The ride to the airport is silent save for whatever songs play on the radio and her humming along every now and then. The kiss she gives me at the terminal is quick and dry.

I don't look back.

I sit on the couch, legs shaking, my hands restless in my lap. I jump at the sound of every car that passes. None of them is Lucinda.

I try to remember the way she looked, the way her voice sounded when she said her last words to me. I think of how long her locks would be now, if there may be a few strands of gray there.

I wonder if Lucinda is happy, if she's finally reached the level of success she was after in her career all those years. I wonder if she ever made time for love, if she ever will. I wonder if someone calls her honey, if someone calls her mama.

I wonder if she knows I am here, that on the first night of the seventh summer Lucinda hasn't come to me, I am sitting and I am waiting.

Haiti's Daughter

Amanda Earl

Séraphine fussed with her out-of-control hair. Her friends told her she should let it go natural, but she found straight hair esthetically pleasing, so she battled her fuzzy frizz, using hair products galore. Not that she didn't love women with natural hair; she found them a total turn on, wild and free. Some even said they were better in bed, better coochy lickers, for example.

She didn't have time to fiddle with straightening this time, so she used a few elastic bands to hold her hair down, as if that could ever work. Smoothing down the frizzy puffs surrounding her like a black angel's halo, she took a deep breath, picked up her camera, and entered the auditorium foyer. Her assignment was to photograph the Haitian Creole poet, Mercedes Saladin.

Her radar went off as she spotted gorgeous black women everywhere, sporting cornrows, straight hair, big 'fros, ponytails, locks, beaded hair. A woman about her own height wearing a yellow short short dress caught Séraphine's eye. She held the attention of the crowd.

"We should introduce you to Mercedes before that group monopolizes her completely, Séraphine."

The photographer turned around to face the organizer of the event. She'd known him for years and was grateful he'd given her the photo gig once again, but the beautiful poet distracted her.

"Oh, hi Georges, so that's Mercedes . . ." Séraphine walked closer, paying no attention to the words of the festival director. She couldn't take her eyes off the poet.

Mercedes looked up. Their eyes caught. Séraphine's body tingled. That smile. Incredible. Soft pink, kissable lips. Séraphine's cunt grew tight and moist at the thought of those lips on her lips, and then on her lower lips. Her legs trembled. She unscrewed the lens cap of her camera, pressed the zoom, steadied her hand and snapped.

Mercedes' mouth opened, lips glistened, and eyes sparkled tiger eye as she looked straight into the camera, right into the photographer's soul; or that's how it felt to Séraphine. Mercedes was a good ten, maybe even fifteen years older than her, but a spicier woman she'd never seen. Coriander skin and berry lips. Scarf wrapped round her head. Muscular, sexy Tina Turner legs showing beneath her mini.

"Jeezus, it's hot in here, don't you think?" Georges said.

Séraphine had forgotten all about him and the room, but realized she was sticky with heat. Never mind that it was only April, snow still white on the pavement outside, a few crocuses and daffodils poking through the softening ground. It felt like a steamy tropical oasis in July.

She closed her eyes, imagined a beach, the waves rushing in. Mercedes undoing the top of her bikini, fingers stroking her breasts until the nipples grew hard.

Realizing she'd moaned out loud, Séraphine opened her eyes, back to reality. In the foyer, men loosened ties and wiped hot cheeks. Mercedes, on the other hand, was looking fine, giving off vibes of calm, cool, and queer, oh so very queer, praise the heavens.

The murmurs of the crowd ceased as Séraphine found

herself slinking over there, like some kind of panther in heat. She didn't feel sleek though, but nervous, very nervous. Mercedes extended her hand; the two of them touched for the first time. Séraphine cooled down and breathed in Caribbean Sea breeze and sweet earth musk. Both women held themselves still until the bystanders walked away. Even Georges left them alone.

"We should get a drink," Mercedes said. There was no arguing with that voice. It was confident, knowing, and relaxed, flowing along Séraphine's body like unexpected rain in a tropical forest, green and hot. Mercedes hadn't let go of Séraphine's hand and the two of them walked together this way. Séraphine didn't say a word, just let herself be taken. Mercedes handed her a glass of white wine, her fingernails lightly pressing the back of Séraphine's hand.

"I've heard about you, Séraphine Dufour, but no one mentioned you didn't speak."

Séraphine took a big gulp of her drink.

"I'm not usually silent."

"And I'm not usually this forward. After the reading, come to my room."

Yes, oh yes, Séraphine thought and tried to still her shaking hands. Soon it was time for the poet to read. The photographer had to arrange the shots, but she didn't want to surrender Mercedes to the audience. A fierce need overcame her to hang on to this woman, not to let her get away. Ever.

It wasn't like she didn't have wham-bam-thank-you mams. She certainly didn't have serious relationships. In between bouts between the sheets with pretty ladies, she relieved herself with vibrators, dildos, and lesbian porn. But this was somehow different. Maybe it was just the exoticness of it all. A chick from another country. Hell, she sometimes fantasized about Iman for God's sake. So what? Séraphine tried to shake it off.

The moderator introduced Mercedes. He talked about how she'd been a member of the Sosyete Koukouy, or Society of Fireflies, how her own mother had been jailed for her writing during Duvalier's dictatorship and then had to go into hiding when Baby Doc took over. This was a strong woman from a long line of strong Haitian women. Séraphine wanted to introduce her to her own mother, if her mother ever accepted that Séraphine was a lesbian, but of course she didn't. So they hadn't spoken since she left home.

Mercedes read not just from her own poems but also the poetry of other Haitian writers. As she listened to Mercedes's low voice recite poetry in the Haitian Creole language she'd heard so much as a child, Séraphine's heart ached.

Mercedes: lover, mother, writer, powerful woman, spell-binding sex goddess, voodoo princess even. Séraphine hungered for her, for all these parts of her. Even the ones she just imagined.

Séraphine took shots of her in her guava-colored dress, swaying as she read, moving her hands and modulating her voice in mountains and ocean waves. The room was quiet, falling under her spell. Séraphine photographed the audience, totally captivated by this woman.

At the end, they gave her a standing ovation, a rarity at any reading. Mercedes walked off the stage, her face flush, her movements graceful, but hurried.

"Let's go," she said. "I'm starving."

"But, what about the reception? Don't you have to attend?"

"I need to get out of here. I need to be dancing, drinking, eating, making love. Come with me."

Séraphine scrambled to keep up with her. At the coat check, Mercedes donned a light jacket.

"You don't have anything warmer? You'll freeze, Mercedes."

"I guess you'll have to keep me warm then." Séraphine could feel the blush start on her face, move down over her neck and onto her chest. Yes, they would be warm enough all right.

"Take me to your favorite restaurant. Some place spicy."

"We can take the metro."

"Ah yes, it'll be good not to be on a tap-tap bus." Mercedes smiled. "It's so different here. Smoother and maybe a bit more tentative. Must be the lack of ocean. If I close my eyes, I can pretend the sound of the subway is the sea. Makes me miss home."

"Then maybe you'll like the restaurant, the chef's Haitian."

They grabbed the metro and headed over to the Sugar Cane. In the subway, they sat close, Mercedes's thigh touching Séraphine's. Mercedes put her hand on the girl's leg.

"You've got a beautiful figure, Séraphine. Your skin glows, ma chérie, did you know that? What a body you have. I look forward to exploring every inch." So quietly she whispered, as if no one else was around. As if they were in bed.

Séraphine wanted to take Mercedes's hand and shove it between her legs so she could feel the heat, the moisture she was causing.

"Maybe we should go to my place, it's the next stop."

"We will, but first we're going to have dinner and you're going to tell me all about yourself, ma chérie bébé."

"Me? There's not much to tell. Everything I am is through this lens." She opened her photography bag and took out her camera, aimed it at Mercedes, who stared intently at her, her brown skin shimmering heat in the fluorescent light of the subway car. Séraphine took another photo of Mercedes's reflection in the window as they emerged out of the tunnel into the night. Mercedes, the blur of her yellow dress reflected in the window as they sped along.

"I think of you as someone who's always moving. The

way you were on the stage, swaying. All that energy as you read. So much power."

Séraphine snapped again then put away the camera. Mercedes took hold of the girl's wrist.

"In Haiti, you have to keep moving. You move for food; you move to avoid being shot; you move to avoid the police. Especially with my writing. I have to be so careful. Even coming here, it's a risk. They let me come, but I have to watch what I say. Listen to my poems. I speak in code."

"How are you surviving? Isn't it dangerous?"

"For tonight I just want to be here with you. Haiti is my mother, Séraphine, and she's me too. I'm proud of her, of my ancestors who beat Napoleon's army back with machetes. We need to protect her, to cherish her, to cherish and nurture ourselves.

"I came here to this festival to tell everyone not just about the horrors but also her beauty and the devastation of the land, what we need to preserve, to protect. A country is more than just what you see in the news. To see ugliness alone, how can anyone feel hopeful, even want to help us? My poems, they show the hope and the strength of the people. Haiti will never die. She's a multitude of voices, a choir, singing out. God hears and so do you."

Séraphine's eyes filled with tears. Mercedes stroked her face. Séraphine moved closer to her.

"Mercedes, my grandparents came from Haiti. They had nothing there, no job, no chance of education for my mother and her siblings. So they came here. Some of my family moved back to Haiti in the 90's, but my parents stayed. It's in my blood too. Sometimes I feel kind of like we abandoned you there."

"Your family sends money and food back home, don't they? This is a beautiful country, child, a rich country. We need what you provide from here."

"We've always sent food through a distributor, it's true. Even when my mother was working in a factory, making $7.50 an hour. Once a month ma tante would order for us—rice, beans, juice—enough to feed fifty people. They say Haitians outside Haiti send over a billion dollars worth of food and money annually. I give some money from my photography earnings as well. It still doesn't seem like I'm personally doing enough though."

"It helps, ma chère. Haiti is part of you. Wherever you go, she is with you. And look at you, so beautiful, tall, and healthy. Like this country, vibrant and lush. When I write a poem about you, you'll be Montreal, daughter of Haiti. Smile, ma belle, let's have this moment."

The two women walked into the dark April night, past the narrow brick houses with their spiral iron staircases, the quiet sound of their footsteps on the pavement punctuated only by a car alarm. Séraphine was comforted by Mercedes's hand in her own. In the distance they heard the soulful music of Emeline Michèle as they approached the restaurant. Mercedes took Séraphine in her arms and started to dance. Séraphine could feel Mercedes's warm body against her own as they moved together. Mercedes laughed and twirled Séraphine round and round then plunked herself down on a low concrete wall.

"Come here."

Séraphine moved to sit beside her, placing her camera bag on top of the wall.

"No, sit on my lap." Séraphine's face grew hot and the heat traveled down her body as she complied.

Mercedes undid the buttons of Séraphine's coat and slowly slid her hand inside, touching the pulse at Séraphine's neck, then pushing her hand against her heart. The young woman's warm breaths created clouds of desire in the cold night air.

"You're heart's beating so fast, fifille." Mercedes leaned down, parted Séraphine's shirt, and put her lips against her chest. "You smell so good, like a ripe mango, ready for me to open. And I need to open you up, pull you apart, devour you."

Séraphine's lips parted as she let the heat of Mercedes's lips warm her cold lips with a kiss. Their tongues touched. Mercedes's hands wandered over Séraphine's silky caramel skin. Séraphine was wet, so wet, the juices soaking her cotton briefs. Mercedes's fingers reached down, unzipped Séraphine's fly, and undid the button.

"I need to touch you there, just for a minute."

They heard footsteps. Mercedes pulled Séraphine close to her. They huddled there in the dark, protecting each other. The footsteps moved farther away. Mercedes slid her hand beneath the waistband of Séraphine's briefs. Séraphine opened her legs wider, felt herself letting go, yielding to the woman's hand, which covered her hairless mound.

"You wax down there, baby? So smooth. Let me touch you. Open your legs more, ma chère."

All Séraphine could do was obey. Mercedes parted her lover's swollen sex lips.

"You're so wet. I need you to touch me, too. Touch my breasts."

Séraphine pulled apart Mercedes's light jacket and reached inside the dress, her hand moving inside the older woman's bra. She wanted to pull it off, cup the heavy breasts, suck the dark nipples into her mouth, but she contented herself with stroking them to hardness. So hard and straight in her fingers. She squeezed until Mercedes cried out. Séraphine humped against Mercedes's hand as a finger slid inside her and a thumb pressed ever so gently on her clit.

In the background the music grew louder. Séraphine tugged on Mercedes's nipple, leaned her head down. She had to taste, couldn't resist any longer.

"Do it. Lick my tit. Suck."

That was all it took. She moved the bra cup down farther. Mercedes's large, swollen breast spilled over the cup. Séraphine nuzzled the nipple, licked around and around. Mercedes put another finger inside her, then pumped it in and out of her cunt. Séraphine sucked the wet nipple into her mouth, smelling the musky scent of arousal coming from Mercedes's cunt. She wanted to touch it so badly, to stroke it, to make love to it, to lay Mercedes out on the cold concrete wall and bury her face in her cunt, lick up every drop of juice.

"Keep moving, just keep moving against my hand," Mercedes whispered in a sing-song voice. Séraphine's cunt tightened as she humped Mercedes's hand. Right there in the open. Mercedes was going to make her come. Hard. Any second. There it was. Her cunt tightened against Mercedes's fingers, circling them, drawing them in deeper, deeper.

"That's it. Come for me, Séraphine. Now. Do it." Manman tanbou and boula drums echoed against the nearby brick walls, their beat increasing, Creole rhythms of rapture.

Séraphine moaned loudly as she let it all out. Released herself. Clenched her cunt around Mercedes's fingers and then let go.

"Karésé'ou té karésé'm," sang Mercedes quietly as Séraphine came. They kissed and kissed and kissed and kissed.

"You're amazing, Mercedes. Oh God."

"So are you ma petite, so are you . . . I'm starving." Mercedes brought her fingers up to her mouth and licked. "As good as you taste, I need something a bit more substantial. Let's eat."

In the crowded restaurant they found a table near the window, realizing they'd been fucking in full view of the patrons. The waiter smiled as he took their order, bringing them a bottle of wine right way: chilled, white, cold.

Some of the patrons were drinking Prestige beer. Mercedes frowned. "That brewer gets rich while the poor suffer. It's a Haitian beer. I'll never drink it." So much Séraphine didn't know, didn't really know how to deal with.

They ate chictai, red beans, and rice. They talked. They held hands. They became friends over sweet potato bread and fried bananas. Séraphine kept snapping photos of Mercedes in between bites.

"You know, when we first saw each other today, I had no idea what it would be like, Séraphine, to be with you. I only knew I wanted you."

"No, neither did I. So now, I'm asking you the question: do you come to Canada often?"

"Let's finish and go. Do you want to come back to my hotel?"

"You're not answering. Will I see you again?"

"I don't know, okay? The festival brought me here. When I travel, it's from funding from the country I go to. I don't even know if the authorities will let me leave Haiti again."

"So why go back?"

"I don't have any choice. All we have is now, Séraphine. It's how I survive at home, day by day. Do you want to be with me now or do you think it's better to grieve and mourn over an unknown tomorrow?"

Séraphine and Mercedes stood up.

"I want you forever, but I'll settle for now, if that's all we can count on. I want to take you back to my place. Not your hotel, not a strange bed, but mine. I want to remember you there, smell your scent after you leave."

Outside the couple embraced.

"Is it far? I don't know how much longer I can wait."

"No, Mercedes. Not far. I live in Mile End. We can walk."

They passed bagel shops, newsstands, and homeless people. Mercedes shivered and gave a man on the street money from her purse.

"I hate to see that here too."

"It's everywhere, more here now than when I was younger. I'd stop and take a photo of him—that's what I do, show the poverty of Montreal to the world—don't know how else to handle it either. God I feel so helpless, Mercedes. Tonight all I want is to forget, to be with you."

"Yes." The two kissed once more. Finally they arrived and climbed the stairs, entering one of the doorways in the house. Séraphine fumbled with her keys, unlocked the door, and turned on the lights, then thought better and started to turn off the switch for the light in the living room.

"Leave it on. I want to see all of you. Take off your clothes."

Séraphine put her camera on a nearby table, then slowly undressed. Mercedes did the same. The two women looked at themselves and each other in a full-length mirror.

"We're so beautiful. Your light brown skin, my darker brown, side by side."

"Mercedes, you're the one who's beautiful." Mercedes removed her scarf to reveal a head of close-cropped hair. Séraphine caressed her cool neck, the back of her head. Mercedes moaned.

"Undo your hair. Let me caress it."

"Oh Mercedes, it's so frizzy and wild. I should just keep it up. It'll get in our way."

"No. I want to see it, feel it. Be wild, let yourself go, Séraphine."

Séraphine undid the elastic fastening her hair and it uncoiled in black curls all around her face.

"You look like the Black Madonna. So innocent. So pure."

"I'm not though." Séraphine wrapped Mercedes in an embrace and the two of them fell to the floor. Being in her own apartment with this beautiful woman made Séraphine feel strong and in control. She kissed Mercedes then moved down along her body, stopping to kiss and caress the shallow valley at the base of her throat. Mercedes's skin suddenly shivered and was covered in tiny goose bumps.

"You're sensitive there."

"Mmmm. Yes. Now let me . . . touch you."

"Just stay put. It's my turn, Mercedes. My turn to make you come."

Séraphine kept kissing lower and lower, her fingers licked at each nipple in turn. She pressed her long black hair against Mercedes breasts, used the end to tickle her nipple into hardness.

"I can't decide which one I like better, the left or the right. Both are beautiful. The right's a bit larger, isn't it, Mercedes?" She took the woman's nipple into her mouth and began to suck. "Like a fine blackberry, so tasty, or maybe more like a grape, so purple, so juicy baby."

Mercedes writhed beneath Séraphine's hands and mouth. Séraphine had never felt this powerful before. She pressed her body hard against Mercedes until they were grinding against one another's mounds, breast against breast. Mercedes didn't shave. The wiry hair on her cunt rubbed against Séraphine's smooth pussy. Her hand moved down.

"I need to be inside you." She put one finger, then another inside Mercedes's cunt. "You're so wet, so wide, so ready for me."

"More, please," Mercedes gasped for breath as another finger, then another penetrated her. Then a thumb. Séraphine's whole hand was inside her, possessing her.

Séraphine squeezed as Mercedes took her fist inside. But she was gentle, oh so gentle. Didn't move at all until Mercedes's cunt clenched around her hand, and then she let Mercedes set the pace with her hips, taking her in, moving her out. In. Out. In. Out. Faster. Faster. Faster. Séraphine rubbed her cunt against Mercedes's leg as the two of them fucked. Rubbing. Moist. So fast now. She had to come. She was going to come again. Mercedes cried out. Séraphine cried out too, a sheen of slippery white come oozing from her cunt onto Mercedes's leg.

Mercedes rolled on top of Séraphine and moved down, parting Séraphine's cunt lips. Then she tasted the juices of her climax. Séraphine looked down and saw Mercedes's almost naked head and moaned as she sucked her clit. She put her hands on Mercedes's head and pulled her in deeper. Mercedes's tongue entered Séraphine's hole. Séraphine felt the point of it at the entrance, its flat sides wetting her swollen cunt lips even more. She wanted Mercedes to swallow her, swallow her whole, like an oyster.

She came. Again. And again. The night would never end. She didn't want it to. They fell asleep on the carpet, body against body, lips against lips.

In the morning, Séraphine woke first. She tiptoed quietly to the bathroom and when she got back, Mercedes was still asleep. Carefully she reached for her camera. She angled it toward her sleeping lover, zoomed in on her smiling, carefree face; that smile, a gift they'd exchanged. A smile she wanted to remember forever. Mercedes kept sleeping so Séraphine covered her with a blanket, and made coffee.

By the time Mercedes woke up, Séraphine had breakfast on the table. Croissants and coffee. She was singing "Give me joy," from one of Emeline Michel's songs they'd heard the night before.

"You should sing more often. You have a beautiful

voice." Mercedes raised herself off the floor, but couldn't help groaning.

"Thanks. You make me want to. Sorry we never made it to the bed last night. I can't believe we slept on this hard floor."

"I slept better than I have in ages."

The two embraced, laughing as Mercedes pushed Séraphine's hair out of the way to kiss her face, then her lips.

"What time is it?"

"It's ten."

"Damn, I have to go. My flight leaves soon. I have to get back to my hotel and pack up quickly."

Séraphine felt the tears start to fall.

"I'm sorry, ma chère." Mercedes took her in her arms, stroked her hair. "Your hair. It's beautiful, Séraphine. You should keep it like that. So natural. You're a natural beauty, my darling. Never forget that. Be proud of who you are. Did you know that the Haitian flag was sewn with a woman's hair? You are Haiti's daughter, Séraphine."

Mercedes stroked and kissed her lover's hair. Séraphine caressed Mercedes close-cropped locks.

The two said good-bye after Mercedes dressed. Whenever anyone asked why she never straightened her hair anymore, she told them it was because she loved Haiti.

Special Delivery

Teresa Noelle Roberts

I went to Bengal Palace for the first time because it was right around the corner from my apartment. I went back again because the food was inexpensive and delicious.

And I kept going back because of the hostess—her soft, welcoming smiles, her colorful saris bright against her honey-colored skin, the way her gold bangles glittered and jingled, the sweep of her thick, shoulder-length black hair.

I never spoke to her beyond polite pleasantries as she showed me to my table, never learned her name, never had any real interaction with her. She was like some exotic bird I could admire, but not touch. But when I found myself eating vegetable korma and chicken tikka and other tasty dishes from the Bengal Palace menu three or four times a week, just so I could stare moonily at her and fantasize about unwrapping her sari, I told myself I needed to get a grip.

The hostess, whoever she was, was a real woman with a real life, not a character from the movie version of *Kama Sutra* (which, okay, was one of my favorite movies of all time; I wore it out on VHS and then got it on DVD). I felt like I was being Weirdo Stalker Chick, and in a way that would make my more politically savvy friends scold me. I knew damn well that the source of my crush was at least as much the exotic-to-me packaging—the pretty saris, the bindi, the delicate gold nose ring that connected to her earring with a fine chain—as the woman herself. Sure, she was attractive, with big brown eyes, pretty features, and a curvy, cuddly body, but would I find her half as intriguing if I saw her in jeans and a sweatshirt?

When I answered my own question with a reluctant no, I decided I'd check out some of the other restaurants in the neighborhood and start using my own kitchen for something besides morning coffee; wean myself off curry and beautiful brown eyes, stop being Weirdo Politically Incorrect Stalker Chick, maybe even see about getting myself a real girlfriend as opposed to an imaginary one.

The only problem with that plan was that I missed the Bengal Palace's food.

Really missed it. Sure, I missed seeing the pretty hostess, but without constantly feeding my crush, that started to fade into an occasional tacky *Kama Sutra*–flavored fantasy.

The craving for the Bengal Palace's cuisine, on the other hand, didn't. I swear they had a stash of heroin that they sprinkled over the food, because it was definitely addictive.

The craving came to a head one rainy night. I'd worked late, come home tired, and determined not to leave the apartment until morning. Nothing in the meagerly-stocked pantry looked appealing, none of my takeout menus called to me. I wanted Indian food and I wanted it ten minutes ago.

I checked the phone book. Sure enough, Bengal Palace delivered. I hadn't noticed before, given how eager I was to see my imaginary girlfriend—but on this nasty night it sounded like a great plan.

One phone call later and dinner was on its way. I changed from my rain-damp work clothes into sweats and got ready for an evening of gluttony and mindless TV.

When I buzzed the delivery person up, I really wasn't thinking about much other than grab food, give tip, close door, pig out. Certainly not about who might be carrying the food to my door. The various slacker-type boys who brought me pizza never made much of an impression, and the old guy from my favorite Chinese place just made me sad—no one should be doing such a drudge job at his age.

But standing in my doorway, holding a bag that smelled like curry from heaven, was the cutest dyke I'd seen in a long time. (Okay, the dyke part was an educated guess. She didn't have I PREFER GIRLS tattooed across her forehead or anything, but my gaydar pinged off the meter as soon as I saw her.)

She had short, wavy dark hair with a few discreet burgundy streaks; a jaunty ruby stud in her nose; loose black cargo pants that did nothing to hide curvy hips and strong thighs I'd love to dive between; a silly bright yellow slicker that actually flattered her smooth complexion, somewhere between the colors of honey and toast; huge dark eyes that were obviously registering my sweatshirt, which sported two cartoon villainesses smooching; and a sweet, but naughty grin as she said, "Love the shirt."

Hot as vindaloo. And, after about five seconds, very familiar.

"Hey, aren't you the hostess . . ."

So I was wrong. In everyday American clothes, she looked even better than she had in the sari. More comfortable. More relaxed. More accessible and less a figure of fantasy.

And—always a bonus—more like someone who might be interested in me.

"I *was* the hostess until last week, but thank God I finally got a job in my field."

I raised my eyebrows. "Delivery?"

"Environmental education. I'm just helping my aunt and uncle out because one of the delivery guys has the flu and they were good to me while I was unemployed." She shrugged. "At least doing this, I can dress like myself. My aunt and uncle are pretty old-country and insisted the hostess couldn't possibly wear slacks."

How had I never noticed that, while most of the Bengal Palace staff had lilting Indian accents, hers was as Middle American as mine?

I mentally mocked myself for my assumptions as she handed over my food.

"Congrats on the job," I said. Then the words slipped out without my brain actually being involved. "But I'll miss seeing you at the restaurant." I felt myself flushing. "You were always so welcoming," I added, trying to backpedal and only making it more obviously flirtatious.

"That was because seeing you always improved my night. You'd smile at me and I'd know you were flirting and I'd feel like myself again, instead of like Generic Indian Girl Number Sixty-Two. It made me crazy that I couldn't really flirt back, but I was trying to be professional, even if I hated the job." Her grin grew broader. "I missed you when you stopped coming in."

Then she seemed to take a deep breath. "Uh . . . you were flirting, right? Or is this when I kind of throw the food at you and run away?"

My heart melted, which put it in the same condition as my panties. The little bit of insecurity made me warm to her beyond lustful appreciation of her good looks. "Oh yeah," I reassured her, "I was flirting! I stopped coming around because I was afraid I was starting to annoy some poor straight woman who was just trying to do her job."

"You weren't." Then she leaned forward and kissed me. Just a gentle brush of lips against lips, but it was full of promise. "I've got to go," she said softly. "Got a car full of deliveries getting cold downstairs. Can I call you? I've got your number right here."

She waved my order slip.

"I don't even know your name!" I was trying to hold her, trying to keep that ripe body and adorable face from slipping away when it was finally in my grasp.

"Amy," she said. "Amy Patel. 293-7524. And you're Sasha Berkowitz. I remember from processing your credit cards." (Knowing we'd both been Weirdo Stalker Chicks made me feel less ashamed.) "I'll call!"

She turned to go, and I sagged a little with childish disappointment. Then she turned back and we melted into each other.

I'd imagined her breath scented with cardamom and fennel, but instead I tasted peppermint Altoids and coffee. Her tongue was fierce, probing, and I could just imagine it dancing on my clit. The damp slicker stood between me and the luscious breasts that the sari and choli top had shown off so nicely, but rubber had never felt so good as it did with her body warming it. And two handfuls of curvy, firm butt did a lot to console me for the slicker.

I'm not normally an instant-sex kind of gal. I like the slow build, the courtship, the teasing and getting to know each other. But in this case, I was willing to make an exception, and from the way Amy's hands were roving over my body, so was she.

Only the sound of a cell phone playing an obnoxious Bollywood jingle pulled us back to sanity. "Oh hell," Amy said. "That's the restaurant. Either they've got more orders for me or someone's complaining I'm taking too long. I'll call!"

"You stop delivering at ten, right? Want to just stop by?"

And she said yes.

I barely tasted the Indian delicacies I'd so craved earlier in the evening. Most of them ended up in the refrigerator to become tomorrow's lunch. Instead of eating and vegging, I spent the intervening time frantically tidying my apartment, changing the sheets, and putting together a suitably sultry mix of music.

Amy arrived at ten-twenty, looking rather like a drowned rat—hair soaked, pants wet to the knees. "The last few deliveries, I couldn't find a parking spot closer than five blocks, not even double-parking."

"Well, we'd better get you out of those wet things," I said, unzipping the slicker, then unbuttoning the flannel shirt underneath it, parting the layers to see the hot, honeyed skin I'd dreamed about so long. The clean sheets turned out to be a wasted effort. We never made it out of the living room.

She was a combination of the anticipated and unanticipated, the familiar and the exotic.

Rounded, firm breasts, their plum-colored nipples peaking under my tongue, just as delicious as I'd imagined.

Skin that tasted like curry (probably from the food she'd been delivering) and Dr. Bronner's peppermint soap.

A stud through her clit hood that matched the one in her nose, and a tattoo of Coyote and Roadrunner on her thigh.

Brazilian waxing, which surprised me almost as much as the tattoo.

The slick, purplish flesh of her vulva, pulsing under my fingers and tongue.

The steady stream of shits and fucks and oh Jesus-gods she let out as she came, even more startling when I remembered the sweet face and shy smile of her hostess persona.

Her tongue, as probing and fierce on my clit as I'd imagined—and just as probing, if more delicate, on the sensitive anal opening where no one had ever licked before.

Me, making noises only dogs could hear and clawing at her dark skin as she tongue-fucked me in ways I'd scarcely imagined, tongue-fucked me into the next day and possibly into another dimension.

Me, having enough brain cells left—barely—not to make

a *Kama Sutra* joke as we lay spent on a pile of sofa cushions and discarded clothes.

Okay, I'd been dumb. I hadn't seen beyond the costume to the real woman underneath it. But Amy, thank goodness, had been smarter than me. And so I'd gotten lucky, gotten a special delivery of hot American dyke inside my spice-scented sari-wrapped fantasy.

Maybe it would work out long-term, maybe it wouldn't. But I wasn't about to risk it all on a *Kama Sutra* joke.

On Her Terms

Sofía Quintero

As per her ritual, she opened a fresh bottle and logged onto the Internet Movie Database. After typing "Nicole Torres" into the search engine, she scrolled down to the bottom of the page to the message board. Someone had started a new forum with the title "Stick a Fork in Her." She clicked on the link:

Nicole hasn't done a Hollywood movie since The Final Stand *last summer, and that was a huge disaster. IMDB says she only has one new film coming out, but you can tell just by the description that it's some low-budget indie horror crap that should probably go straight to video. Stick a fork in her because she's done.*

Nicole took a deep swig of bourbon. It was low-budget indie horror crap. Her agent Charlene called it "the next *Blair Witch Project*," but ten pages into the script Nicole knew it would never make it into theaters. She hated *In the Shadows* but had to do it. Nicole had squandered her pay for *The Final Stand*, where she caused so many delays in production that Initiative threatened to drop her. Nicole took scale for *In the Shadows* and needed every penny to pay both her lawyer and publicist to spin her free from that hit-and-run on Wilshire.

And just as the IMDB.com poster predicted, Charlene told her months ago that *In the Shadows* would go straight to video if Nicole were lucky. She didn't say, "If we're lucky," like she used to when Nicole signed with her six years ago. Then again, six years ago Nicole was Hollywood's latest It girl whose debut film was bought at Sundance for an amount five times its budget, generated three times more at the box office, and garnered her an Independent Spirit Award for Best Female Newcomer.

Nicole scrolled through the next entries on the message board:

I hate to say it, but you're right, and I absolutely love NT. As a Latina and an aspiring actress myself, I always admired how she refused to play stereotypical roles. Even though NT has done a handful of decent movies, she's never been able to match the success of In Her Best Interest.

I used to be a fan of Nicole Torres until she started making a fool of herself, and I'm not talking about the bad role choices. Did anyone see her on Leno when she was promoting TFS*? She sounded like she had tossed back a few too many backstage if you catch my drift.*

Check out this blind item from Eonline! What former A-list actress and party girl has hit on hard times? The exotic beauty who quickly leaped from art house fare to big-budget productions is on the verge of losing her fame and fortune at the bottom of the bottle. Her tendency to show up on the set late and drunk has rendered her persona non grata to most Tinsel Town dealmakers. Is the stunning brunette's battle with the booze an attempt to drown her Sapphic desire? *I don't know about you guys, but I think it's Nicole.*

Drunk or not, I'd get with Nicole in a nanosecond. And I'm a hetero girl. That's how hot she is !!!!!

Just because Nicole plays strong female characters who don't need a man to rescue them doesn't make her a lesbian. She almost married Leandro Solis, and he can have any woman he wants. Do you think he would go out with Nicole for over a year and propose to her if she were a lesbian? Or a drunk? Get real! And even if Nicole were gay, so what? That's her personal business. She's still more beautiful and talented than any of you will ever be. Stop hating on Nicole already!

Nicole snickered and refilled her glass. She appreciated her defenders even if they were naïve. But she had been, too. Leandro was the perfect merkin until he fell for that black stand-up comic who starred opposite him in that buddy cop movie. Leandro played straight almost as well as she did. Nicole gave him that.

Then a new message board that had not been there the day before caught her eye: "The Next Nicole." She clicked on the link and began to read:

Have you guys heard of Christina De La Cruz? I just saw her first movie Tailspin *on DVD, and mark my words, she's going to be the next Nicole Torres. She's already been cast in three major features with co-stars like Terrence Howard, Jake Gyllenhaal, and Anthony Hopkins. She even has that sexy tomboy look that Nicole used to have before she went glam. Check out these stills of Christina from her debut flick.*

•

Nicole huffed and moved her cursor to the link. She could never win with these damned people. When she first arrived in Los Angeles, the tabloids constantly skewered her for her jeans and T-shirts and even the vintage suede Pumas that earned her daps in Queens. Then Nicole hired a stylist, allowed a plastic surgeon to whittle the sides of the broad nose she had inherited from her Afro-Cuban father, and made a standing appointment at the Yamaguchi Salon. The industry appreciated her transformation, and Nicole even made the Most Beautiful list in *People en Español.* But the message boards contained as many insults as they did compliments. Her detractors called Nicole anything from a drag queen to a sell out. Now her own "fans" were already naming her replacement.

Nicole selected the link, and a large photo of a young woman leaning against a motorcycle appeared across the screen. Wearing a pair of black leather pants and a blinding white men's undershirt, Christina De La Cruz straddled a piping red motorcycle. Unlike the crass displays of flesh and fabric of straight girls desperate for male validation, her thong bikini peeked over the waistband of her pants in a shy, subtle beckoning. Christina's long, dark mane waved along the golden skin of her face, neck, and shoulders the way caramelized sugar flowed over the top then down the sides of a creamy, sweet flan. Her lips were plush and red, like the velvet cushions that cradled the jewels Nicole borrowed from Neil Lane and Robyn Rhodes for premieres. Only when Nicole felt the attraction seeping into her skin and spreading through her body did she close the photo.

She logged onto the Movie Review Query Engine and entered *Tailspin.* Over the next two hours, Nicole read every word of the over one hundred reviews. Of course, a handful of critics dismissed the film as little more than an after school television special. They had done the same to Nicole's debut.

They did it to every independent effort to cast a different light on the urban experience besides the testosterone-fueled gore that made false liberals feel cool to praise for their authenticity. But the majority of the critics embraced the film and fell for its ingénue. Roger Ebert even referred to Christina as "the Latina reincarnation of Gregory Peck." But none of the critics likened Christina to Nicole even though they both possessed the same penetrating gaze, lithe physique, and irrepressible edge.

Nicole willed herself to hate Christina, but the attraction—to her beauty, her talent, and even her newcomer status—had already taken hold. She reached for her telephone and dialed Charlene's number. As always, her secretary informed her that Charlene was unavailable. Imagining that her agent was standing right there mouthing "not here", Nicole requested to be transferred to her voice mail. "Charlene, it's Nicole. I see that Initiative just signed Christina De La Cruz." She couldn't help herself. "Thanks for letting me know, seeing how everybody's saying she's the latest version of me. Anyway, I'm thinking that if there's any thing to all her buzz, we should find a project that she and I can work on together. Call me back. Let's discuss."

Nicole hung up, refilled her glass, and searched the Internet for more photographs of this Christina De La Cruz.

When she returned from her grocery run, Nicole found a message from Charlene on her answering machine. She procrastinated by replenishing her bar. After all, Charlene had been dodging her for so long. She could be calling her to say that she no longer wanted to represent Nicole. Or maybe she had an audition or script for her. Or perhaps Charlene finally stole a minute away from her more lucrative clients to scold Nicole for blowing off the Deidre Whittaker audition that she never wanted.

She didn't give a shit that Deidre—the screenwriter for three successful chick flicks—had written a role for Nicole in her directorial debut. Nicole was never offered romantic comedies so the idea of working with Deidre interested her. That is, until she realized that, once again, she would be playing the ethnic sidekick to some white girl who had just arrived in town last week. Nicole complained to Charlene who claimed to understand, but still pressured her to meet with Deidre. "Take the meeting and then say no," she said. Nicole truly meant to meet Deidre, but she had gone to a premiere the previous night, had too much to drink, and just slept through the alarm.

When she could no longer stand it, Nicole poured herself a glass of bourbon in a coffee mug and hit play on the answering machine:

Nic, it's Charlene. Got your message. Fabulous idea. Yeah, Chris signed with Erica Nash once Screen Gems bought the distribution rights to Tailspin. *Anyway, I followed up with her, and it turns out that Chris is your number one fan. So, Friday, Hugo's, ten. And lay off the fuckin' sauce for one night and be on time. The kid just got into town from Brooklyn, and I don't want YOU to be the one to disillusion her.*

Nicole polished off the bourbon in one sip. She began to recap the bottle and then decided to pour herself another cup. She had a good feeling about this meeting. Why not celebrate?

Nicole wasted an hour that morning attempting to dress younger than her thirty-two years, because she had developed a paunch that rendered hip huggers and baby tees disastrous. The last thing she needed was for some paparazzo to snap a photo of her and sell it to a tabloid. With her luck he would sell it to *US Weekly* to run in its "They're Just like Us" section under the caption THEY HAVE BEER BELLIES. So she settled for a baby doll top that hung away from her bulging waistline and Capri-length cargo pants, and arrived at a quarter to ten to find Charlene was waiting for her.

Then Erica arrived and soon Christina followed. Nicole and Christina locked eyes the second she entered the restaurant. Although more petite in person, she dressed all in white in a knit halter top, denim miniskirt and canvas wedges. Nicole stood to offer her hand, but Christina ignored it. "No, you gotta give me a hug," she said. As she held Nicole, Christina said in her ear, "I know you hear this all the time, but don't believe it until now." She pulled back to look Nicole in the face, obsidian eyes to obsidian eyes. "*I'm* your biggest fan."

Then throughout lunch, every time their hands brushed across the table or their feet touched beneath it, Nicole felt fire and knew these fleeting connections were not accidents.

"Nicky, we've got to talk," Christina insisted when she called three days later. "I've found the perfect script."

Nicole didn't even know that Christina had been looking for a script, too. At lunch, she seemed overwhelmed with auditions and interviews. So Nicole began wading through screenplays which read as if they came from the recycling dumpster on the Initiative lot.

She suspected that Christina's judgment was less than sophisticated, but the sound of her East Coast twang made Nicole want to see her. "So bring it to my place tonight," she said. "I'll make you dinner. *Un pernil con arroz y habichuelas.*" Then Nicole laughed and said, "You know you can't find real Caribbean cooking here on the West Coast."

Christina rang her intercom at exactly eight o'clock. She wore white hip huggers, a shredded black T-shirt with the *V for Vendetta* logo over a white ribbed tank top. Nicole chose to wear a cream strapless sundress with a jeweled, fitted bodice and full skirt with beige underlay. "Wow, look at you," Christina said as she crossed the threshold. "All that just for me."

Nicole knew she would do this. She knew once they were alone, Christina would reveal herself. She hoped that she would. But still Nicole played it safe. "What you've got there?" she asked, motioning to the slightly worn screenplay Christina had rolled up in her hand.

"It's called *On Her Terms*," Christina said. She followed Nicole into the living room and sat next to her on the cranberry Zanaboni sofa. "And it's about a professor who sues the university when she doesn't get . . . what do they call it?"

"Tenure?"

"Yeah, that's it!"

"And they don't grant her tenure on what grounds?"

Christina blinked at Nicole as if she should already know. "Because she's a lesbian. And what's so great about the script, Nicky, is that the character's out, right, but the homophobia she deals with isn't all in-your-face. Still Deborah—that's her name—knows what's going on. Just like in real life, that's what I love about it."

"Oh." Hearing Charlene coach her in her head, Nicole restrained from immediately shooting down the project. Instead she would listen, inquire, ask, and then ultimately pass. "So who would play who?'

Christina grinned. "Well, of course, I wanted to play Deborah, but Erica will kill me if I play older. Besides you're the one who's established and experienced and all that. You gotta play her. And I'll play your teaching assistant, Marie. So what if it's not the lead? It's still an awesome part. She's really important to the story."

With a mixture of relief and disappointment, Nicole said, "Well, okay, I'll read it, and we'll see." She started to stand

and say that they should move to the kitchen. But Christina took her hand and pulled Nicole back down on the couch.

"Let's read a few scenes together, you know, to see how it flows," she said. She inched closer to Nicole until their thighs touched and laid the script across their laps. Christina's hair had the almond scent of drug store shampoo, and Nicole smiled at the memory of her early days in Los Angeles. When she had no money, she had anonymity, and with anonymity came companionship with women who didn't notice if Nicole wore Revlon instead of Mac and didn't care if Nicole paid twenty or two hundred dollars for her jeans. Those earlier days of struggle had not been so bad.

"Like this scene where Marie encourages Deborah to sue," said Christina. Then she began to narrate. "*Interior, Deborah's office, day. Marie rushes in and finds Deborah packing her things. She grabs a text from Deborah's hands.* Don't tell me you're going to stand for this?"

"Why fight to stay somewhere I'm not wanted?" read Nicole.

As the scene progressed, Nicole grew captivated by the character's richness and nuanced dialogue. And Christina, clearly having read the script several times and mined the scene for its subtext, fueled the enchantment with her impassioned delivery. When Nicole reached to turn the page at the height of the argument between Deborah and Marie, Christina leaned over and gave her a moist, lingering kiss.

Nicole pulled away, and Christina giggled at her stunned face. "That's what the script calls for." She turned the page and pointed at the next line of direction. "See?" And then Christina placed the script aside and kissed Nicole again.

No! Nicole's reason ordered, but as Christina laced her tongue across her lips, every inch of her body betrayed her ego. With one hand, Nicole caressed her hair while the other eased under her top to caress her breast. As she felt Christina's nipple harden beneath her fingertips, Nicole felt her own ache against her bodice. With a strength that betrayed her petite stature, Christina pressed against Nicole, pushing her onto her back. Their kisses grew deeper, moister, interlaced with gasps of pleasure as they grasped for buttons and zippers. They stopped for Christina to stand and removed clothes while Nicole pulled her dress over her head. She watched as Christina lowered her bikini pants, revealing a mound blanketed with dark curls. Nicole smiled and reached out to stroke the hair on Christina's pussy. She had grown tired of the bald lips of giggly starfuckers, yearning for natural womanliness.

Christina descended on Nicole again, pressing her lips against hers and sliding her toned thigh between Nicole's legs. Nicole hooked her leg around Christina's waist, writhing until she felt the plush sensation of her thigh pressed against her clit. Legs intertwined, thighs against clits, hands on tits, lips parted and eyes closed, Nicole and Christina kissed and gyrated on the sofa, moaning and rubbing until Nicole cried out and burst into spasms.

Still throbbing with release, Nicole poised herself over Christina to kiss her. With one hand she grabbed a fist of her silky hair and the other she pried between Christina's warm legs. Christina exhaled, opening her legs, and Nicole's finger dipped between her silky lips. When her thumb found Christina's clit, it circled and circled the slippery button as two fingers slid inside her milky walls. As Nicole rubbed, Christina sucked her nipples with gasping desire as she humped her hand. Faster and faster Christina wound her hips, drenching Nicole's hand as it rubbed harder and plunged deeper until Christina exploded.

Nicole lowered herself beside Christina on the sofa and kissed her on her forehead. Christina reached over and traced a finger around Nicole's swollen areola. "I told you I was your biggest fan," she said.

They agreed to develop *On Her Terms*, and Nicole took the lead. Her dwindling savings took another hit when she paid to option the script, but she refused to hire the screenwriter for revisions, insisting that she and Christina together could iron out the wrinkles. Whenever Christina took a break from her combat training for her upcoming film shoot in Germany, they met at Nicole's apartment. They divided pages, rewrote scenes, and acted out the revisions. Nicole and Christina knew the changes worked whenever they found themselves grinding against each other on the carpet or across the table, whether or not the scene called for it.

When Christina left for Germany several weeks later, Nicole drove her to the airport. Christina griped the entire way. How she wished she hadn't given into Erica's pressure to make this film, clearly aimed at sixteen-year-old boys. How she hoped Terrence Howard wouldn't hit on her, and how she would lay him out if he dared. How she worried that Germany would be full of racists and homophobes. All Nicole heard in Christina's rambling was *I don't want to leave you*, but all she did was nod her head and pat her knee reassuringly.

When Nicole pulled up the departure curb, Christina said, "You're not going to park and wait with me inside?"

What would be the point? thought Nicole. *I can't kiss you in front of all these people so let's not make a difficult farewell worse.* "I've got a few meetings today," she lied. "But you'll be okay."

"Oh. Okay." They climbed out of Nicole's jeep and pulled out Christina's bags from the back. "Well, this is it."

"Just for nine weeks."

"Yeah."

On the curb they embraced like sisters, and one passerby recognized Nicole and alerted his friend. Still Nicole broke and whispered in Christina's ear. "You come back to me."

Christina pulled back, thrilled to finally get this affirmation. She looked into Nicole's eyes and squeezed her hands. "No doubt."

When Charlene returned from Utah, she insisted that they meet with Eden Morales. Eden's directorial debut *Riveting* had won both the Dramatic Grand Jury Prize and Audience Award at Sundance. "What's the film about?" asked Nicole as she logged on to the Internet, hoping to find an e-mail from Christina.

"It's a love story between two women set in Hell's Kitchen during the 80's," said Charlene. "One's black, the other's Hispanic, and they meet at a construction site, and . . . Well, just think of it as a female, urban *Brokeback Mountain*!"

"Jesus Christ . . ." Nicole hated Hollywood shorthand and its ability to reduce complex storylines to marketing clichés. But she hated something else more. "Just because this Edith . . ."

"Eden."

". . . Eden Morales already did a gay-themed film doesn't mean she's the right person to direct *On Her Terms*."

"Well, you can't say that until you meet her." Clearly, Charlene wanted desperately to sign Eden Morales, knowing that the opportunity to direct *On Her Terms* with Nicole and Chris in the leads would keep the rising auteur away from CAA, ICM, and William Morris, and even her own colleagues at the Initiative Agency.

So they met at the Ivy. Nicole took an immediate dislike to Eden and her buzz cut, nose ring, and 1940's army green work dress. But her look book eerily captured the movie just the way it projected across Nicole's imagination. And throughout lunch the budding director was respectful but never reverential, and Nicole couldn't help but admire that. She had to battle her growing fondness for Eden.

An hour later, Eden left them to confer. Charlene raved about her as Nicole turned to the last page of her look book which contained her bio. Every other word was lesbian, queer, or LGBT.

"She's perfect for this project," said Charlene. "That bitch Rebecca Steiners at CAA was all over her at Sundance, but *On Her Terms* is our trump card. Now I'm not crazy about all of her ideas, but I think Eden would be open to . . ."

"No," said Nicole.

"What do you mean 'No'?"

"I mean, no. Just because she's . . ." Nicole dropped her voice. "Just because Eden's gay doesn't mean she's perfect for this project."

Charlene said, "Hey, I never said that was why she was perfect, but—"

"Look, it's obvious that she's loaded with talent, but you know better than I do that we have to take other things into consideration."

"Such as?"

Nicole shoved the look book across the table so hard, the linen tablecloth bunched. "She's just too . . . out. Even though this is a low-budget film, Charlene, it has real potential to cross over."

"Yeah, but I figured that Eden being . . . *you know* . . . would actually be an asset."

"But you kill all the crossover potential the second you attach an unknown, out lesbian as the director," said Nicole. "Get a director like Ridley Scott, and this small character-driven film becomes a studio picture and maybe even a box office hit. But if you attach someone like Eden Morales, then this just stays a little film that Nicole Torres and Chris De La

Cruz took for scale to keep their indie cred. Jesus, and we're all Latina, too. The answer's no, Charlene."

Charlene took a sip of her Perrier to help her digest Nicole's rationale. She set the glass down and took a deep breath. "Nicole?"

"Yes."

"Are you sure you're totally comfortable with this whole gay thing?"

"Jesus, Charlene, would I have optioned the script if I were homophobic?"

Charlene scoffed. "Nicole, don't give me that shit. Plenty of actors put their politics aside for a meaty role. Carroll O'Connor played Archie Bunker for twelve years, and they say he was more liberal than Rob Reiner!"

"I'm talking business here, not politics," said Nicole, although she knew Charlene was right. "I can't afford for *On Her Terms* to be just a lesbian cult classic, and if we attach Eden Morales as director, we pretty much guarantee that this film will be ghettoized in art houses." The guilt began to wrap itself around her, and Nicole resented Charlene. She resented her for not lobbying harder for Eden and convincing that part of Nicole Charlene did not even know exist. "Don't get me wrong, Charlene. I like Eden Morales. Her talent's undeniable, and I'd love to work with her some day. Just not on this film."

Charlene sighed and summoned the server. "I'm sorry, Nicole, for suggesting . . . I didn't mean to offend you."

"Forget about it." *Please just forget about it*, Nicole thought. "If anything, I appreciate your honesty."

"It's just that . . . well, Erica told me that she thinks Chris might be gay, and I worry about her."

"Really?"

"We're not sure if she is or isn't, but sometimes I get frustrated with the industry's *open secret* policy. If we're such a bastion of liberalism . . ." The server arrived with the bill.

Charlene reached into her purse and said, "I just wonder sometimes what if one of these girls was my daughter or sister or something."

Charlene surprised Nicole. She wondered if she were to come out to Charlene at that moment what, if anything, would change about their relationship. Would Charlene show Nicole—her own client—the same concern and compassion she just had for Christina? Or would she finally drop her, citing issues Charlene had managed to ignore before, much like the tenure committee does to Nicole's character Deborah in *On Her Terms*.

"I can't tell you anything about Chris De La Cruz's private life, but gay or straight, the girl wants to be a star. This is the role that can make her one. With her talent, she deserves that opportunity." Nicole finally felt honest again. "Let's find a director who can make that happen for her."

Christina called. Her voice sounded faint but clear, and Nicole ached to trace her fingers across her lips.

"How's the film?" She could never remember the title of the sci fi-slash-heist flick Chris had flown six thousand miles to shoot. Nicole wondered whether she blanked on the title because she found the concept asinine or because it would keep Christina away from her for another seven weeks.

"God, they had me hanging from this fuckin' wire during a fight scene for, like, five hours. The thing was digging in my crotch, and the whole time I'm hanging there thinking, dude, this is why I'm into women." Christina laughed. "And how're things going with our movie?"

"Charlene and I met with some director who just won Sundance. Really talented, very nice. Just not right for *On Her Terms*."

"You're not talking about Eden Morales, are you?"

Nicole's stomach fluttered, and she considered lying. "That's her. How do you know about her?"

"I saw *Riveting*. It's off the chain!"

"But it just premiered at Sundance."

"This chick I know is friends with the editor, and she sneaked me the rough cut. Even then I knew it was going to be fire. Have you seen it?"

"No," said Nicole. "Not yet."

"Aw, man, you gotta see it." Then Christina said what Nicole had been thinking. "I can't wait to go into production with our movie." She paused, then said, "I miss you so much, Nicky."

"I miss you, too." But the silence that followed seemed weighted with something much heavier than longing. "So . . . you're having fun? You know, when you're not being strung up by your crotch."

Christina gave a short laugh and then Nicole heard a gruff voice behind her. "Shit . . . Look, Nick, I have to go." Nicole noted that she had defeminized her name, and she smiled with approval. "I'll call you first chance I get, okay babe?"

"You do that."

Over the next week they exchanged bittersweet telephone calls and long e-mails. Then Charlene awoke Nicole with the news one morning. "Looks like Erica was right about Chris De La Cruz," she practically sang.

Nicole yawned and rubbed her eyes. "What are you talking about?"

"Gawker, Perez Hilton, a Socialite's Life . . . take the gossip site of your choice. What can I say, Nicole? You were so right about Eden. Had we attached her to direct . . ." As Charlene babbled, fear seized Nicole and thrust her out of bed and toward her computer, "But I'm not worried about it so don't you be, okay? I've got a call into Cameron Crowe's people, and word is he's looking for something like *On Her Terms*. The way I see it, between you and Chris, I can't imagine who *won't* see this movie when it's released," she cackled. Then Charlene added, "Although I have to say, I'm glad I'm not Chris De La Cruz. Poor kid. But, hey, that's Erica's problem."

Nicole logged onto the Internet and rattled Christina's name into the search engine. She swallowed and slowly tapped out *lesbian* then punched the return key. The first three results came from three online tabloids all with variations of the same headline:

De La Cruz Fuels Lesbian Rumors
Christina De La Cruz Goes Dirty Dancing in Lesbian Bar
Actor De La Cruz and Singer Sontag Gal Pals?

Jealousy drove her to click on the third link:

Actor De La Cruz and Singer Sontag Gal Pals?

Her star has only begun to rise yet preternaturally talented Christina De La Cruz has already landed on the pages of tabloids across the globe. Cruz, 22, whose breakthrough role in the gritty indie film Tailspin *won her a slew of awards and even briefly generated Oscar buzz, was spotted in a lesbian nightclub in Berlin canoodling with songbird Serena Sontag, 27, lead singer of the internationally popular rock band Never Scared. The sexy couple were photographed grinding on the dance floor of the Schoko in Kreuzberg.*

Pinned in the middle of the article was a large photograph of Christina, her breasts pressed against Serena's and their lips so close that Nicole could feel Christina's breath on her own face. Serena had her back to the camera, but the purple streaks in her dirty blonde dreadlocks and her trademark tattoo of a rainbow flame on her lower back gave her away. And the look on Christina's face. It was the same look of impending ecstasy that Nicole recalled when she touched herself under the covers at night.

Nicole continued on to the next paragraph below the photo:

"At first, Christina was working the room," dished our source. "She was just having fun, flirting with this girl then that one. But then Serena arrived and asked to be introduced to Christina, and it was like every other woman in the club just disappeared.""

De La Cruz is in Berlin shooting the sci-fi action film The Polaris Connection *with Terence Howard and director Kathryn Bigelow. A native of the city, Sontag is reportedly here working on her solo album. While Sontag has always been out and proud since* Never Scared's *chart-topping debut in 2002, De La Cruz has been skirting questions about her sexuality from the start of her career, describing herself in interviews as "straight but not narrow."*

"Well, there should be no doubts about it now," our spy said. "The way Chris and Serena just tuned out everyone in the room was really sweet. And very sexy!"

Our source was unable to confirm if the stunning duo left Schoko together.

Nicole's phone rang, and she only answered it to escape the gossip. "Hello?"

"Nicky."

"Chris?"

"Yeah, I hope I didn't call too early. What time it is over there?"

"Almost ten in the morning."

"It's seven o'clock at night over here. We broke for dinner, and I had to call you."

"Really?"

"Yeah. Something happened the other night. I mean, nothing really happened, but I still didn't want you to hear it from someplace else."

"I know, Chris."

"You do?"

"Yeah, it's all over the papers and the Internet." Nicole visualized Christina and Serena rubbing against each other as the bass thumped all around them, and other women, inspired by their lust for one another, taking to the dance floor. They encircle Christina and Serena who are lost in each other's skin, in each other's smell, in each other's breasts, and all the women grind around their nucleus, pulsating as one in a rhythmic orgy. As Nicole's own nature rose, so did her fury. "How could you do this, Christina?"

"I didn't do anything, Nicole, really! Okay, I got a little buzzed and went too far with Serena on the dance floor. But that's all that happened, I swear. I even told her about you."

"You what?"

"We went to the café afterwards and just talked. She was really cool, Nicky. You'd like her."

"Do you realize what this could do to your career?"

"What?"

"Did you think that because you were in another continent, you could go to a club like that and the media wouldn't find out?"

"Damn, Nicole, you sound more upset that I was at a lesbian club at all than if I had been with another woman in my hotel room."

"You need to grow up and be more discrete."

Silence followed. Nicole thought they had lost their connection but then Christina said, "Look, I gotta go." And before Nicole could say good-bye, she hung up.

Several hours later, Nicole received Christina's e-mail:

Dear Nicole,

First, I want to say that I'm really sorry I hung up on you. I've been feeling bad about it ever since. I'd call you back, but I'm afraid you won't answer, and I can't say I blame you one bit.

So that's why I'm writing you. Since I've come here, I've been thinking about a lot of things. Everything really, like my career, my life, you. I love you, Nicole, and I want to be with you forever. And I want the world to know how I feel about you. I want us to be in this world as we truly are together.

We can do it, Nicky. I know you think I'm young and idealistic or whatever. But it's like this song Serena has on her new album. It goes something like although things are not the way they should be, they're not the way they used to be either.

Call me.

Love always,

Chris

Nicole immediately dialed Christina's number at the hotel. The phone rang and rang, and Nicole imagined her at some sidewalk café chatting with Serena Sontag. The voice mail finally answered.

"Chris, I want you to call me as soon as you get this no matter what time it is. I got your e-mail, and this isn't just your life and career you're talking about but mine as well. Under no circumstances can you do this."

Nicole hung up and waited. She waited for Christina to call and prepared for anything. For Christina to whine, to plead, and to rebel as the younger ones usually did. Nicole waited for Christina to call and attempt to convince her to come out with her and live happily ever after, to argue that even if Nicole's career ended, her life would finally begin, and to try to make her believe that, yes, things were not yet as they should be but were still not as they once were. Nicole lay in bed and waited for Christina to call to submit and then to seduce.

Christina never called. A week passed, and while the tabloids offered no more reports of Christina's adventures in Berlin, Nicole did not hear from her. Nor did she contact her. Instead, she drank her bourbon and monitored the message boards for clues. The boards were on fire as Christina's small base of fans debated whether or not she was a lesbian, whether or not it mattered, and whether the entertainment world would finally have an out lesbian celebrity couple of color in the Nuyorican Christina and the biracial Serena. Not a word about Nicole, perhaps because their project had yet to be announced, as they hoped and waited for a studio to come aboard once they wooed an A-list director.

Even when Christina returned from Germany in April, Nicole did not contact her. Driven more by fear than pride, she called Charlene asking her to confirm via Erica if Christina remained committed to *On Her Terms*. Within days she received her answer.

"Christina's out," said Charlene. "I mean, out of the project. I think the Serena incident freaked her out. She told Erica to tell me to tell you that she's sorry, and that she hopes you understand."

"I do," said Nicole, her heart shattering precisely because she did understand. She hated herself for understanding. "No hard feelings."

"But guess what?" said Charlene. "I kinda saw this coming so I started calling around, and . . ." She paused for the punch. "Jessica Alba's very interested! She's tired of doing all the T and A and having her talent questioned. Jessica thinks this is the perfect role to prove she's got chops. You know if we get her, the studios will be all over it."

"Then make it happen," Nicole said. She had no doubts that Charlene would. Nicole saw the future of *On Her Terms* as if it were on the pages of a tabloid site on her computer screen. The buzz over Jessica Alba's controversial role. The comeback stories about herself. The studio's For Your Consideration ad campaign in the pre-Oscar nominations editions of *Variety* and *The Hollywood Reporter*. And at the center of her wildest dream, Nicole still foresaw the empty void that Christina had briefly filled.

"Turn on your TV set." Charlene called the last Monday morning in June. "Christina did it now."

Under the weight of her pounding hangover, Nicole could barely sit up in bed and find her remote. She clicked on the television to find news coverage of the previous day's pride march through the West Village in New York City. Wearing a grand marshall sash across her body, Christina spoke into a cluster of microphones.

". . . I'd be lying if I said that I wasn't a little worried about the impact on my career, but I've got three films coming out next year . . ." She paused to giggle at her choice of words, and some reporters laughed along with her. "And I think the world can handle it. And if not, oh, well. It's not like there aren't a thousand other things I can do."

"Did Serena inspire you?" asked a reporter with a gossipy slant.

Christina sneered at her. "Serena's been a great friend and of real support, but actually someone else inspired me to take this step. Because of her, I discovered how I wanted to live, and no matter what happens, I'll always be grateful to her for coming into my life and teaching me what it truly takes to be happy." Christina paused, her eyes blinking. "So who needs Hollywood? I've got my health, my family, my community. . ."

She turned around to gesture toward the throng of parade watchers who erupted in cheers. "We love you, Christina!"

Christina laughed, blew kisses at them, and yelled, "I love you, too!" She turned back to the reporters, shrugged, and grinned, "That's all a gal needs." Then Christina climbed back onto the float and drifted away down Eighth Street, smiling and waving very much like a Hollywood star on the rise.

Nicole clicked off the television and crawled out of bed. She grabbed the bottle from the nightstand and carried it into the kitchen to toss it in the recycle bin. She beat the temptation to log onto the Internet and scour the message boards and gossip sites for more information about Christina's pronouncement. Instead Nicole brewed a pot of coffee while she showered, then settled on the cranberry sofa with her steaming mug and the latest draft of *On Her Terms*. Although Jessica Alba had pulled out of a Joel Schumacher blockbuster and agreed to scale to sign onto the film, Nicole could only commit the lines to memory when she envisioned Christina in the role of Marie.

Just Be

Andrea Dale

I was convinced Sarita was going to leave me.

The hushed phone calls, the hanging up when I came into the room.

The fact that we hadn't had sex in over a month, and over a month before that, and probably more but I'd blocked it out. And even those times had been rushed.

The suitcase I found in her closet yesterday morning when I was looking for a scarf I thought she'd borrowed, although she hadn't mentioned any trips to me.

But it had all probably started before that; maybe it was the night I was late to her birthday dinner, rushing into the restaurant from a study session that had run long, and her looking up from the table, her luminous brown eyes glowing disappointment in the candle flame as everyone at the table fell silent for a moment.

We'd known my going to law school would be a burden on us both. At the time, we'd made the decision together, discussed the potential problems, worked out solutions. I'd gotten scholarships so money wouldn't be a big issue; I'd be too busy to spend frivolously anyway. We'd have to cut back on traveling, but there would be summers. That sort of thing.

Going back to school, especially this kind of intense studying, was harder than I expected. I guess when you're thirty you don't have the kind of resilience you do in your late teens and early twenties. You don't have the momentum of coming out of high school straight into college, or cannon-shot from college into grad school.

Sarita and I barely saw each other, and when we did, my head was spinning with torts and USC sections, and I was rambling about fellow students whom she'd never met.

And the screeching halt in our sex lives? Well. Nobody would have expected us, with our reputation of being screwing-like-bunny dykes, to be falling asleep with no more than a brush of a kiss and a snuggle. Every damn night.

I'd abandoned her, and she was probably just being her usual wonderful self by waiting until after my stress-crazy finals to tell me that it was over.

I don't know how I made it through finals. I remember waiting to be handed the Constitutional Law test, on the verge of tears from thinking about my life empty without her, and then the paper was in front of me and my world narrowed to articles and amendments.

Hours later, I looked up, and my stomach twisted again. You'd think I'd feel relief that finals were over. Instead, I was sure they spelled the beginning of the end.

I grabbed a Snickers bar from the vending machine—I didn't remember eating breakfast, and I'd skipped lunch in favor of some last-minute cramming—and headed to my car.

Sarita was standing by it. My steps slowed even as my body tingled. With her dark East Asian complexion, she could pull off fire-engine red like nobody's business. The little stretch lace tank top hugged her high breasts. She'd paired it with khaki shorts and a pair of red thong sandals. Her toenails were the same shade of red as her shirt. Sexy right down to the details. Did she have to look so good just to dump me?

"Hey," she said when I got close, and stepped forward into a kiss.

Out of familiar habit and familiar desire, I responded, letting myself focus on nothing more than the feel of her soft mouth moving against mine, her teeth gently nipping my bottom lip before she stepped back.

"Will your car be okay here over the weekend?" she asked.

Confused, I nodded. The student lot was open 24/7.

"Good. You're coming with me."

I followed her, too brain-fogged to form a coherent question. She asked about the tests, and I told her how I thought I'd done (Contracts, pretty well; Criminal Law, hard to say). It wasn't until we pulled onto the freeway in the opposite direction from home that I had the foresight to ask, "Where are we going?"

"Yosemite," Sarita said, flashing me a grin.

That was entirely beyond my current comprehension level.

"You need a break, sweetheart," she said. Her hand on my knee wasn't helping, but I tried really hard to concentrate on her words. "You've been studying your ass off, and now finals are over and you deserve a vacation. We both do. You get to decompress and we get to re-acquaint ourselves with each other."

I took her hand from my leg and pressed my mouth against her palm. It was the only way I could express my gratitude and relief. And then I did something I wouldn't have thought possible.

I fell asleep.

I stayed asleep until we were pulling up to the ranger station to pay our entrance fee, bleary and blinking and needing to pee.

I apologized to Sarita for not helping with the driving, but she waved my contrition away.

"You were exhausted," she said. "I'm glad you were able to sleep. It means you're starting to relax and let go."

We stopped to stretch and pick up a few last-minute supplies and change into hiking gear, then continued on into the park. Apparently Sarita had thought of everything, including packing all the stuff I'd need. That explained the suitcase in the closet, and the phone calls.

Despite my nap, I still felt groggy and overwhelmed, like I was dizzy and wandering around in a fog. Strapping on the packs and hiking up to the meadow went a long way to clearing that fog. We didn't speak much, just occasionally to point out an eagle overhead or to comment in awe over the views. All of Yosemite looks like a postcard, a surreal, impossible beauty.

Kind of like Sarita. Dazed and confused as I was, as the hike progressed and the weight and stress of school peeled away, feelings I thought I'd lost resurfaced: Arousal. Desire. Lust.

It wasn't just the brisk air that quickened my breath and hardened my nipples. Oh no. Watching Sarita's lithe form moving gracefully up the path was doing wonders for my formerly buried libido.

The sun was no more than a blushing glow behind Half Dome by the time we had the tent set up and the fire going. Since it was late, supper was simple: canned stew, fresh sourdough bread, and cherries for dessert.

In the flickering firelight, I watched the cherries stain Sarita's lush lips a deeper red, and I quivered right down to my clit.

She looked up, and saw me watching her. She must have seen the look in my eyes, because she smiled, tossed the pit in the fire, and leaned over to kiss me.

Like the kiss at the car, it was slow, gentle, gradually

deepening. Dimly, I realized that I understood the cliché of air to a drowning man. I breathed in the feel of Sarita against me and felt alive again.

The skin of her bare arms was satiny under my hands. Suddenly I wanted to be naked, feel my body against hers: soft belly, hard hipbones, sharp nipples, silken hair above and coarse below. I wanted it so badly that my hands shook.

"You taste so good," Sarita whispered, licking the hollow of my breastbone. "I've missed the taste of you."

"I've missed you, too. I'm so sorry—"

She pressed her lips against mine again until she was sure I'd stopped trying to talk, then said, "Ssh. Don't talk. Just be."

I let tears of wonder drain back into my throat and kissed her, cupping her beautiful face in my hands. Her tongue darted in and out of my mouth, teasing and playful, and my pussy contracted as I thought about how that teasing touch would feel on my clit.

We tumbled back onto the sleeping bag we'd cleverly laid out already. Sarita kneeled over me, unbuttoning my shirt and leaving trailing kisses along the exposed skin, then deftly undid the front hook of my bra. Cool air slid over me before she took my breasts in her hand and warmed first one, then the other nipple with her wet mouth.

It had been so long since we'd touched that my cunt ached from the sudden rush and swell of desire. I think we might both have had it in our heads to take this slow, to savor and celebrate. Our bodies, however, had other plans.

I reached up to brush my palms across her breasts. She was braless beneath the tank top, and her nipples distended the fabric. She hissed as I pinched, first gently, then harder. Her hips twitched, which pressed her crotch harder against mine.

"Sarita!"

It wasn't quite an orgasm, or maybe you could call it a mini-orgasm. I know I shuddered with pleasure, cried out her name. Whatever it was, it was enough for her to expertly strip me of my shorts and part my thighs with her long-fingered hands.

Then her mouth was on me, and she licked and sucked my swollen clit, and that was enough to send me off on a real orgasm, one incredibly long one or maybe a string of them.

She kissed me, her face covered in my juices, and moments later I was between her legs and returning the favor, two fingers stroking her deep inside as I licked her until she screamed.

After that we slowed down, stroking and whispering and luxuriating in having all the time in the world to make love.

Some time after that, with a waxing moon high in the sky and stars like you've never seen, we threw half the sleeping bag over us and finally talked.

I admitted I'd thought she was leaving me. She was shocked, protesting until I kissed her quiet just as she had done to me earlier.

"The look you gave me when I was late to your birthday dinner . . ."

"I was worried about you," she said. "You'd been working so hard and not eating, and you walked in and you looked so pale and gaunt . . . I wanted everyone else to go away so I could feed you and take you home and put you to bed."

"I'm sorry things got so crazy," I said.

"I'm sorry I couldn't do anything to make it easier," she said.

Then we both laughed, because we knew we were being silly apologizing for things we couldn't control.

We'd find a way to work it out. Communicate better, take

the occasional weekend or even just a day or an evening to reconnect during the most stressful times.

As the embers pulsed orange and hot in the fire ring, I looked up and watched a bat swoop overhead.

And just let myself be.

The Getaway

Tawanna Sullivan

This trip to the country was impromptu. Sarah had come home from the police station, literally thrown some clothes into her gym bag, and was riding shotgun. Nicole's foot was heavy on the accelerator and it wasn't long before Baltimore was a distant blur in the rear view mirror.

They rode in silence until they lost the frequency for their favorite easy listening jazz station and a steady stream of overdubbed bass poured through the speakers. Sarah turned off the radio and finally exhaled. "Thank you for this. I just needed to get away from there."

Nicole nodded, never taking her eyes off the road. "It's no problem. My aunt owns a bed and breakfast in Brockburg. I let her know we're coming. Are you okay?"

"Yeah."

"Are you sure? It was bad enough finding Michelle's body, but I didn't think the police were ever going to let you go."

Sarah winced as she remembered the gruesome discovery. She had gone to the theater directly from church and found her ex-girlfriend with her head pushed into Maggie's litter box. Someone had knocked Michelle unconscious with her precious Vagi, an award for best performance in a lesbian-themed one-woman play, and left her to suffocate in the ammonia-stenched hell. The killer had hit her so hard that the little silver clit had fallen off the statue and rolled into the orchestra pit.

"It was terrible. The police think I only pretended to find the body. According to a note found in Michelle's pocket, she was supposed to meet some mystery person at 11:30. They think I slipped out of service during offering, killed her, and then magically appeared back at the organ in time for Sister Franklin's solo."

"I'm sure there were at least one hundred witnesses who will testify that you never left service." The women at Mt. Holy Redeemer always kept too close an eye on Sarah for Nicole's taste. It was amusing at first to see the female members of the young adult choir looking hungrily at their director, with their lips and legs always parted just enough to invite temptation. There was a fine line between adoration and nuisance; hormone addled youth crossed it every time.

On second thought, Nicole really couldn't fault them. When talking to Sarah, it was quite easy to find your gaze slipping from her eyes and resting on her bosom. Nicole took a quick look over at her beloved. The tears had stopped and the chest no longer heaved, but fully erect nipples threatened to poke through her cotton tank top. Was she excited or was this just some weird biological response to stress?

Sarah thought Nicole was taking a side-eye glance of her legs and shifted them accordingly to give a proper view of her thighs. "They say I have the strongest motive. She ruined my credit and threatened to out me to my boss, but I have better sense than to kill her before rehearsal."

"Don't take it personally." Nicole reached over and patted a newly available knee. "I'm sure the police interrogated the rest of the cast. Some cop gave me the third degree when I showed up at the theater looking for you."

"Yeah, they talked to everybody. It just looked so bad that I arrived first. Damn me for being punctual."

Actually, the police were interested in her because she had said something outrageously stupid: "I was surprised that she was dead, but not disappointed." It would have been a cute throwaway line in a comedy. Baltimore law enforcement was not so easily amused.

In fact, Detective Campbell had suggested she not leave town. That's why this jaunt on the open road was so exciting—she enjoyed being a bad girl. Instinctively, her fingertips grazed Nicole's forearm while she daydreamed about them fleeing the scene like a modern day Bonnie and Clyde. We can get away with this, Sarah thought.

"What's the status of the play now that the director is dead? I imagine *Little Ms. Ride My Hood* will be a hot ticket. The whole production can be in her memory."

"I don't know. We still need a lot of work and I don't know if Karla, the assistant director, can whip everyone into shape. You should have seen Lynette go into hysterics when she found out Michelle was dead. She didn't fool anyone."

"Are there other suspects or do you definitely think it's someone from the show?"

"Half the lesbian population of Baltimore hates—hated, Michelle. She knew how to play on your sympathy with that poor, starving artist act. So dedicated to her craft that she couldn't afford the luxury of having a steady paying gig. When the money dried up, she moved on to the next patron."

"Did you know about her reputation before?"

"Yes and no." Sarah ruffled her fingers through her locks to hide the flush of embarrassment making its way across her cheeks. "There were some rumblings overheard here and there, but you expect that from ex-girlfriends." A memory from the morning resurfaced and she had to fight a fit of nervous laughter. "Poor Maggie was standing next to her litter box meowing at Michelle's head."

"Try to put that behind you. I've got some things in store that will help take your mind off it."

"Like what? Cow tipping?" After another stretch of quiet, Sarah got tired of counting cows and cornfields. "What time is it?"

Nicole glanced down at her empty wrist and shrugged. "Want to stop and stretch your legs for a minute?"

Sarah nodded and they pulled over at the Wicomico River scenic overview. Except for where waves lapped at the banks, the river appeared as calm as a lake. The valley beyond was a patchwork of different farmlands and crops.

Nicole sat on the trunk of her Impala and pulled Sarah into her lap. "Clear water and fresh air. This would have been a nice spot for a picnic."

Gray clouds rolled over them and brought a soft, spring shower. "A soggy picnic." Sarah leaned back and drew Nicole's arms around her. "This feels good though." Lips brushed against the back of her neck and sent a tingling ripple throughout her body. "Nic, don't start something you can't finish."

"Who says I can't finish?" Nicole caressed her shoulders and kissed her collarbone.

Sarah tilted her head to the left, giving full access to her earlobe. "Not out here, someone could see us."

A squirrel darted out into the landing, shrugged at them, and disappeared into a cornfield. "I don't think he's going to tell anybody."

Sarah studied herself as a hand found its way under her skirt and between her thighs. When fingers reached the entrance of her hot, pulsating center, she reached back and grabbed a handful of Nicole's braids. "Wait," she whispered. "I need to tell you the truth. To confes—"

Fingers alternated between stroking her inside and spreading her juices all over her clit. Between quakes of pleasure, Sarah fought hard not to lose her train of thought. "I tampered with the evidence." In that one moment, everything stopped. Hands retreated. No more cool kisses on hot skin. "Nic, I—"

"Shh." Nicole leaned back and watched raindrops land and drizzle down her lover's back. Maybe this was just part of a game. Sarah always liked to bring a bit of her acting class into the bedroom. Nicole bent her forward and pulled up her skirt. Then, she unzipped her pants and let her dildo rest against the newly exposed booty. Okay, she thought, let's play.

Sarah was relieved to feel Delilah pressed against her but the slap that followed caught her completely off guard. Fear mingled with excitement and she found herself quickly approaching the edge of orgasm. It had been so long since she'd been properly punished.

"You little slut." Each word was punctuated with a stinging spank. With years of Catholic education under her belt, Nicole knew how to deliver strokes without leaving marks. "Did you promise Michelle pussy? Lure her there . . ."

"No!" Sarah spread her thighs and Delilah slipped and slid across her lips. "That's not what happened."

"Why?" Nicole whispered. "Why did you do it?" She pulled Sarah upright and squeezed her nipples. She pulled them roughly as Delilah bounced rhythmically against her clit.

"You. I took it to protect you."

Sarah tried to say more but her words dissolved into moans. A hard bite on the shoulder tipped the tide of passion and her knees began to buckle. She felt light headed as if her soul was rising up in a bid to flee, but it couldn't escape. It was then that Delilah finally slipped inside her and set off an explosion that rippled through every inch of her body. Sarah heard herself crying . . . felt them both collapsing against the side of the car . . . sinking into the soft, rain drenched grass.

Nicole was dumbfounded. She had been so careful: picking a time when she knew Sarah would have an unshakable alibi, wearing gloves once she got inside the theater discarding her clothes to get rid of all traces of litter and cat hair. "Sarah, I'm sorry. You weren't supposed to know."

Sarah rolled over on top of Nicole and kissed her. "It's okay, baby." She pulled a gold watch from her pocket. "The clasp is broken, but I'm sure we can get it fixed in Brockburg."

Sunlight had returned and glistened in Nicole's tear-filled eyes. Sarah kissed them. "Don't worry, baby. I'm going to take care of everything."

For All My Relations

Jean Roberta

Lynette had been missing for a week when she was found behind the Royal Arts Centre, naked and tied up. She had been left in the bushes in the surrounding park, on a January day when the temperature hovered at forty below zero in Fahrenheit as well as Celsius. She was found too late.

"Jesus," I said to Amanda. We were watching the image of a covered shape on a stretcher being loaded into an ambulance by paramedics on the TV news. Police were looking for the last man who was known to have seen her.

"Did you know her?" I asked.

"A bit, yeah. She worked for Crystal and Sapphire when I was there. She took on too many guys on the side, though, just to collect the agency fee. That's not safe."

Crystal and Sapphire were legendary, and their fame went a long way toward convincing most of our johns that all whores were dykes and vice versa. The two madams (*Mesdames*? I had taken some French in high school), one black and one white, had arrived in our simple town from a more worldly city five years before, and opened the first escort agency here.

A woman who could cheat on Crystal and Sapphire would have to be shortsighted, to say the least. It didn't follow that she deserved a slow, painful death.

Amanda and I cuddled together on a motel bed, watching TV in the nude. "Gotta go," she said as she stretched a shapely leg off the edge of the bed and stood up. Her waterfall of long, shiny black hair swung down her taut back as she walked to the bathroom. I watched her little squaw bum (her words) swaying slightly as she walked away from me. Most of Amanda's skin was a healthy shade of almond-tan, like that of Lynette in her missing-person photos. I was fairly sure that Lynette's skin must have looked different (mottled lavender, like mine on very cold days?) when she was found.

For an instant, I was jolted by an irrational fear that Amanda would disappear into thin air.

I thought of the myth of the Vanishing Indian as a kind of human dinosaur that had supposedly been dying off for at least two hundred years because he (she? it?) couldn't survive the spread of civilization. But in the Canadian prairie town we lived in, which was civilized enough to have computers in every government office and crystal meth on the street, 20 percent of the population showed some native blood, some more (Amanda with her hair, skin, cheekbones, and shape) and some less (me with my pale face, wood-brown hair, hips, and ass).

Each of us appealed to some man's taste. Each of us could attract too much attention from a human predator.

Amanda came back to me. "'Manda," I asked her, "don't you think it would be safer to get a straight job and stick to that?"

"No. Maybe I'm a fatalist, but I don't think it does any good to live in fear. Do you think waitresses never meet guys like that? Or cashiers? We can't even be sure he was a trick. Lynette had an ex-husband somewhere. It might have been him, eh?"

"Jesus. Fucking men. I swear their testosterone drives them insane."

"We just have to stay three jumps ahead of them. And watch each other's back."

Amanda was generous enough not to remind me that the kind of rabid white man who called her and Lynette "fucking Indians" usually tried to rescue me from the error of my ways. At least they were chivalrous as long as they thought of me as a white woman who was available to them but still a few cunt hairs above their idea of a real whore. It was a narrow road to walk, but it had kept me out of danger so far.

Amanda seemed to run on sheer determination, helped along by native wit. She wrapped a warm, strong arm around my waist. "Why, are you scared, honey?"

The faint musk from her armpits and the comforting scent of her hair were all round me. As I sat on the bed, her breasts were just at my eye level. For a moment, I had the impression that her big brown nipples could watch me back. It wasn't a scary thought, but I blinked it away. I didn't want to be as crazy as the poet Percy Shelley, who had once (by his own account) run screaming from his wife Mary under the same impression.

Amanda was waiting for my answer. "No," I said. "Not right now. I don't want to think about men on our day off."

She pressed her mouth against mine in a long, hot kiss. She seemed more aggressive than usual, as if to assure me that she wasn't planning to disappear (not without a fight, anyway, and I knew she had some skills in that area) or to assure herself that she could protect us both from all harm. Her breasts pressed against mine as she gradually but firmly pushed me back against the bed. She ended up lying on top of me with our legs tangled together, our feet on the floor.

I could feel her heart beating next to mine as her hair surrounded my face like a curtain. Somehow the sweetness of the moment made me feel like laughing. As she held me, I was reminded that most of her weight was in her arms, chest, and shoulders. In some ways, her body was so different from mine that we could always discover something new when we explored each other.

I remembered how I had felt when we play-wrestled and she laughed at the lack of power in my punches. I had been humiliated but impressed when she had demonstrated a real punch that broke a wooden board in half. And then I had been half-proud, half-ashamed to see how fast she could jump away from my kicks. I had shown her that my strength was in my legs, my thighs, my hips. Together, I thought, we could be as powerful as a team of Amazon warriors.

That was another proud nation that had supposedly vanished; assuming the ancient Greek men who described the Amazons hadn't made them up.

Amanda rolled one of my hard, deep-pink nipples between her fingers. "You need some attention, baby?" she teased. I moaned in answer.

"Perky little things," she snickered. She lowered her head to pull my nipple into her mouth and suck hard, gently grazing my sensitive skin with her teeth.

I could hardly speak, but I couldn't let her description stand. "Not that little," I told her, breathing hard.

She raised her mouth from me and licked her lips. "Not now," she agreed.

Her mouth and hands on my breasts felt so good that I wished I still had milk to give her. She would have appreciated the gift. Amanda and I were both mothers, doing what we had to do to support our fatherless kids. It was one of the things that bonded us at a level deeper than words.

She continued squeezing, stroking, and tickling my breasts, watching my reactions. "You get any tit men, honey?"

I laughed. "Yeah, but they're disappointed. They usually advise me to get implants."

Amanda looked serious. "Are you thinking about it?"

"Nope. My regulars don't complain. Besides, if I had complications from the operation, it would cost me more in the long run."

Amanda smiled. "I'm not complaining. How's your clit doing?"

"Mm. It's awake now," I told her.

"Wants to play, doesn't she?"

"With you, 'Manda."

"Little whore," she snickered, making it sound like an endearment, or even a term of respect. "You'd get wet for anybody. It's one of your best features. But I want you to eat me out first. I want to get some before I fuck you doggy-style."

Amanda was good at that, and she had brought all her toys to this motel where we hoped no one from work would find us. Blaine, our pimp, didn't mind if his girls got together for fun; in fact, he encouraged any development that might raise morale among the six of us and make us better at pleasing our johns, especially the ones who liked girl-girl scenes. But he knew that private lesbian affairs could make girls uppity and create conflict with the rest of the stable. Blaine hadn't warned us in words, but we knew he was watching us like a hawk. So were several of our coworkers, who managed to be jealous and homophobic at the same time.

"Show me," I told Amanda. She rolled off me, arranged herself on her back, and spread her legs wide apart, showing me a triangle of black hair. Its warm fragrance wafted to my nose. I saw some beads of moisture, like dewdrops, shining on the matted hair that had been pressed into coils by her tight panties. When I moved my face in close for a look, I saw that each wet drop against blackness contained a little rainbow. I knew where the pot of gold was located.

I spread her outer lips apart to find her swelling button and the slick, dark-pink folds of flesh that so many men had visited. I didn't care. Like a theme park or a scenic natural site, Amanda's cunt never lost its power of attraction.

"I want to taste you," I told her. "Are you sure it's safe? I want us both to stay healthy."

"I never let guys kiss me, honey," she told me. "Not at all, and they don't get to touch me there without some latex in between. I get tested regularly. I'm safe."

How far could I trust her? I wasn't sure. Like her, though, I was somewhat of a fatalist. Fate plays a role in everything, I thought. I decided to take the risk.

I held her hairy lips apart while I reached her plump clit with my pointed tongue. I licked all around the touchy head first, then sucked it all into my mouth, imitating her treatment of my nipples. She moved her hips, showing me that I was on the right track.

I sucked hard, then backed off just when I thought she was in danger of coming too fast. She tangled a fist in my messy shoulder-length hair, and tugged my head just hard enough. I felt Amanda losing her self-control as my face grew wetter with her juice. I hadn't worn much makeup, knowing what we were going to do, and I felt my face being washed clean, down to the bare skin.

I carefully slid one of my thin fingers into her opening, following her inner curves while trying to avoid too much contact with her flesh. (She had complained about my sharp fingernails, even though I refused to grow them as long as some of my regulars wanted them.)

"Jackie," she whispered in my ear. It was my working name, and she liked it. She seemed to think it brought out my resemblance to Jackie Kennedy as a young widow. "Harder," said Amanda.

I slid a second finger in beside the first, then a third. I felt the little mouth of her cervix, and rubbed it with my longest finger. "Mmm," I hummed on her clit, sucking hard. I scraped her with my teeth as gently as possible, feeling her clit vibrate in my mouth.

"Oh! Fuck! Baby!" she yelled at the ceiling, thrashing so hard that I could barely hang onto her. I didn't need to ask what that meant. Her whole cunt seemed to be clenching, as though trying to swallow my fingers and tongue.

Men be damned, I thought. At that moment, she was mine.

Amanda gradually settled down, like a thunderstorm subsiding into pools of rainwater. I kept my mouth on her clit until I felt it subtly relax, then I slid up to kiss her salty navel, her breasts, her neck, and her open mouth. She welcomed me as I pushed my tongue in past her lips, giving her the taste of her own womanhood.

We kissed for a long time before we reluctantly pulled apart. "Jackie," she told me, "you know how to give it. You are so going to get it."

"Bring it on," I bragged.

We lay together for a few more minutes, feeling each other's breath and body heat. Then she raised herself up on her elbows, pushing me up too. "Come on," she said. "Up on all fours, bitch." She grinned to soften the message.

"This bed is too soft," I complained. I was still too shy (if that was the right word) to tell her that I couldn't hold myself steady enough on a soft mattress to enable her to work up the amount of friction I wanted.

"Then get on the floor," she said, willing to oblige me. "The carpet won't hurt your knees, will it?"

"Probably not," I answered. Or if it does, I thought, I won't complain.

Amanda was already off the bed, rummaging through her leather backpack. I sank down to the floor, planted myself on all fours, and studied the raised pattern of the Perrier-green carpet. When I turned my head, I could see her walking toward me, wearing her leather harness with her purple silicone dildo, the one that made me laugh whenever I saw it. It produced other reactions when it was invisible, plunged deep inside me.

One of her hands slid slowly over both my protruding ass cheeks. I knew that her other hand was stroking her whimsical cock, preparing to guide it into me. She lowered herself gracefully until she was kneeling behind me, checking my wetness by snaking two fingers between my cunt lips and casually stroking my clit. "You ready for me?" she asked, already knowing the answer. I appreciated her willingness to talk to me while she was an unseen presence behind me, poised to strike. Sex from behind, even when I was familiar with the person and the method, always included an element of surprise.

She fed her cool cock into me, a few inches at a time. We had done this before, so she knew how to aim it up and in, slowly but firmly, as I pushed back to get as much as I could. "Good girl," she said, pulling back slightly. I squeezed around her cock, feeling it sliding against my wet folds as it held me open.

Amanda reached under me to tickle my clit, then settled both her hands on my hips to hold them in place as she worked up momentum. I moaned as we rocked together. Soon I could hear a faint slurping sound every time she pumped my wet cunt.

"O-ohh," I moaned.

"Come for me, baby," she told me. "I've got you."

I saw colors in my mind when I came, squeezing her cock over and over. She held herself still until my breathing had slowed down.

I stayed on all fours for a while after she had withdrawn from me. "You okay, Jackie?" she asked, stroking my hair.

"I'm fine," I told her. "I'm just catching my breath." Everything about the motel room, including the faintly musty smell of the carpet that rose to my nose, felt comforting. For the meanwhile, this space belonged to Amanda and me, no trespassers allowed.

She helped me up and wrapped her arms around me. We swayed together for a moment before climbing back onto the bed. "You want a rye and Coke, honey?" she asked.

"Sure," I answered. "From your bag?"

"Where else? Do you see a bar in this room?"

"But it won't be cold," I pouted.

"Look around and use your brain, woman," she smirked. "There's ice on the window ledge." I looked out, and saw it shining like diamonds in the winter sun.

Before long, we were each holding a glass of rye and Coke with little broken icicles in it. "To us," said Amanda. We clinked glasses, and then she pressed hers to each of my nipples, making me squeal.

"We should start our own agency, Jackie," she told me. She sounded serious. "We could be bigger than Crystal and Sapphire. We could have different names for different kinds of scenes, like Multiples for the guys who want two girls, or Ties That Bind for the guys who like bondage. And we need to reach women who won't go to the gay bar but they'll pay for a dyke who can show them a good time. And I mean, they'll pay well."

I admired Amanda's ambition, which didn't surprise me. I knew she had wanted to outshine the two founding divas ever since she had left their agency, but I didn't really believe in the myth that a whore could earn a fortune by specializing in female customers (janes?). I couldn't imagine many filthy-rich dykes living anywhere near us, and I couldn't imagine them spending their lives in the closet so many years after the

Stonewall Riots. Yet Amanda wasn't the only one in our town who believed that sugar mamas with a taste for cunt were an untapped market.

I knew, more or less, where Amanda's view of the world came from. She had grown up in a famous (or notorious, depending on one's viewpoint) local crime family. There had always been guns, stolen goods, dope, and lots of booze in the houses where she spent her childhood, but according to her, she had never been neglected or abused. She had spent summers on reserves with her extended family, learning to dance pow-wow, and she had made good use of funding from the Metis Association to take a few college classes. Late nights spent studying to get a degree didn't appeal to her, however. Amanda was the Canadian prairie version of a Mafia princess.

I didn't really know how to start bridging the gap between us. "'Manda," I said. "I don't want to stay in this business. My daughter is seven now, and I don't think she knows what I do, but she'll figure it out in time if I don't get out. I don't want her to be exposed to this stuff. And I really don't want to lose her to a foster home if someone reports me to Social Services or I get busted. Aren't you worried about what could happen to you?"

"I'm a Dustyhorn," she bragged. "And I'm related to the Stonechilds. Nobody wants to get on the wrong side of us. Why do you think the cops leave Blaine and us alone?"

I wished I could share her sense of immunity from legal harassment. "It still makes me nervous, honey," I told her. "You know I just have to finish my thesis to get my Master's degree. What do you think will happen if anyone at the university hears something about me or sees Blaine's photos?"

Amanda guffawed. "Everybody knows those professors are all big johns, but they think they have an image to protect.

Do you think any of those guys are going to make a big stink about you? They've got too much shit of their own to hide."

She playfully rolled me onto my stomach and ran her fingernails lightly down my back. She squeezed my ass cheeks, kneading them like bread dough. "Everyone has some shit to hide," she reminded me. I could hear her pulling a latex glove onto one hand like a doctor preparing to examine a patient. I shivered.

She was doing something above me, probably adding lube to her gloved fingers. "Everyone is so sensitive back here," she told me, easing a smooth, cold finger into my back passage. "Just relax, my girl. You can't hold tension in there while someone is fucking you in the ass or you'll get hurt."

I gave in to it, wiggling slightly as she delved into me. Despite my best effort to unlock the gate, my sphincter clenched, trying to expel the invader.

Amanda held herself still, stroking my back. "You can take it, honey. Just open up. You've got such a nice ass. Don't any of your johns offer to pay extra for it?"

I took a deep breath and let it out slowly. "Oh yes," I answered. "A lot. But I don't let them."

"That's it," Amanda crooned in my ear. I had heard her use the same tone with her four-year-old son. "I won't hurt you. If you learn how to do this, you'll be a better escort. You can be pickier and make more money." I moaned, even though I wasn't paying attention to her words.

As in childbirth, I discovered that focusing on my breathing was the key to staying relaxed. Amanda's touch was magic, and my ass was enchanted. Tingling warmth spread all through my guts, sending sparks into my clit even before she petted it.

This time, I came like lightning. I jerked into a fetal position, almost dislodging Amanda's fingers as my anus squeezed them in uncontrollable ecstasy. I must have howled like a coyote in heat because she said "Sssh!" several times. "You're too loud." She sounded delighted.

After she casually dropped her used glove on the floor, we lay on our sides, wrapped in each other's arms. "You loved that," she gloated. "You love getting fucked, Jackie. You just need to stop being so uptight about it."

"'Manda, I don't want to give up hope. That's the thing you're not hearing. I always wanted to be a writer and a prof. I want to teach literature to adults. I know that doesn't make any sense to you, but it's what I want to do."

Amanda kissed me. "You're such a smart girl," she said soothingly. "You could do whatever you want."

She wasn't willing to look at the truth that lay between us like a wall of ice. She didn't want to admit out loud that we could never build a home together without hurting ourselves or each other. And our kids, who probably wouldn't remember each other when they were grown.

"There's a sweat lodge coming up on the White Buffalo First Nation," she told me. "I know the medicine man who's running it. Anyone can go. Do you want to go with me, honey? We saw Lynette's body on the news, and I'm sure her spirit needs help before she can be at peace. There's evil out there and it's going to stay with us unless we deal with it. We need to cleanse ourselves."

I remembered the stifling heat of a previous sweat lodge, a kind of earthly experience of hell designed to force the participants to face their fears and overcome them by sweating them out. I remembered the elder's repetition of the comforting phrase "all my relations," meaning not just a family like the Dustyhorns or even a nation or race or the human species, but everything living on the earth. Everything related by the spark of life.

"Yeah," I said. "That's a good idea, 'Manda. I'd like to go with you. As much as anyone can like a sweat lodge." We both laughed, hearing an undertone of grief that wasn't there before.

We still wanted to eat and play with each other a few more times before we were finished. We had the rest of the day to make memories before we had to pick our children up from the babysitter and go back to our separate lives.

Enchanting Evalina

Lisa Figueroa

It wasn't until I got into my car after work that I noticed the flyer stuck under the windshield wiper. Why didn't I ever see those things before I closed the door? I'd had a rotten day at work and just wanted to go home. After arriving at work late, I'd started a fire in the microwave warming up my lunch, lost an important account file for my company's most valued client, and my ex had called three times wanting to borrow money again.

Sandra, my ex, had this peculiar idea that I was supposed to continue supporting her after we broke up, or rather, after she left me because she thought I was too boring and normal. Sandra fancied herself a Wicca enchantress, burning candles to the Goddess and chanting spells for money. Now she swore she'd get back at me somehow. So, I figured she was the source of all the bad luck sticking to me like the abundant cat hairs lining my couch. I yanked the advertisement free from the wiper then settled back in my car seat ready to crumple it into a tiny ball, but my attention was involuntarily drawn to the artful lettering and picture of a giant eye in the center of the ad. It was a very pretty eye despite its size and all-knowing gaze. I read its offering with interest, my displeasure temporarily forgotten.

Skilled Curandera. Services include: Limpias, tarot cards, candle dressing and jewelry to ward off evil. Stuck in a rut? Feeling down? Searching for answers? I can cure what ails you. Walk ins appreciated or call for an appointment—Señora Evalina.

There was a number and an address not far from work. I decided to drive by and check it out.

The curandera's business was a small, pink stucco house on a large property enclosed by a chain-link fence. Overgrown trees lined the sidewalk and cushioned the house on either side, creating cool shade and an aura of mystery while hiding the backyard from view. I had the sensation of walking into an enchanted forest; half expecting to see elves and gnomes peaking back at me as I approached the front door. There was a plain cardboard sign hanging on the doorknob with the invitation OPEN, PLEASE COME IN in both English and Spanish.

I opened the door and was greeted by a fluffy white cat with peridot-colored eyes that meowed at me as if announcing my entrance. I guess I had anticipated a black cat since a curandera was a close cousin to a witch. At least, that's what my grandmother always said. A woman soon followed the cat; a beautiful woman, who, I realized with a jolt, had similar green eyes. She also had long, dark brown hair, high cheekbones that added to her exoticness, and lovely full lips, which parted into a smile.

"Hello, I'm Evalina. I see you've already met Luna," she said as I struggled to pull my attention away from her mouth.

"I'm Josefina, but call me Jo. I hope you're not busy," I said.

"It's a perfect time. I don't have any appointments until later tonight. How can I help you?"

"I've been having some bad luck lately. I broke up with my ex and things at work haven't been going that great."

"I take it your ex is not wishing you well. I do sense her hovering around like a bad odor."

I nodded, blushing at her perception that my ex was female and not male. What else did she know?

"Let's go into the kitchen and start with a reading." We sat at a table across from each other. "Give me your hands," she said, taking them, palms up, into her smaller ones, her fingertips brushing along the lines. I realized we shared the same sweet caramel skin tone as her light touch made the hairs on the back of my neck stand up. After a moment, her eyebrows wrinkled in surprise and she tilted her head to one side. She released my hands and I braced myself for bad news.

"What's wrong?" I asked.

Evalina smiled. "Nothing at all. In fact, your luck is going to change for the better. What you need is a limpia, a cleansing to rid yourself of bad energy. Since this is your first time, I'm going to give you some items to take home with you."

She went to a cupboard and withdrew several small bottles, one larger bottle, and a tall, glass alter candle. The smaller bottles contained oils and she poured a few drops of each into the candle as she chanted some kind of prayer or spell. I wasn't sure which. After she finished, she wrapped the candle in clear Saran Wrap and placed it with the larger bottle in a brown paper bag. "Now, you'll finish the limpia at home. Light the candle first then take a bath using the cleansing oil. Empty it all into the water and soak for at least thirty minutes, the longer the better actually. After that, I promise things in your life will improve."

I frowned, wondering if it could be that easy. Evalina handed me the sack and as our hands touched again I caught the sweet scent of her, flowery but exotically tinged like night-blooming cereus. She walked me to the door with Luna trailing behind us and I stood cradling the bag, not wanting to leave. There was something comfortable about the house and its energy, and especially, Evalina. "How much do I owe you?"

"I'm giving you a special deal today, a free limpia. Don't you agree, Luna?"

She giggled and picked up Luna, who purred loudly as she nuzzled her. I longed to trade places with the cat as I watched Evalina's fingers stroke the silky fur and Luna's eyes close in pleasure.

"Thank you for everything."

"Any time." I walked toward my car and looked back over my shoulder. A part of me expected the house and Evalina to vanish in a puff of smoke. But she just waved and smiled at me before disappearing inside and closing the door.

By the time I made it home, my head was clearer and everything that happened with the curandera took on a surrealistic quality. My own cat, Bella, a gray Siamese, meowed her displeasure at her late dinner as I made a sandwich for myself. We both ate while I reflected on my visit with Evalina. She'd been so lovely and kind. It had been a long time since I'd found a woman so attractive. As usual, a magical woman had entranced me. Although, Evalina seemed the genuine deal, not a wannabe like Sandra, who skimmed through books on witchcraft and made bad guesses at tarot cards. I hoped more than truly believed the limpia would work. Maybe I was becoming jaded like so many other dumped lesbians, or could it be I was simply afraid of believing in something again?

I only finished half my sandwich, too much in a hurry to get started on the limpia. Bella joined me in the bathroom, warily watching the tub fill as I undressed. I glanced at myself in the mirror and flexed my biceps, pleased at their definition along with the smallness of my breasts and narrowness of my hips. My androgyny gave me a flexibility that drew both femmes and butches to me, but although butches had their charms, I was mostly attracted to femme women. Evalina, with her soft voluptuousness and mysterious charisma, was a perfect example.

I poured out the contents of the bath oil, letting it mix with the cascading water as a heady scent of flowers and spices rose on waves of steam. After I lit the candle and turned off the light, the bathroom took on an eerie glow. I sank into the warm, soothing water, delighted by its silky, slippery feel. After the stress of the day, my muscles began to relax and smooth out and my thoughts returned to Evalina. I closed my eyes, imagining her in the water with me as I leaned my head back comfortably against the edge of the tub. I must have dozed off because I blinked open my eyes, forgetting where I was as I flailed about and splattered foamy water on the floor. The radiance of the candle had amplified in the moist air, and when I looked at the foot of the tub, I was astonished to find Evalina.

She wore a thin robe tied with a sash and her hair was pinned up. I opened my mouth in surprise, attempting to speak, but she brought a finger to her mouth and shook her head. She smiled as she pulled the sash and opened her robe, letting it fall to the floor, revealing her lush body. Her breasts were larger than I thought, heavy globes with small, pert nipples, and her slender waist tapered into full hips and shapely legs. She gracefully lifted her leg to step into the tub and I was treated to the view of her pussy. My clit contracted and began to throb.

Once she was completely in the tub, I reached for her and she met my embrace with equal fervor, wrapping her legs around my waist to straddle me. Our mouths opened to each other, warm tongues exploring and tasting each other's sweetness. Her nipples repeatedly brushed against mine as if seeking attention. They didn't have to try hard. I released

Evalina's mouth and encircled her right nipple with my lips and tongue, sucking fiercely. She gasped in pleasure then leaned back, granting fuller access. I latched onto her left nipple, keeping it in my mouth as I opened my thighs. Instantly, our slippery pussies united. Evalina worked to grind hers into mine as her knees tightened around my waist and I grabbed the cheeks of her backside to help her. Our clits flicked and chafed together as we kissed, in between groans of pleasure that grew increasingly louder.

I shifted my position, leaning backward to force Evalina to relax her thigh grip, and she held on to my shoulder for balance. I kept one hand on her ass and with the other, massaged her pussy. Evalina reached down into the water and found my own pussy, her touch making me cry out. She entered my lips with several fingers as I entered hers. We fucked each other vigorously, fingers plunging deeply, splashing with abandon as we sought out the ultimate pleasure. Finally, Evalina shouted harshly and I echoed her, our bodies writhing in the midst of mutual orgasm.

She lay on top of me as our breathing eventually returned to normal and our bodies were at rest. However, with her yielding, warm weight against me, I felt my clit growing hard again. I opened my eyes as she kissed me, but then she pressed her fingers to my lips and shook her head. She got out of the tub before I could stop her, quickly getting back into her robe. I made a move to follow her, but she smiled, turned, and blew the candle out.

I woke up once more in darkness feeling disoriented. My pussy was sensitive; the feel of Evalina's fingers still indented on my clit. The water had grown cold, so I got out of the tub, fumbling in the dark for a towel and turned on the light. Bella sat up, stretched, and yawned. Had she been here all this time? I looked around, wondering if my encounter with Evalina had been only a dream. One thing I did know for sure was that I felt wonderful; in fact better than I had in a long time and ready to face the future.

I dried off slowly, then hung up the towel as Bella jumped on the sink wanting attention. I stroked her back and noticed a card next to the candle: *Dear Jo, if you're reading this, then the limpia worked. Call me if you'd like to see me again and I don't mean for business. Love, Evalina.*

I smiled and Bella purred.

Monisha

Jolie du Pré

Sitting on my sofa I look out the window and watch the snowflakes fall from a white sky. It's cold outside, yet thanks to my landlord my place stays at one temperature—hot. Sweat beads on my chest as I open a window in search of relief.

It will be Christmas soon. My family stopped speaking to me ever since I came out, so I don't have a lot of presents to buy. I want to go outside into the cold air, get a latte, and read the paper, listen to corny holiday tunes, and get the hell out of my apartment.

I walk into a coffee shop. A jazzy instrumental comes out of the speakers to the tune of *Silent Night*. She's behind the counter. Tawny skin and a face full of freckles. Brown dreadlocks. Large breasts. Big hips.

She turns around and bends over to get some cups. I stare at her full behind and imagine us naked: she on her stomach, my dark chocolate hands on her caramel ass.

"Happy Holidays," she says. She's standing up now, facing me and smiling.

"Happy Holidays. What's your name?" Flirting has become my hobby ever since I went on unemployment.

"Monisha. Yours?"

"Gladys."

"Do you come in here much, because I've never seen you before?"

"No, but I will now."

She blushes. I've taken a lot more chances these days, hitting on pretty girls who work behind counters whether they're straight or not. If I bomb, I just get what I need and leave. But when Monisha hands me my latte she looks me in the eyes.

I grab a paper and sit down. Every so often I stop reading and look at her face. She catches my gaze and smiles. I smile too.

"I'll be back tomorrow," I say to her as I leave.

The music is still of the holiday variety, but bluesier, sexier. The smell of the coffee is stronger, invading my senses. I feel good. Monisha is behind the counter wearing a half apron tied around her waist instead of a full apron covering her front. Her large breasts barely fit inside her blouse. When I come up to the counter my eyes fall to them, 'cause I can't help it. She notices immediately and she smiles, putting her fingers on her necklace and then lowering them to graze the start of her cleavage.

"Would you like some cherry in your latte?" she asks. Cherry in my latte. Cherry in my latte sounds real good.

I take my drink and sit across from her this time. No paper. Stare directly into her face. She's blushing. She can't concentrate on her customers because she keeps looking at me. I drink the rest of my cherry latte and imagine my tongue in her mouth, down her neck, on her chest.

It gets crowded. She wants to look at me some more, but she can't. I leave, but she knows I'll be back tomorrow.

In the morning I go into the coffee shop, but I don't see her. The manager says she has the day off. I leave the shop and chastise myself for not giving her my number or my e-mail address.

But later I see her at a bus stop, sitting with an older woman. Her mother?

"Gladys!"

"Hey!"

They're bundled up in their winter coats, inside the bus shelter, trying to stay warm.

"Momma, this is my friend Gladys. Sometimes she comes into the coffee shop."

Her mother looks at me and smiles. "Merry Christmas!"

"Thank you. Merry Christmas to you, too."

"Big plans for the holiday, Gladys?" Monisha asks.

"Nope."

"Just dinner with family?"

"No family."

"You're alone?" Her mother asks, her face furrowed with concern.

"Yeah, but it's cool. I'm going to get one of those hams. Listen to music. Eggnog. It'll be nice."

Monisha is staring at me. Her mind racing. My pathetic statement was about to get me an invitation. I can feel it.

"Momma, can Gladys have dinner with us? I'd hate for her to be alone on Christmas."

"Certainly, we'd love to have you over."

So now I was having Christmas dinner with the coffee girl. The bus arrives. Monisha grabs my hand. "If I don't see you in the shop tomorrow, call me there. I'll give you my address."

Then they're off.

I ring the doorbell and Monisha answers. She gives me a hug and presses her globes hard against my chest. "It's good to see you," she whispers into my ear, pulling away from me when her family comes in. I smile at them and try not to focus on my throbbing clit.

We eat Christmas dinner at one of those really large tables. Monisha and I sit side by side surrounded by her mother, brother, sisters, and an aunt.

"What do you do for a living, Gladys?" the aunt asks me. The rest of the family looks at me as I grab some turkey.

"I'm in between jobs right now."

"Lord have mercy, I wish Monisha would find a better job," the mother says. "Stop wasting her life away in that store."

"Momma, please!" Monisha shouts.

"You could have been in your third year of law school by now."

Monisha looks at me and rolls her eyes. I smile and reach my hand under the tablecloth, resting it on her knee.

"Do you work at that store too?" the mother asks.

"Gladys said she's in between jobs, remember?" Monisha responds.

"Well . . . it's lovely that you're here, Gladys," the mother says. "Of course it would have been nice if Joe were here."

"I don't want to talk about Joe," Monisha says. She opens her legs a little wider. I move my fingers slowly up her thigh.

The phone rings. Her brother gets up to answer it. "It's Joe."

Monisha pulls my hand from between her legs and hurries over to the phone.

"The wedding is in April, right Georgia?" Monisha's aunt asks the mother.

"Yes, when he's home from Japan. He should be here now. It's not right. I don't know why he agreed to work so far away anyway."

Monisha was getting married—déjà vu. I got tangled with two other married chicks in my past. They seemed to find me.

After dinner they all head into the family room to watch a movie. I look around for Monisha, but she's gone, so I get my coat and walk outside.

Then I hear a car honk. "Gladys!" Monisha is in the car, shouting at me. I run over and get in.

She drives as if she's being chased, doesn't look at me at all, eyes peered on the road.

Light becomes dark. We stop at a deserted park. She turns off the car and looks at me. Two seconds later my tongue is in her mouth.

She pushes me off, climbs over to the back seats, and pulls the seats down. Then she takes off her coat and lays on her back, ready for me. I pull off my coat and climb over as well, resting my body on top of hers. We kiss hard on the lips. I lick her neck and then I pull her shirt open, grabbing her breasts in my hands.

Now I'm on my back and she's on top. She brings her chest to my face and puts a breast in my mouth. She knows I want them. I grab her tits and lick the nipples. Then I put her on her back and pull her pants off.

She's wearing red satin panties. There's a wet spot between her legs. Staring at it, I start to throb. I slowly pull her panties down her thighs and spread her legs. Placing my hands under her bottom, I grab the flesh of her ass and then I bring my face to her clit, sucking it into my mouth and licking it as fast as I can.

It's winter. It's cold. But inside the car fire rages. She wraps her legs around my waist as I push my face into her. Soon she grabs my head and explodes, coming in spasm after spasm.

Then she has me on my back again and she pulls off my pants and panties. My pussy is wet and very little is needed to bring me over the edge. She puts her fingers inside me and moves them in and out while she sucks hard on my clit. I come in no time, my juices all over her fingers.

We kiss each other and hold each other tight. Near midnight she drives me home.

"They'll be worried about you."

"I know," she says. "But I don't care about that right now."

She pulls in front of my apartment and kisses me.

"Goodbye," she says.

"Goodbye." I get out of the car. She reaches over and puts her hand on the passenger window, looks at me then drives away.

A week later I get a job in a different state. Two weeks later I move.

I don't return to the coffee shop until months later when winter has turned into summer. They tell me she's gone, say she moved to Japan.

The shop has an array of new drinks, perfect for quenching your thirst, but none of them interests me. I stand in the center of the shop and imagine the smell of cherry latte and the taste of her on my lips.

ABOUT THE CONTRIBUTORS

Nan Andrews would like to be considered a Renaissance woman, but given how poorly women were treated back then, maybe she should be considered a Renaissance man in drag. Her story, "Finally", can be found in *After Midnight: True Lesbian Erotic Confessions* and the story, "A Little Help" in *CREAM: The Best of the Erotica Readers and Writers Association.*

Jacqueline Applebee is a black British woman who enjoys writing erotica at inopportune moments. She is a secretary by day, but has also earned a living making sex toys and silver jewelry. One of her fondest memories is of serving tea at SM Pride to an admiring crowd.

Cheyenne Blue combines her two passions in life and writes travel guides and erotica. Her erotica has appeared in several anthologies, including *Best Women's Erotica*, *Mammoth Best New Erotica*, *Best Lesbian Erotica*, *Best Lesbian Love Stories*, and on many Web sites. Her travel guides have been jammed into many glove boxes underneath the chocolate wrappers. She divides her time between Colorado and Ireland, and is currently working on a book about the quiet and quirky areas of Ireland. You can see more of her erotica on her Web site, www.cheyenneblue.com.

Tenille Brown's work is featured online and in several print anthologies including *Glamour Girls: Femme/Femme Erotica*, *Ultimate Undies*, *Sexiest Soles*, *Caught Looking* and

Ultimate Lesbian Erotica 2007. She obsessively shops for shoes, hats, and purses and keeps a daily blog on her Web site, www.tenillebrown.com.

Rachel Kramer Bussel (www.rachelkramerbussel.com) is senior editor at *Penthouse Variations*, writes the Lusty Lady column for *The Village Voice*, and hosts In the Flesh Erotic Reading Series. She has edited a dozen red-hot erotica anthologies, including *Naughty Spanking Stories from A to Z* 1 and 2, *First-Timers*, and *Up All Night* and is the author of the forthcoming novels *Everything But* and *Eye Candy*.

Andrea Dale's stories have appeared in *Best Lesbian Erotica*, Fishnetmag.com, *Ultimate Undies*, and *The MILF Anthology*, among others. As Sophie Mouette, she and a coauthor wrote *Cat Scratch Fever* (Black Lace Books, 2006), and as Sarah Dale, she and another coauthor have sold *A Little Night Music* to Cheek Books. In other incarnations, she is a published writer of fantasy and romance. Her Web site is www.cyvarwydd.com.

Dylynn DeSaint lives in Mesa, Arizona with her partner. A freelance writer, Dylynn enjoys writing short stories and erotic fiction during her lunch hour at the library where she works. An avid people watcher, she finds inspiration for her stories at coffeehouses, airports, and annual treks to New York City.

Amanda Earl's fiction appears in *The Mammoth Book of Best New Erotica*, 2006 and 2007, and *CREAM: The Best of the Erotica Readers and Writers Association*. Her erotica can also be found on BlueFood.cc, Oystersandchocolate.com, Goodvibes.com, UnlikelyStories.com, and Xodtica.com. Amanda lives juicy with her husband Charles in Ottawa, Canada.

Lisa Figueroa is a Chicana writer from the Los Angeles area who received an M.A. in English/creative writing from CSUN in 2001. Her writing has appeared in *The Harrington Lesbian Fiction Quarterly*, *Sinister Wisdom*, *Erotic Interludes 3*, and will be forthcoming in *Best Lesbian Romance, 2007*. Besides writing, she loves spending quality time with her beautiful, amazing partner of six years and their three adorable cats.

Isabelle Gray is the pseudonym of a graduate student and writer whose work can be found in numerous anthologies, including *First Timers: True Stories of Lesbian Awakening*, *Best Date Ever*, and many others. She only wishes she knew how to change her own oil.

Michelle Houston has had stories published in over a dozen anthologies, including *Heat Wave*, *Three-Way, The Merry XXXmas Book of Erotica*, and *Slave to Love*. She is also an e-published writer. You can read more about her, find out her contact info, or see more of her writings on her personal Web site The Erotic Pen (www.eroticpen.net).

Jolene Hui is a writer/actor who loves to watch scary movies and TV, eat sweets, and dream of the day when she will get her Chinese crested hairless and standard poodle so that she can finally have the family she always desired. One of Tonto Press's first authors, she has also been published by a variety of monthly, weekly, and daily newspapers, *Medium Magazine*, and Cleis Press. She currently resides in southern California.

Winnie Jerome was born in San Francisco. She now resides in the Monterey Bay area and writes in her spare time.

JT Langdon is the Taoist, vegetarian, lover of chocolate responsible for nearly a dozen erotic lesbian novels, including *Hard Time*, *For I Have Sinned*, and the *Lady Davenport's Slave* trilogy, as well as having stories in such anthologies as *Heat Wave* and *Blood Sisters*. Despite numerous requests to leave, some made with the business end of a pitchfork, JT continues to live in the Midwest. Visit the author online at www.jtlangdon.com.

Shanel Odum is a lover of words, art, and music. She is currently a Brooklyn-based scribe.

CB Potts is a full-time writer living in upstate New York, about half an hour away from where "Test Your Luck" takes place. She writes erotica of every flavor, as well as mainstream journalism and ghostwriting work. Learn more at www.cbpotts.net.

Born in the U.K., **Terri Pray** now resides in Iowa with her husband and two children. Her work ranges from the sweet to the wild, fantasy to erotica, and anything else she suddenly has the urge to try.

Sofía Quintero is the author of *Divas Don't Yield*. Under the pen name Black Artemis, she also wrote the hip-hop novels *Explicit Content*, *Picture Me Rollin'*, and *Burn*. Sofía is the co-founder of Chica Luna Productions and Sister Outsider Entertainment, both devoted to the creation of socially conscious popular media by and for people of color.

Jean Roberta teaches first-year English in a Canadian prairie university and writes in several genres. Her erotica appears in over forty anthologies, including two collections of true lesbian stories from Alyson Books: *Up All Night* and *First-Timers*. In the early 1980's, she survived as a single mother by working for two escort agencies. This story is dedicated to the First Nations women of the prairie, who have endured so much.

Teresa Noelle Roberts writes erotica, poetry, romance, and speculative fiction. Her erotica has appeared or is forthcoming in *Best Women's Erotica* 2004, 2005, and 2007; *Secret Slaves: Erotic Stories of Bondage*; *FishNetMag*; and many other publications. She is also one-half of the erotica-writing duo Sophie Mouette, whose novel *Cat Scratch Fever* was released in 2006 by Black Lace Books.

Tawanna Sullivan is the owner of Kuma2.net, a Web site that encourages black lesbians to explore their sensuality and sexuality through writing erotica. She lives in New Jersey with her domestic partner Martina.

Fiona Zedde moved to the United States from Jamaica as a sweet, yet misunderstood, preteen. After spending a few years in Florida fooling around with incendiary women of all types, she moved to Atlanta, where she currently lives with her partner. Fiona is the author of two novels, *Bliss* and *A Taste of Sin*, both published by Kensington Books. Find out more about her at www.fionazedde.com

ABOUT THE EDITOR

Jolie du Pré (www.joliedupre.com) is a writer of lesbian erotica and lesbian erotic romance. Her stories have appeared on numerous Web sites, including Scarlet Letters, Word Riot, and the Galleries of the Erotica Readers & Writers Association; in e-book at eXtasy Books and Ocean's Mist Press; and in print in *Hot & Bothered 4—Short Short Fiction on Lesbian Desire* edited by Karen X. Tulchinsky, *Down & Dirty Volume 2* edited by Alison Tyler, *Best Bondage Erotica 2* edited by Alison Tyler, *The Heart of Our Community* edited by Sachel Peters, *Luscious* edited by Alison Tyler, *CREAM: The Best of the Erotica Readers and Writers Association* edited by Lisabet Sarai, *Got a Minute? Sixty Second Erotica* edited by Alison Tyler, and *Best Lesbian Erotica 2007* edited by Tristan Taormino.

Jolie du Pré is the founder of GLBT Promo (www.glbtpromo.com), a promotional group for GLBT erotica and erotic romance.

ACKNOWLEDGMENTS

Thanks to everyone at Alyson Books, especially Shannon Berning, Anthony LaSasso, and Joe Pittman. Thanks to Robert for being there for me. Thanks to Lisa and Paula for their encouragement. Thanks to Shaynie for an everlasting connection. And thanks to the readers, writers, and publishers of the world who support lesbian erotica.